The Quest

Books by Manolis

The Medusa Glance, Ekstasis Editions, 2017
The Second Advent of Zeus, Ekstasis Editions, 2016
Chthonian Bodies, paintings by Ken Kirkby, Libros Libertad, 2016
Images of Absence, Ekstasis Editions, 2015
Autumn Leaves, poetry, Ekstasis Editions, 2014
Übermensch/Υπεράνθρωπος, poetry, Ekstasis Editions, 2013
Mythography, paintings and poetry, Libros Libertad, 2012
Nostos and Algos, poetry, Ekstasis Editions, 2012
Vortex, poetry, Libros Libertad, 2011
The Circle, novel, Libros Libertad, 2011
Vernal Equinox, poetry, Ekstasis Editions, 2011
Opera Bufa, poetry, Libros Libertad, 2010
Vespers, poetry by Manolis, paintings by Ken Kirkby, Libros Libertad, 2010
Triptych, poetry, Ekstasis Editions, 2010
Nuances, poetry, Ekstasis Editions, 2009
Rendition, poetry, Libros Libertad, 2009
Impulses, poetry, Libros Libertad, 2009
Troglodytes, poetry, Libros Libertad, 2008
Petros Spathis, novel, Libros Libertad, 2008
El Greco, poetry, Libros Libertad, 2007
Path of Thorns, poetry, Libros Libertad, 2006
Footprints in Sandstone, poetry, Authorhouse, 2006
The Orphans - an Anthology, poetry, Authorhouse, 2005

Manolis

The Quest

Ekstasis  Editions

Published in 2018 by:
Ekstasis Editions Canada Ltd.   Ekstasis Editions
Box 8474, Main Postal Outlet   Box 571
Victoria, B.C. V8W 3S1   Banff, Alberta T1L 1E3

LIBRARY AND ARCHIVES CANADA CATALOGUING IN PUBLICATION

Manolis, 1947-, author
    The quest / Manolis.

Issued in print and electronic formats.
ISBN 978-1-77171-283-5 (softcover).--ISBN 978-1-77171-284-2 (ebook)

    I. Title.

PS8626.A673Q47 2018   C813'.6   C2018-901322-2
                                                                          C2018-901323-0

Canada Council   Conseil des Arts   Funded by the   Canada
for the Arts   du Canada   Government
                                             of Canada

Ekstasis Editions acknowledges financial support for the publication of *The Quest* from the government of Canada through the Canada Book Fund and the Canada Council for the Arts, and from the Province of British Columbia through the Book Publishing Tax Credit.

Printed and bound in Canada.

C O N T E N T S

Romania — Early Years

Since his early childhood Pericles had listened to the stories his grandfather told, stories on a far-away island called Crete, and tales of mythological beings.

He was influenced by his grandfather even before he went to the Hellenic Community School to learn the basic use of the Hellenic language. Besides what his Greek-born parents told him, his grandfather had undertaken the serious role of a tutor. Pericles' life in Romania was quite different from the one his grandfather described, but as he grew older he began to understand this other world and was determined that one day he would travel there.

Pericles' grandfather was a huge man almost two meters tall with wide shoulders like the walls of a house and gigantic hairy arms and hands. He had jet black hair and eyes always dark into which one could observe an undying fire, a power that scared anyone who came near him, prompting them to think they had to deal with a beast. Each day he wore his traditional Cretan attire of dark blue breaches and black boots high up almost to his knees. On his stubborn forehead he always displayed the black traditional scarf with fringes falling onto his forehead which one could think was made of steel, a springboard of thunder and lightning. He was an old man, an inexhaustible source of information, a brook endlessly babbling, a wise owl always advising, a fresh spring flowing in the heart of summer. He was the one hundred year old oak on the hillside basking in the vast valley of experience and relating back to the young boy stories of grandeur and everlasting pride.

Pericles imagined Crete, the island they came from, to be just like his grandfather, a woman with dark complexion with dark blue breaches and black boots to her knees, with the scarf on her forehead and two knives in her belt with silver plated handles. When the old man talked, his voice, deep, subterranean, it was as if it came from the bowels of earth, shaking the house to its foundations as if it was answering to his grandfather's call. One would think they were two beasts in a duel. Indeed, who else could ever stand up to this huge man, his grandfather? Whoever knew him tried their best to stay clear of the *big man* as they called him and they would always avoid arguing with him. Even Alexander, his son, wasn't the exception, and every time he heard the old man yell he would walk away like a dog with its tail between its legs.

Whenever his grandfather was angry he would stay up all night and walk in his room from one side to the other with a regular stop by the window where he would focus to the south where he imagined his Crete was located. He would stare the void for long time as if in the darkness of the night he could discern his village, smell his roots. He could see the relatives he had left behind when he immigrated to this forsaken place in Romania. He would stand there, at time motionless, as if frozen by the cold he felt in his heart, as if unable to move before the power enforced onto him by the image of his island, even though it existed only in his imagination. Crete was like a scimitar outstretched, shaped like an eloquent eyebrow. Crete captivated him, filling him, made him feel immortal. During such nightly occurrences he stayed there until the morning star would appear, the sign he waited for and then he would go downstairs. He would throw some cold water onto his face and drink a glass of milk, then go to his regular chair outside on the porch where he would wait until everyone else was up and ready to face the day's responsibilities. No matter what the weather was one would always find him there sitting with his eyes focused to the south where he imagined his Crete was located. He was always found in that position as if he was looking at his island, as if he was walking on its soil, as if he was drinking his Cretan wine in his back yard, as if he was living in his island, as if he

8

was there.

No matter what the day of the week it was, the old man was always there until his grandson woke and come to sit close to him. This made the old man feel reborn, as if he was graced with a new life. These were the times when he would tell Pericles story after story about his island, about his life that passed like fresh water from a mountain spring and he would drink it, never feeling quenched. He told stories about the people and the blue sea, the olive groves and the orchards of oranges and lemons and the boys who would go around all day long with slingshots in their hands and adventure in their minds. He would tell his grandson about the cicadas with their endless singing all summer long, about the sea that at sometimes turned angry with waves the height of a house ready to gulp everyone in its way. He would tell him about gods, lots of gods, not just one like they had these days but lots of gods and above them all, Minos the greatest, the wisest and the most just of all. He would tell Pericles about the young men who ran and took part in sport competitions, the boys who danced and jumped like eagles until it seemed the mountains were leaning down to admire them. He would tell him about the young women who eyed the boys and felt a slow burning fire in their bodies. He would tell him about wars, a lot of wars which they fought until the day of liberation when they celebrated and partied for forty days and forty nights non-stop.

Pericles listened quietly and his childish mind was filled with young men and with women as beautiful as the gods and good mannered, simple people joyously going about their daily lives and high snow-capped mountains that spoke like men and went down to the valleys and danced during the celebration for their freedom. And the boy imagined Crete to be an orchard with bloomed flowers and fruit trees where gods walked and talked and made jokes with the mortals and it was always spring and summer, unlike the cold place where they lived.

Today as they were sitting in the veranda overlooking the other side of the long street his grandfather narrated to him the story of a brave young man, Diomedes, who in one single fight killed one hundred enemies. It was the time, he said, when the barbarians had come to their land and abducted the most beautiful Helen and they took her to their city and that the Cretans put together an army of men and run against the barbarians to take back their beautiful Kore. His grandfather told him how people were all good to each other, how they together challenged death. This was the first time Pericles heard the word death.

"Pappou* where do people go when they die?" he asked.

The old man, being unprepared for such question, coughed not because he needed to clear his throat but to quickly come up with an answer; then turning to the direction of the boy he said in a very quiet voice:

"Eh, they die, they go to the after-world. They go to meet their family, their parents."

"Pappou, how do children come to life?"

"From their parents, but leave this aside, when you grow up you'll understand these things, and let me finish the story."

"Yes, the story pappou" the boy answered and tuned his ears to the voice of his grandfather who narrated the rest of the story.

But that same night as Pericles sat with the dim light of the oil lamb on the wall he pondered these two mysteries: there was a big valley, red in color, where men sprang from when the proper wind was blowing and the sun was rising. Then he imagined a snake at the edge of the valley that meant death would come and take the old people when the time was right. But what was the role of god in all this? He asked himself. He couldn't find an answer and decided he would ask his teacher at school.

A few days later Pericles found his grandfather in his well know place at the veranda looking toward the south where he imagined Crete was located. The old man, a motionless statue, was silent, enclosed to himself and solitary, as if living in a time past. As he sat with teary eyes, his expression was that of an angry man, an expression the boy remembered from other times. And the boy also knew that only when he came close and sat beside him would his grandfather tell him his favorite stories.

---

* grandfather

But this time young Pericles preferred to sit on the other side of the veranda to which the old man, as if a statue might regain motion and become alive without turning his head his grandfather called him:

"Come, Pericles, come sit with me or are you afraid of me, eh?"

Pericles lowered his head and walked to his grandfather's open arms. After squeezing the boy a little, he caressed Pericles' head and while still staring to the south he let a sigh leave his lips. Soon after, as if he regretted showing his sadness he took his pipe from his pocket and got busy cleaning and wiping it with his kerchief, something he didn't do often as he rarely smoked unless he was alone on the veranda, never when Pericles was present.

"Once upon a time there were two brothers the name of one of them was Pericles, like you and the other Menelaus. They had two other brothers, Themistocles and Euripides, but the two were different because they were twins. Just like the twins Mrs. Fourakis had a year ago, you remember?"

"Yes, pappou" the boy said.

"*Endaxi**... So, these two brothers were very close, as if they were two halves of one rose and when they grew up they always did things together; they were inseparable day and night. They were so close their parents used to say about them, 'these two are so close that when one dies the other will die shortly after' The years went by and when they grew and became almost adults they started having the responsibilities of their household. Along with their other two brothers they took care of the animals and the orchards since their father was an old man by then. Pericles and Menelaus were responsible for the big family flock of goats which they took grazing up on the mountains and the other two brothers Themistocles and Kostis took care of the orchards. One day Pericles was on his way home when he met Irene the most beautiful girl of the village, daughter of Homer Daskalogiannis, and from that day his life changed. He dreamed of Irene, and always talked of her. He sang the traditional folk songs of the area and always made sure Irene would hear him or learn about

---

* Good

how he sang for her. The image of her body, slender and calligraphic drove him mad and he dreamed that someday he would marry her."

The old Cretan stopped to let a sigh float in the air of the veranda, as if to release him from a weight he carried deep inside his heart, as if he wished to become lighter than a bird and fly over the mountains to reach southward to his island where his glance travelled, like all other times when he wished he could see his island, his Crete. There with the fragrance of their jasmine plant coming from the flowerbed only five feet away from the veranda he searched in his mind to meet Irene again, like that time by the fresh water spring when she looked at him and smiled at him for the first time.

"*Cursed let it be, the old age*" he thought, "*Let fate be cursed for always bringing old age and death*". That thought calmed him down and he turned toward his grandson, caressed his head and carried on with the story.

"Ah, I forgot to mention, the twins were in a way completely different from each other. Menelaus took from his mother her angelic heart. He was a timid church-going young man who always prayed, always observed the religious holidays and if he heard someone curse the holy icons or God he would get very upset and he wouldn't talk to that person for a long time. He never worked on a Sunday or any other holiday. If he happened to be on the mountains with their flock of goats on a Sunday he always sat on a big boulder and gazed down toward the fertile plain toward the village which was visible to his right, and farther away to the left and north toward the glaucous playful sea. Other times he would grab his knife with the black handle and he busied himself crafting a cross or an icon or the face of a saint on a piece of wood or the bark from a nearby cypress. Menelaus was a nature lover and he would never step on an insect. There were times when he would make crumbs out of his bread and place them on his favorite boulder to attract ants which would come and feast on them.

If he was in the village Menelaus never went to the orchards to help his brothers on a Sunday but he would get up very early and get ready to go to church. When he came back from church he always read pamphlets and other church books. His twin brother Pericles was the opposite. He was different, unique. He took after his father's side and he was wild, a rebel, always against every possible established idea, habit, or custom. He was always strong willed and had an athletic body, strong muscles, huge hands and arms, very tall with dark complexion, a brave man, generous, strong and capable of lifting double the weight of things you load on a donkey. He was always wild and rebellious, a big drinker, good dancer, graceful, like an ancient god. Whenever there was a party or any other celebratory festivity the Pericles was always the first and best who took part in it and as the days went by he was known to everyone around the area and in each and every village on that side of Crete. People would say, "A celebration without Pericles isn't a celebration!"

"What did they mean by that grandfather?" the boy asked.

"It meant that everybody wanted him to be in their celebration, my boy, because Pericles was a different kind of firebrand. If someone asked him to go to church he would always answer: 'I'm not for churches, I'm not a saint...' and he would stop the conversation from going further. He didn't like the priesthood, I mean to say. These twins were truly two different characters. They were on the mountain once, herding their goats, when something happened. Pericles who couldn't sleep all night because of his love for Irene and angry at himself for reasons unknown, got up and walked outside their small shepherds' room to the big boulder, his brothers favored spot facing the village down below. Above him was the starry sky, serene, asleep, quiet, immense, gleaming by the luminous stars and around him quietness, silence and only a couple crickets arguing about their love affair. He sat there for a long time mesmerized by the darkness of the world above him and below toward the village until at one moment he got up, pulled his knife from his waist, and sliced his arm, and felt his blood flowing from his arm and dripping to the ground. He swore: 'God of the Oath, God of the Cretan men, to you I swear, no one ever will come between me and Irene!' He thought nobody heard him and only the ears of the night and those of the God of the Oath were awake to hear his cry but he was wrong: Menelaus, inside their small room, was also awake and heard his call and his cry, his threatening promise. He said no word, only he turned to the other side of the cot and tried to go to sleep and when Pericles came back into the room he pretended he was in deep slumber.

The young boy was shaken by the last words and interrupted his grandfather, "Pappou, who was the God of Oath? Wasn't Minos the highest God in Crete?"

The old man smiled, "Yes, of course Minos was the best. No, no Minos wasn't alive those days."

"Minos was dead grandfather?"

"Ah, yes, of course he had died."

"But do the Gods die grandfather?" The boy was surprised because he remembered comments by the priest of the Community church, father Aristotle, at the Sunday school, comments that referred to the Almighty God.

"Eh, yes, they die sometimes, they get old like people. They get sick and they die…But leave this aside, you'll understand it better when you grow up and let me finish the story." His grandfather said and slowly stirred in his chair but without letting his eyes leave the face of his grandson whose attention was tuned to every word the old man said.

"Yes grandfather, the story." The boy repeated while his interest was aroused once again.

"That summer Pericles went with his father to the family of Irene and asked for her hand; everything went well and they got engaged since Irene liked that huge man and dreamed of having children with him. Everyone was happy for the engagement and the upcoming wedding except Menelaus, his twin brother, who was also in love with Irene. He had never divulged his feelings to anyone because he remembered his brother's oath that night up on the mountain and for this reason he kept his feelings to himself. One time around the end of August they had all gone to Saint John's celebration to the other side of the peninsula to a small church where they went every year. It was an annual celebration that usually lasted three days. People from all the villages in that part of Crete would travel on foot or with their donkeys or mules to the site around the church, where they set up camp and spent the following three nights and days celebrating, eating, dancing and having a good time on the occasion of the church festivity. Every year when the dance would start Pericles was always first in the line leading the dances for hours. Irene was there as well with her parents, and she blushed looking at Pericles doing his exquisite moves as if the musicians played their music to follow his dance steps. At one time Pericles' eyes caught his beloved Irene's and suddenly his legs seemed to grow wings and his feet wouldn't touch the ground any longer but he was like an eagle, like an ancient god floating in the clouds dancing and making everyone present to live the moment. He asked the lyre player to quicken the rhythm and as he danced he became a fascinating image of a young man beating the elements and his body defying nature becoming free. Once the dance finished he ordered the one they called *pidihtos*, 'the jumping one' which was a very fast dance that involved a lot of jumping. One had to have good health and good legs to dance it."

The old man took a deep breath. He let his glance travel from the boy's face to the road where a couple of men were walking and in loud voices debated something obviously very important. Then his glance would fall back to the boy. Then as if taking from the boy's sweet eyes power the glance of the old man got fixated to the south where he thought Crete was located and he imagined he was there, at the Saint John's festivities. He was again the leader, first in the line, dancing the *pidihtos*. One word would be enough for him to get up there on the veranda and start dancing like he did back then.

"*Ah, the ravaging of age. Let it be cursed,*" he thought and a faint smile appeared on his face as if he had already beaten the years that had passed and he had already finished dancing his *pidihtos*.

The boy's eyes flashed and as he admired the bravery of the young men of Crete. He desired to also do this, to be in Crete and at the Saint John's celebration and take part in the *pidihtos* dance. He wanted to be as brave as the men of Crete, to show to all others that he is Cretan too, like his grandfather, a desire that reflected in the eyes of the young boy of twelve which the old man sensed. A faint smile appeared on the grandfather's face knowing this young boy one day will be another great man of his lineage, another brave Cretan who will carry the name of his family with pride. He smiled a wide happy smile that his grandson was getting what he wanted him to receive.

"Yes they all danced the same way until Menelaus got up and he said he wanted to do the same. But although his brother Pericles tried to talk him out of it Menelaus wanted to do exactly what his twin brother had done minutes earlier. But his health wasn't good and his heart couldn't take the stress and after he went into a paroxysm and his whole body shook as if the strongest electric current run through it he collapsed. They took him to the closest hospital but he was very sick. He lasted only four days and then he died. But before he took his last breath he wanted to talk to his brother Pericles who had walked into the room of the hospital. Everyone left them alone and it was then that Menelaus informed his brother that he also was in love with Irene, that he had also wanted to get married to her but when that night he heard Pericles' oath he kept it to himself and never showed any sign of his deep love for her. He died in the arms of his brother — together in birth together in death. None ever heard any word from Pericles as to what they had talked about in the room when they were alone. Pericles didn't even say anything to his Irene, who he married a few months later."

"And Menelaus died, pappou?"

"Yes he died, my boy"

"What happened after?"

"Pericles married Irene."

"How many children did Pericles have pappou?"

"Just one"

"What was his name?"

"Alexander, like your dad."

"Why did he name him Alexander, pappou?"

"It's traditional my boy, for a son to give his firstborn the name of his father"

"Grandfather, do you have any brothers?"

"Why?"

The boy shrugged his shoulders.

"Yes I have, but go now. Go play with your friends and next time I'll tell you another story. There I see Demetrius coming this way. Go and play with him."

Although Pericles preferred to sit and hear another story from his grandfather he said nothing else but got up to welcome his friend Demetrius who with a broad smile upon his face came through the front gate playing a soccer ball in his hands as if teasing his buddy Pericles. And it had the expected effect since Pericles got up and the two boys set up their goalie and shooter game in which Demetrius was the goalie and Pericles was shooting against.

The old man seeing his grandson leaving the veranda sighed and let his eyes run to the south, towards his Crete, and a faint smile appeared on his face again. "Next time I shall be more careful" he thought "at least until he grows up a little more."

Voyage to the New Land

It was a very rough voyage. Waves four meters high hit the boat on the starboard making it toss from right to left while every loose item on the deck, things the crew didn't tie down before the tempest hit, slid from one side to the other. So did the people, whether they were in the small salon in the back of the ship or dared still be outside on the deck when the roughest waters of the Aegean that always occurred between Crete and the Peloponnese started slamming the ship. The deck personnel frantically ran around trying to calm the people and secure the various items so they wouldn't be tossed over each other or injure any of the passengers.

Pericles eyed his wife Irene and his nineteen year old son Alexander who had already gotten sick and had emptied his stomach twice. What a daring voyage they had ahead of them! But what else could he do in a country devastated by wars and famine, a country trying to find its footing in the world? It was better for them to take the chance to travel to a foreign country than stay behind with no future for his son. Their voyage was long and adventurous as they would travel on board this ship from Kissamos to Monemvasia in Peloponnese; from Peloponnese to Piraeus and from there to Romania and to their destination, the port of Konstanza where a lot of Hellenic ships travelled those days. Pericles knew a man there, a distant relative on his mother's side, and his eyes were fixated on getting there, rain or shine.

It took them almost a week, from Kissamos to Peloponnese, to

Piraeus a very busy port, the biggest harbor in Hellas with ships coming in and going out almost every hour of the day and night. They had boarded a ship named *Alexander the Great* and were standing on the deck watching the bustle and commotion of the longshoremen running in all directions trying to finish all necessary duties and make sure the boat was in every respect ready to sail out of the harbor; their voices, the bustle and speed with which each thing was done, the antithetic smells of the water's salinity and the cawing of the hungry gulls fighting over morsels of food created a havoc drowning out the people's farewells. Above them the cloudy sky poured down heavy rain that soaked the ground turning the harbor into a shining, glittering surface into which the clouds reflected and the sky was so heavy that its weight sat upon the people chests almost as heavy as their sins sat onto their consciences.

With his eyes Pericles said farewell to the sacred ground they were leaving, his heart overtaken by the joy of adventure and the melancholy of departure not knowing whether he'd ever see these images again, knowing this could be the voyage of his life. Suddenly he felt his heartbeats palpitating in tune with the sound of the engine the ship as it plied its way out of the harbor of Piraeus into the dark waters of the Aegean Sea. The endless voyage commenced without a clear view of the designated port of arrival.

The *Alexander the Great* took them across the Aegean through the Straights of Hellespontos to the Straight of Marmaras and from there farther northward along the Bulgarian coastline to the port of Konstantza in Romania where they met his distant relative, Agamemnon, a ship chandler. Agamemnon took them to his house and early the next morning he presented them to the Greek Consulate of the port city, a young man of Greek descent Apollo Nikolitch, who did his best to help them arrange the necessary papers. They were invited as farm workers by the ship chandler's brother who lived in the city of Craiova, unfortunately far away to the west of Romania.

The second morning after they reached Konstantza they boarded the train for the long six hour trip across Romania. Agamemnon had provided them with food for their travel and said that, God willing they'd reach Craiova early in the night. At the train station of Craiova,

Homer, the ship chandler's brother received them and took them to his house. They were finally and legally in a foreign country, Pericles had a job, and the countryside was a good place for them during these difficult days, a safer place for his son.

Craiova was a peaceful city where one could discover barber shops, bakeries, two big markets where they could buy anything and everything, and movie theaters where the cinemas of Italy and Russia were sending their best productions. The Craiovans visited these places every Sunday matinee and enjoyed the modernistic attitudes of the young starlets with who the young men of this city fell in love.

Like any other city there were plenty of pigeons all around the grounds and during the early days of spring the chirps of birds would change the impeccable silence by singing unabatedly for fays on until summer came to metabolise the atmosphere and turn the streets into a joyous party with wheat- ears dancing competitions and revelry unlike any other one had experienced.

Pericles and Alexander worked like horses trying to make ends meet, since those days everyone lived in poverty; a reality as harsh as death yet they accepted it as it came, whether dressed in glitter and sparkles or in rags and disheveled hairdos. It was their life and they did the best to explore its outer layer. They also met other members of the Hellenic Community of Craiova, perhaps one thousand people directly from Hellas, along with their children born in Romania. The children attended the school of the Community where the teacher Mr. Aristides, a Macedonian, taught them the Hellenic language and traditions.

The newcomers lived on a farm that belonged to Mr. Homer, the ship chandler's brother. He lived in a big farm house and next to it there was a second one, smaller in size where the newcomers settled. Both farm houses were well built of cement columns and brick, with the exterior stuccoed and painted while the roof was made of tiles which were made of clay just as the houses back in Crete. Homer's family consisted of himself, his wife Helena, a daughter, Aspasia, two years younger than Alexander, and an eleven year old boy called Hephestos.

When Alexander reached his early twenties he got engaged to

Aspasia and her father, as tradition dictated, gave her a new house as a dowry which he built on the property a hundred yards away from the other two. In this house two years later a baby was born who they named Pericles to honour his grandfather.

The same year the Second World War started, and after a four years ordeal, the Communists took control of Romania. The borders were closed, and nobody was allowed to leave without the proper approval of the central committee of the ruling party. But Pericles and his family had settled for good in this country and now they knew they couldn't go anywhere under these new rules. On the other hand they learned that in their homeland a civil war was taking place with brothers killing brothers. This made Pericles feel thankful that they had left. He imagined if they still lived in Hellas how his son would have to choose between one side and the other, the leftists on the mountains fighting against the national army supported by the west. No! No matter how bad Romania was, the civil war wasn't any better.

School Years

Years later when the old man's grandson, also Pericles, grew and started going to school he learned many things about the country of his parents and his grandfather from the teacher of the Community school, Mr. Aristides, and the boy's borders became a lot wider and their motherland became larger. It was called Hellas, and it wasn't confined only to Crete as his grandfather had told him, but it was a lot larger and it had hundreds of small islands in the Aegean and Adriatic Seas. His teacher, Mr. Aristides, taught them many other things about the beautiful islands of Hellas, its archeological sites, and the invincible Hellenic spirit that has spread all over the world. He learned about the glory of Hellas, the Trojan War and there weren't, Mr. Aristides insisted, only the Cretans who went to take back the beautiful maiden Helen but the whole of Hellas got involved in the war that lasted ten years.

Pericles read everything that came to his hands: books in his school, books that his teacher gave him. He tried to learn about the country his grandfather came from, his roots but also about books of world literature, works such as the Jules Verne stories, Victor Hugo and literary books from Russia and other countries. All this was good for a while but it turned out not to be enough for Pericles. He wanted to know everything possible and what he couldn't read he imagined, and his imagination was as creative as the imagination of all the famous Hellenes whose names he heard from his teacher, men such as Aristotle and Plato, Odysseus and Agamemnon, Hercules and his ten wonderful deeds, Theseus and his travels to Crete, Alexander the Great and his unsurpassable adventures. And during these moments, Pericles imagined that he was fighting against the Persians in Marathon and in Thermopylae; there were times when he could stay for hours dreaming of adventures and battles and he always knew that Hellenes were the victors in all these battles and they always received the famous laurel wreaths on their glorious heads. In this state of mood he would get up and grab the sword he had made of wood and he would go to the streets fighting and defending his motherland from invaders. Invisible or not was irrelevant to him. His imagination gave life to every hero or enemy and when he was in such a mood and by chance one of the other boys, especially the Romanian boys, would challenge him he was capable of breaking the boy's head with his sword or by throwing a stone at him.

One day on his way to school he remembered the story of Alexander the Great, the famous hero who defeated the Persians in many battles and extended the borders of Hellas almost to India where the sun rises every morning. It was said that Alexander placed two soldiers to guard the sun and they lighted it every morning during the days they wished to be sunny and other days, when they didn't feel to do so, the sun wouldn't rise, and for this reason it was said, every cloudy day people believed that the guards of the sun weren't in a good mood and they didn't let it rise up on the horizon. Suddenly and almost unconsciously Pericles would raise his eyes to see whether the sun was up that morning. This had become his habit every morning — to look and see whether the guards of the sun were in good mood and the world was sunlit and pleasant which meant that the day would be full of games and laughter.

Pericles learned at school that Alexander had a couple good friends, Hephaestos and Cleitos who were with him every hour of each day. Together they fought and laughed and sang together. They killed all their enemies and since Pericles liked that story, he decided that he would select two of his friends, just like Alexander did, two who would be with him every day. Together, along with the other Hellene boys from school, they would defeat the Romanian boys against whom they quite often fought. He thought of who to choose, but he couldn't make up his mind because Hermes, his neighbor, was a bit chubby and couldn't be a good leader because he wasn't able to jump over a fence. Pericles wanted his close buddies to be flexible and agile. On the other hand, Aristotle, the butcher's son, was too skinny and short so he didn't fit such a big role either. Even Homer, the priest's son, and Demetrius, the postman's son, weren't much better. So he decided to put them to the test: they had to fight against each other, with swords and spears like their ancestors and the best would be selected to be his close confidants, while the others would be the plain soldiers of his army.

During the first recess at school, he gathered all four of them and when Aristotle said he didn't want to follow Pericles pulled him forcefully and led them to their secret meeting place. When they reached the spot behind the fence of the school grounds he ordered them to get their swords from the shrubbery and he disclosed his plan to them. They listened and as he looked at all of them with his stern eyes, they couldn't refuse to take part in the competition. Hermes was to fight with Aristotle and Homer against Demetrius while Pericles stood up on a big rock to supervise the whole battle. But as soon as they started, Aristotle put his sword down and Demetrius did the same. Pericles got very angry with them since they didn't have the courage to fight it out and he was ready to beat them with his own hands. Then he changed his mind and called them cowards, which was an insult that made the two boys blush with embarrassment. They didn't dare say a word, afraid that he would beat them, therefore they decided to leave. Pericles hugged the two remaining strong friends and they became his close buddies and confidants. They were supposed to do anything their leader told them to do: what weapons to craft, and how to organize and beat the Romanian boys the first opportunity they had. As soon as the other two boys, the cowards, distanced themselves from their three buddies, they started calling Pericles names.

"You aren't a Hellene. You aren't a Cretan; yhua, yhua, yhua..." This made Pericles angry and he ran after them. When he caught them, he forced them to the ground, took off his belt and hit them repeatedly until they started crying. He took their belts and tied their hands behind on their backs and forced them to walk to the class-room.

When the teacher saw this spectacle he was left with a gaping mouth while the other children laughed at the sight and mocked the "cowards". Pericles regretted that he made such fools of them, but when the teacher tried to find out the reason for what he had done, he said whimsically: "They were good boys, too."

Mr. Aristides, the teacher promised not to penalize anyone, but after he asked them to take their seats he started a story about the people of their motherland who always fought amongst themselves.

"From all the Gods who lived in our home-country," the teacher began, "the greatest of all was Zeus. He was the father of Gods and he also was wise, very strong, wild and persistent."

"Teacher, teacher" Pericles interrupted.

"Yes Pericles. What is it?"

"The greatest God was Minos, the wisest and strongest of all."

The teacher must had known from where such a comment came and decided to leave things as they were.

"Yes, in Crete Minos was the greatest and wisest God. But in the whole of Hellas they believed Zeus was above all others."

"You mean outside Crete?" Pericles was ready to fight his battle, knowing that his grandfather would back him up.

"Yes, outside Crete" the teacher conceded.

But even with this compromise of the teacher, Pericles wanted to get to the bottom of this, and when he would go home he'd get his grandfather to clarify it.

"And there were," the teacher continued, "besides Minos and Zeus a lot of other Gods, men and women. Some were young, others old with gray hair. One of them was the God of the sun the other was God of the underworld, God of music, of the rain, and women who were Goddesses of the house, the Earth, of dancing and of music and a strange Goddess whose name was Goddess of Discord! This one was an evil Goddess and very well rooted in their homeland and no one had the strength to get her out of the country. While the people fought against the barbarians who attacked their country, this God-dess kept a low profile and no one saw her, but soon after the battle was over and the enemies were defeated this strange Goddess appeared as from nowhere and with evil words she would make the people fight against each other."

After the school day finished, Pericles ran to the house eager to learn from his grandfather who was the greatest and strongest God in Hellas. He had kept the words of the teacher in his mind to make sure he could relate them to his grandfather. He doubted that his grandfather was wrong and the teacher right, but he also wanted to know how could they believe that Minos wasn't the greatest and strongest God of all? It was impossible!

When he arrived home, he run to his bedroom, he threw his school bag away and went to look for his grandfather.

He saw him in the garden tending his vegetables. "Pappou, pappou!" he called.

The old man turned and seeing him, he laughed admiring the youngster.

"Here comes my pride. Here comes my brave young man. What's on your mind? Why you yell? Did someone beat you at school?"

Pericles laughed. "Beat me? Nobody dares pappou" the boy said sternly and pushed his chest forward like a boxer ready to defend his title.

The old man's eyes flashed as if a fire was burning in them, the Cretan fire the old man carried inside him and this moment upon seeing his grandson fired up and ready to take anyone he couldn't but admire the boy's reaction which satisfied him because he knew this boy wouldn't take any punches without giving it back in equal or double number. This boy was a true Cretan and he hoped that one day Pericles would go to find his family's roots and pay respect to them.

"Then what happened that made you look so upset?"

"Pappou, the teacher said that Minos wasn't the greatest and strongest God. He said it was Zeus. Is it true?"

His grandfather noticed the eyes of the boy had darkened even more that their natural color. *How could the teacher be right?*

"Come, come here and I'll tell you," His grandfather said. "I'll tell you all I know and you decide, okay?"

26

"Yes, pappou..." the boy agreed and sat on a chair next to his grandfather who was trying to figure how to talk to the young boy about these issues. Yet suddenly a story unfolded in the mind of the old man.

"Minos was the God of Crete and at the same time the king and ruler, the first ever king. He had his palace in Knossos and a special palace on top of Idi, the highest mountain. From there he could keep an eye on everything that happened on the island: its people, the animals, the crops, the sea, everything. Nothing escaped him and because he was a just God he always helped the ones who needed help and he kept company to the ones who needed company and he was the first who wrote laws in books and enforced them. He was the first who helped his people defeat their enemies and the savages and barbarians who sometimes attacked the island. He also was the first and best judge who enforced the laws and taught the inhabitants of the island the art of letters, poetry and story-telling which made our ancestors who also flourished during Minos' reign very smart and for this reason they brought to him the best of their annual crops. They sacrificed their best animals to him and in return he granted them another plentiful year. And, I forgot to mention, Minos was the best in the crafts and arts. He was a farmer and a warrior, a craftsman and a pot maker. He was specialist in wine making and dancing. He was the best seafarer and taught the Cretans to build boats which they used to travel all around the sea as far as Athens and Macedonia where the teacher Mr. Aristides comes from."

Pericles was left with his mouth gaping upon hearing all these great things about Minos the best God of Crete. His imagination was wild and he thought he could see Minos here in front of him full of glory, tall, strong, wise with gray hair like his pappou, like the Gods he saw at the church every Sunday.

Then he asked: "And Zeus? Who was he, pappou?"

Now how could he explain this to the boy? Up to now it had been easy. What could he say now?

"Zeus, yes," he said, "He had his kingdom on Olympus and he wasn't the king of Crete but king of the Gods of Olympus and there were a few, I have to say. Zeus' throne was on top of the highest mountain of Hellas and from there he governed the people. They say that he was a wild God, crazy and a he had a lot of women, not like Minos who was a family man with one wife. Zeus had a lot of wives and he had a lot of children with them. Some even say Minos was the son of Zeus, but to tell you the truth I don't believe it."

"Yes, pappou, the teacher said that to." The boy said, remembering the teacher's words.

The grandfather felt trapped like a lone old wolf surrounded by an enemy wolf pack, he felt small and incapable of answering the simple question of his grandson.

"Well if the teacher said that, perhaps he's right. But tell me, who you think was better. Zeus or Minos?"

Pericles stood and putting his hands behind his back like an orator about to unfold his speech. He stood close to his grandfather, looked deep into his eyes and, like his teacher, Mr. Aristides who always stood close when he spoke to his students, he began. "Since Minos was the son of Zeus and the father always knows more, but you said our Minos was the wisest. No one was of the same quality to him and he was a family man, not like Zeus who had many wives, therefore Minos was the best of all."

After the young Pericles ended his oration he went to sit next to his grandfather who placed his arm around the boy's shoulders as if confirming their understanding.

"Bravo Pericles, I couldn't have said it any better myself. But I'd add this: don't doubt the abilities of Minos because he was Zeus' son. They say that the son always reaches farther than the father, and if this wasn't the case the world wouldn't go ahead but backwards; I remember in my days in Crete when a child, a boy, was born the maid who delivered him would raise the boy in the air, turned him to the four corners of the world and she would wish him: 'Farther than your ancestors, you never forget that' and this was a good omen and an order. So bravo my son, bravo! I'm proud of you."

High School Years

A few years went by. Irene, the old man's wife died. They buried her at the Hellenic Community Cemetery as it was customary. When Pericles was fourteen years old and was in high school he also attended the high school classes of the Hellenic Community School still under Mr. Aristides. One day upon his return from school he asked his mother when they planned to go to Crete to meet his relatives, his cousins, his uncles and all the others. But his mother couldn't tell him anything with a degree of certainty since she didn't know for sure. However sensing the seriousness of his question she left the casserole she was attending and coming close to Pericles she showed him to sit down. Her eyes almost turned teary since she didn't really know what to tell him, his father and his grandfather would be better in this.

"I don't really know, son, but when your dad comes back from work we'll ask him, okay?"

But this wasn't enough for the young man who got up almost turning his chair to the side and before his mother could finish what else she had in mind Pericles with his eyes turned fiery red, his voice sounded between gasping and choking. His arms created strange shapes in the air while he yelled at his mother.

`"You don't know anything! You and dad and my grandfather, you always say the same thing over and over again and I just can't wait anymore. When I grow I'll leave, even if I have to go no my own. I promise I'll leave soon as I have what I need!"

His mother also stood up and opening her arms she tried to hug him, to calm him down, but Pericles wasn't one you could calm down so easily.

"Come now, come time will pass fast, and we'll leave, you'll see" she said, being taken aback by his reaction. Her son was in like his grandfather, rebellious and insubordinate, ready for a fight against an impersonal enemy, like his grandfather ready to punch someone for something one has said, a reaction soon after to be regretted. *God, who is this boy?* She thought *what kind of man has he become? Exactly the same like his grandfather...a tough rough Cretan, that's who he is.*

Pericles raised his arms in the air as if he wanted to hit something, as if he wanted to fight for his right, his voice came out almost hissing "You all call me the same 'Come now, come now, little boy'. I'm sick and tired of these same words. I've grown up and I'm not your good little boy, I'm not your little boy anymore, no I'm not."

At that exact moment his grandfather came in from his garden and seeing him in that state he quickly understood what was going on, and knew what he must do.

He said to Pericles, "What is going on? Why you are so upset? Come here, let us sit here." He showed Pericles the chairs in the veranda.

"Come, let us sit over there, relax, I'll answer what question you may have." And taking him by the shoulder they both walked to the veranda where the old man showed his grandson to sit. He also sat and after he let his eyes travel toward the excited expression of his grandson he said.

"There was a time when..." The old man started to speak when the boy stood up, his eyes still red fiery.

"No, no more stories, pappou. No more fairy tales. I don't want any more fairy tales."

The old man sat back in his chair, stretched his legs, gazed the young man. He recognized that Pericles wasn't much different than himself at that age. Time had passed and his grandson was a young man. The old man recalled all the difficult times he had put his mother and his father through when he was the same age, the mischievous pranks, the time he beat up the neighbor's son for calling him a midget because he was very short at a young age. Now he felt for his grandson who wouldn't take fairy tales anymore, his grandson who wanted to know the truth of things, the raw truth!

"Alright then, if you don't want fairy tales, so it is. But tell me what happened and why you got angry with your mother?"

"Nothing"

"If nothing happened why were you yelling?"

Pericles was silent. Then he said "I just asked mother when we would go to Crete."

"And, what did she say?"

"She said she didn't really know."

"She was right. Nobody really knows these days how easy or difficult it is to get the necessary permits to leave. "

"But why pappou? Aren't we free to go? " Pericles got up as if to show him that he was ready for such a voyage.

"No, it isn't as easy as you think, son. You have to be patient."

Seeing that he couldn't get a better answer than that the young Pericles agreed.

"Okay"

"There you are. But come, sit down, I want to tell you this story. Not fairy tales anymore. A true story, *kala**?"

Pericles relaxed as the old man reminiscent and narrated the story.

"I was newlywed. I remember when your grandmother and I went to the Chryssoskalitisa church which was at the south side of Crete and was dedicated to Virgin Mary — a monastery where a first cousin of mine was the leader of four nuns and one monk. A big group of villagers, young and old, married and single started from the night before around midnight to reach the church by the following morning before the sun would rise and bring up the heat of the day. It was a serene night with the bright moon in the sky guiding our steps up and down the mountains. I remember we sang the traditional songs as we tried to help the young men to get their minds away from the skirts of the girls. We took turns singing one after the

---

*endaxi-good

other the famous *mandinades*.* I remember that the women were riding donkeys and mules while we men walked and our voices came and went like waves on the wind carrying it all the way down to the sea where the church was located. Even the old folk with their missing teeth sang to keep up with everyone and to give all of us courage so we didn't think of the road that was ahead of us. After all it was a long and tiring walk since the path we followed would take us over a mountain, a very dangerous gorge and through three other villages until we would get to the monastery grounds the next morning."

The eyes of the young man flashed his pleasure listening to this story while his imagination took him along the grandfather's memory.

"I was always close to your grandmother who was riding our donkey. It was almost daybreak when we reached an open plateau before we made our final descent to the monastery grounds. From this vantage point the church was visible on top of a huge rock. Looking at it from this point one would get the impression that the church was afloat on the waves like a white dove rushing from side to side depending on the whims of the winds. When we got down to it we discovered a bunch of rooms, cellars, storage rooms and gardens where the nuns with the monk were growing their own products and on top of the huge rock the holy building like a lone sentinel keeping away from things human.

There were a lot of people around putting tents up and others cooking. You know how people cook when they are away from home: they put down a couple of rocks and in between them they light their fire. The casserole is put on top of the rocks and there you have a makeshift kitchen. All the festival goers had to organize themselves for the overnight stay and also provide the children and everyone else with food. Some had brought their own animals for slaughter, others would share with relatives, and others would just make do with what their friends would provide for them."

The old man stopped for a minute and keeping his eyes on his grandson he tried to figure whether the boy was paying attention to

mandinades-traditional folk songs

the story. But the young Pericles was fully into it with the eyes of his imagination seeing everything from the church to the surrounding area where all the commotion that people and animals were created

"These events have been going on for eons and people know what to expect and how to go about their day and night in such festivities." The grandfather carried on.

"Seeing the church, and the people around going and doing one could almost feel King Minos was there too, along with the other men, and he was going from cellar to cellar and from storage room to storage room counting and taking measure of all the supplies and goods the monk and the nuns had stored. Soon after we arrived we went to the church where we all lit our traditional candles. Then we went back to the spot where we would camp for the night and my father, the leader of our group, gave the orders of the day: the women were to take care of the food, the young men were responsible for the sleeping facilities and the men were to go along with him to greet some of his friends and relatives who were around the grounds. When the oldest of the group says something, there was no way anyone could debate or question his orders. My new wife, your grandmother, God bless her soul, along with the other women got involved with the task of arranging the cooking, to find wood for the fire, put together the cooking site, cut the meat we had brought from home and boil it. After the meat was boiled, they would make pilaf, a traditional dish that always went next to the boiled meat, the meat being most of the times goat meat. The rest of us followed my father and went from tent to tent greeting and drinking the moonshine, we called it *tsikoudia** in Crete, another traditional offering which would always appear as if from no-where. The people, whether known to us or not, always offered and exchanged a good word with us, the visitors, and we did the same by visiting other tents around the campgrounds."

At that moment Pericles' mother appeared at the veranda door having on hand a tray with a sweet offering, her famous, *nerantzaki,*†

---

*moonshine
†*sweet made of bitter orange peels and syrup*

made of the peel of bitter oranges, a traditional Cretan sweet usually offered in a small plate along with a cold glass of water, exactly as his mother brought them this time one for her father in law and one for her son. The young man took his plate in hand and after taking a spoonful of the sweet offering and after taking a good portion of his water he turned to his grandfather waiting for the story to continue.

His grandfather sensed the eagerness of the boy to hear the rest of the story and for this reason he quickly gulped his sweet *nerantzaki*, he had a good gulp of his water and looking deep in the eyes of the young man he continued.

"There was another tradition or custom that took place in this monastery every year, like the Saint John's church on the mountains, remember the story I told you some time ago? People would dedicate their newborns to be baptised in this monastery during the annual festivity. They would bring along with them all the family members and a big number of friends who'd party for the occasion. It wasn't unusual to have up to a dozen christenings in one single day and that of course meant a lot of extra invitations and a lot of extra drinking and partying. It took us two hours to do our round of greeting and drinking which meant that by the time we went back to our tent it was time to eat our festival meal. We were almost full of food and alcohol by then. After this quite filling meal my father thought it would be a good idea to go around the cellars to check if there was anything else there that we hadn't tasted that morning so we could grab it and take it to our tent. So we followed his half-drank steps. Every step he took the soil beneath his boots retreated by an inch or two out of respect for the weight of the man.

In one of the storage rooms we discovered my cousin, the leader of the monastery with his group of nuns, friends and the lone monk having the time of the lives and of course we couldn't go anywhere without having some of their food and wine. The day went like that and not without the traditional songs and dances as the lute and the *lyra* players had arrived and they got on top of two tables and the dancing kept on until late very late in the night. We finally went to bed, some under a tent, others exposed to the faint breeze coming from the sea and others in the cellars and storage rooms where they had put their blankets."

"How did you spend the night, pappou?" The boy asked.

"I and your *yiayia** slept under our tent, my boy," the old man said and stirred in his chair as if feeling next to him the body of his wife, back then when they were young and felt each other's touch everywhere they went. A sigh left his chest and the young man upon hearing turned and gazed his grandfather who was almost teary. However the grandfather pushed aside his melancholic mood and carried on.

"Morning came, and slowly we all got up and prepared for the liturgy. This was the way festivities such as that one took place in Crete, and it was a tradition upheld for centuries. While we were in the church a boy ran into the courtyard and yelled as loud as he could. 'Nikolas has drowned, Nikolas has drowned!' We noticed a few other boys running towards us. When we asked them where this happened one of the boys pointed down to the sea where his friend, Nikolas, and a few other boys had gone to swim. 'The water whirl took him! The water whirl!' the boy cried and I remember that I, along with other men, ran toward the edge of the parapet of the courtyard that faced the sea. I thought I saw the boy in the water. I ran down to the shore, took off my shoes and with no second thought, I jumped in the water. As I jumped, I thought I heard a voice say, 'With my blessing'. Did I hear these words or did I imagine them? I didn't know. Was it the grace of the Virgin Mary who blessed me to be successful and save the child or was it my imagination?"

He stopped his narration as if to recollect and re-hear the words to re-discover what happened that morning, but Pericles wanted to hear the rest of the story and grew impatient.

"What happened to Nikolas, pappou?"

The old man looked deep into the eyes of the young man and it was as if he was seeing himself as a youth. He smiled and carried on with his story.

"Oh, yes — to the boy Nikolas who I thought I saw in the water. It took me a few minutes to reach the area where the boy must have

---

*grandmother

been and it wasn't easy to see him while swimming but suddenly my mind told me to dive my head into under the water so perhaps I could see him better. And true enough, I saw him just a few meters away. I swam to him and grabbed his arm. I slowly brought him out to the shore where others had arrived and were waiting for me. They all helped to bring Nikolas back to life to the joy of his parents who for the rest of the day and for a long time after that wished me the best for saving Nikolas. The rest of the day passed by and we drank and ate and had a lot of fun with our family and friends and very late toward midnight we took the road to return to our home."

As the old man spoke, the boy kept looking at his grandfather and one could feel the admiration in his eyes and the joy on his face realizing that his grandfather had been a hero that day. He was proud of having such a brave man as his grandfather! Pericles was silent, although his eyes and face said so many words unspoken by his lips.

Rebellious Youth

The days went by one after the other, and became months and years. Pericles had grown into a young man and besides helping his father at their grocery store he attended his last year in high school. He also kept on learning to speak and write the Hellenic language under the guidance and constant advice of Mr. Aristides his teacher. He constantly read and he also borrowed books from the small library of the city, books that referred to Hellas, to its mythology and history, to the ancient era as well as the current days, in which books he learned of the war days and how the Hellenes stopped the Italians during the 1940 campaign. Besides these sources of information, his parents always added their own knowledge to his and especially his grandfather who had his own point of view regarding everything in life and which he made sure he transferred to the mind of the teenaged Pericles.

Often his grandfather reminded him to not forget to go to Hellas when he would become an adult. Pericles always responded that he hasn't forgotten and that one day he will accomplish it.

It was this year, Pericles' seventeen years of age, when he learned of Communism and what it meant and also what it meant to be free and do as one pleased without the interference of the government. This was something new and the concept of a free society and communism were two antithetical concepts that divided the world into two camps — the eastern camp under the influence of Russia which supported and promoted communism, and the west under the influence of the United States of America which supported and promoted a free society. For the first time in his life, Pericles also heard about dictatorship and what it meant for the citizens of the unlucky country that was ruled by such a government.

When he went home after school he raised these issues with his grandfather, trying to add something else to what he already knew. But the old man wasn't in the proper mood to start such a discussion. Pericles decided to corner his father later on, during dinner time to see whether he would add something to what he already knew. They were all sitting in their usual seats: his mother to his right, his grandfather across from him and his father to his left. Although he felt that no one was in a mood for discussion Pericles, not having any other way to start a conversation, turned and asked his father: "When we'll go back home, father?"

His father smiled but said no word.

"When dad?" Pericles insisted.

"Soon. As soon as we have the funds and secure a visa from the government."

"You mean we aren't free to go when we want?"

"Well, first of all you have to grow a little older to be able to travel without any problem then we have to have some money for the voyage. Then of course we also need the permission of the local authorities in order to travel outside the country."

"What do you mean 'get permission'? Aren't we free to go when we want?"

"Well, it all depends on how soon we can prepare our papers and get the government's approval. It takes time, you know"

"Let's start preparing the papers."

"It's not so easy. Sometimes they refuse to approve visas."

Pericles stood up. He walked around the room as if trying to find a new direction, as if wanting to get out and run away, as if he was kept inside a place he wanted to escape from. His eyebrows almost touching each other and his face turned red, his arms in constant movement, yet he had hard time finding the words he wanted to say. Then suddenly a burst of words came out of his mouth, were they his words or someone else's?

38

"They refuse the visas? You mean we aren't free to go when we want?"

His mother, seeing he was upset, extended her arm as if around his shoulders but Pericles wouldn't have any of that.

His grandfather, tried to calm him down. "Settle down! Relax, don't be so angry," his grandfather said, "It's not anybody's fault. It's the system — the law. You can't do anything about it at this time. Come now, settle down. I'll tell you when we'll go back home."

Pericles' eyes went around to his father and mother, then to his grandfather. The old man's words made him feel a little better and he settled down without saying any other word.

"Promise me that you'll never yell and get angry at your parents anymore. Promise me you'll never say anything about our plans to go back home to anyone."

Pericles lowered his head and grabbing his fork started eating his food again. He raised his eyes to meet his grandfather's and nodded his agreement.

"Yes grandfather, I promise."

"Good, after we finish our supper you go to bed. Tomorrow is another day."

"But you didn't tell me, grandfather."

"Tell you what?"

"You didn't tell me when we'll go back home."

"Soon, very soon."

Pericles face frowned again not being able to get a clear answer from his grandfather but he said nothing else. Something was telling him things weren't exactly as he thought they were… when he finished his supper he got up and went to his bed hoping that 'soon' would come sooner.

The next morning Pericles got up late. He went to the bathroom, brushed his teeth, took a shower and standing before the mirror he noticed his eyes were still red from tiredness and last night's excitement. He went to school, but he felt something wasn't right. Everything seemed wrong to him. After his regular school day and on his way to the Hellenic class he met three of the Romanian boys.

"Stupid Hellene," Pericles heard them saying.

"Romanian *malaka*,*" he answered.

The Romanian started getting close to him in a circular way enclosing on him and the boy who looked he was their leader jumped forward and tried to throw a hard fistful against Pericles who ducked and responded with a hard hit of his own against the boy's cheek; next moment the other two attacked him and although he managed to throw a few fistfuls against every one of them he also ended up with a few fist hits on his body and face where he ended up having an obvious mark that bore witness to his fist fight against the Romanian boys.

In the classroom he was still agitated and twice Mr. Aristides told him to keep focused. But his mind was still mulling over "They don't give permits" which made him even angrier than before.

During recess he went to the office of his teacher and found him sitting at his desk "Teach, I want to ask you something."

His teacher got up and walked to Pericles who was standing by the door of the office.

"What is it Pericles?"

"Is it true that the government won't give us permits to go back to Crete?"

Mr. Aristides, remembering the difference of opinion he'd had with Pericles' grandfather regarding the god Minos and because he didn't want to create another issue this time he said: "I don't understand, Pericles, what your parents told you?"

"I asked when we would go to Crete and they said that the permit takes a long time to be approved and that sometimes they don't give permits at all."

"I see."

"Is it true, sir? They don't give permits?"

"No one knows what they might do because they do these things on a case by case basis and they don't follow any rhyme or reason. They may issue the permits easily, but they may delay them too," Mr.

---

*Asshole

Aristides explained.

"But aren't we free to choose where to live?" Pericles asked.

"Well it's not a simple black or white, you see. We are free, but the authorities have a big say in the concept of freedom too. But don't worry you'll go when the time comes. You'll see." Then, noticing Pericles' bruised cheek, he asked "What happened to you? Who hit you?"

Pericles started to walk away without saying a word, but Mr. Aristides called him back. Pericles went back, with his head down and in a few words he explained to his teacher what happened to him on his way to school. After hearing the story Mr. Aristides extended his arm around Pericles' shoulders for the first time.

"I want you to promise me something" he said, "You'll never get into a fight with the Romanian boys again, okay?"

Pericles's face turned saddened as if it was his fault he had a fight with the Romanian boys, and almost like a whisper he said the words "*Kala* teacher."

"You're all almost adults now." Mr. Aristides gave him a stern look.

"You have to stop fighting."

"But if the other boys start the fight, what can I do?"

"You can always try to avoid them, because even that may be a reason why the authorities could refuse to give your parents the permission to leave. Do you understand?"

Pericles walked away from him not knowing what to say, but his teacher's comment sank in his mind and deep inside he promised himself to be extra careful and never provoke the Romanian boys to a fight.

The rest of Pericles' day went peacefully and on his way back home he made sure he avoided the Romanian boys. When he reached home his mother upon seeing his bruised cheek let a yell and began to cry. Then leaving her food preparation she took a clean cloth which she wet and tried to clean up his face applying the cold cloth on the bruise.

"What happened to you? Who did this to you?".

"I got into a fight."

"With who? Why?" his mother insisted.

41

"The Romanian boys who always pick a fight with me, you know. Since the days of the elementary school, don't you remember?"

"Yes I remember but I've told you many times to avoid those boys, when you will stop fighting them?"

"I will. I'll never fight them again. I promised my teacher too."

All this time his grandfather was watching from where he sat. A faint smile spread on his face. When Pericles took a chair and went to sit close to him, the old man said, "In the name of god, is it true that you have decided not to fight with the Romanian boys anymore?"

Pericles laughed. "Yes grandfather, but tell me why you said, 'in the name of god'?"

"It's just an expression you don't have to take it seriously."

As they sat next to each other, the old man felt his grandson eagerness to hear a new story, not a myth, but a good story from Crete.

"Come now, let me tell you about a buddy I had when I was young."

"Yes pappou, but a real a story, not a fairy tale!"

"Yes a true story. Years ago I had a good friend. His name was 'Tall Theseus' because he was the tallest man in the whole of Crete and the most non-believer man I knew. He never went to church, he never observed the Christian holidays and he never observed any of the good willed ways of most people. When he'd meet someone on his way he would say 'go to hell, *malaka*', instead of greeting him politely irrelevant of whether the person he had met was an officer of the community or a simple villager, he put everyone in the same basket. When he got married he forced his relatives to get the priest to his house to execute the sacrament since he refused to go to the church. And if someone invited him to a christening or a wedding in the church he stayed outside until the ceremony finished. His poor wife often argued with him but his mind was always made up and she had to do as he wished. I remember I asked him once 'Why don't you come inside the church Theseus?' to which he said 'I'm not for churches, I am not for these things and I don't like to listen to the priest. You, the Christians, go and observe what you like but leave me out of these things."

While this conversation was going on his mother was cooking: she was preparing potatoes with green beans in the casserole, a dish Pericles always loved and along with a few olives and a good piece of bread he was usually very happy and content. The smell of sauteed onions and garlic reached Pericles's nose and his appetite was even stronger now. His father would come home in about an hour when they would have their evening meal.

The old man stirred in his chair, fixed the scarf he had always tied over his eyebrows and crossing his black boots turned towards Pericles who was anxiously waiting to hear the rest of the story.

"Theseus and I were good buddies. We went fishing together, we hunted, we worked in the fields together and often we talked of various things. I have to say, this was a man, my good friend Theseus, different from all the other guys in the village. I remember one time we worked for the local co-op when, after the annual grape gathering, after all the grapes were turned into must which was stored in the big storage containers, we got the order to clean up all the facilities. We worked for a few days, up and down the huge cement storage tanks with brush and soap and water hoses. Theseus had as his share of the work on the tanks to the east and I the ones to the west side of the co-op. As I was busy with my share of the work, I didn't pay attention to what Theseus was doing until I noticed I couldn't see him anywhere. I was curious to see where he was and what he was doing so I stopped my work and walked over to his side. But still, I couldn't see him anywhere, until as I walked by a storage tank I heard him calling from inside one tank full of grape must. I leaned down onto the opening of the tank and saw him floating in the must. He must have fallen into it moments earlier because you couldn't survive in the must for too long. To make the long story short, I called for help and a few guys came to the rescue. We pulled him out, and just in time, because he was almost dead from the fumes of the boiling must. Afterwards, after he spent two weeks in the hospital and when I met him for the first time I joked with him 'Theseus,' I said to him, 'every single molecule of your body got drunk, from the top of your head to your toenails!' And we both laughed. This was my buddy, the tall Theseus, who after that incident was a different man. I remember

43

him, always kept him in my thoughts. He didn't react the way he used to, after the incident he was always aloof. I remember once we were sitting at the edge of the cement roof of the local café, away from the others and in secrecy he explained to me what happened to him the day he fell in the must. When he was so desperate and he thought he would die, he called upon the help of Saint Irene, to whom we have a small chapel at the edge of our village. He called the Saint to his assistance. He trusted me with this confession, but he had me swear never to say anything to anyone. When he told this to me his eyes were teary and he was afraid the other men at the café would see him cry. He felt embarrassed, but he admitted that he went through a very difficult time. He also promised the Saint that once he got out of the wine storage tank and if he survived, he would take a big candle matching his height to offer it to the chapel of Saint Irene."

The old man paused as he recalled in his mind his good buddy, tall Theseus, and their times together in the village, back when they were both equally crazy and best friends. As the people in the village would say 'One finds his match.'

Pericles couldn't restrain himself and let a loud laughter. His grandfather looked at him with a serious glance. "Why you laugh? This wasn't a laughing matter. This was the moment of tall Theseus' deliverance, the moment the giant turned into an ant, the moment of his passing through the gate of perception unlike no other ever had."

"I noticed how practical your friend was," Pericles said.

"What do you mean?"

"Well, all his life he didn't care for churches or God, but when time came and he was almost dead, he remembered them and asked for help."

"Well, it's a way of looking at it" his grandfather said.

"No, it's the reality, pappou, even if this event hadn't taken place and tall Theseus hadn't asked for help at that moment, I'm sure he would have done so with his last breath. I'm sure he would ask for forgiveness."

"Why forgiveness?"

"For being a non-believer and not a church goer as you called him. But you didn't finish the story grandfather. Did he go to Saint Irene's chapel with the candle?"

"Of course he did," exclaimed his grandfather. "But I haven't told you the funniest part of the story. This will surely make you laugh. Not only did he promise to bring a candle as high as himself to the icon of Saint Irene, but he also promised to do this naked."

From across the room where Pericles's mother was cooking she let a surprise yell leave her lips and Pericles laughed imagining a tall man naked and walking into a church full of men and women.

"Naked? Did he truly do this?"

The old man extended his hand and touched Pericles' head a gesture of tenderness he often did. His gentle touch was as if the light breeze coming from the fields caressed the boy's hair, as if the sun winked at him. Pericles sniggered.

"Don't laugh," his grandfather said. "Just think what it means to be human. As I said earlier, Theseus the tall, the man who would never go to church or observe any Christian traditions, was willing to make a laughing stock of himself…to bow down to everything, to let go of everything he stood for, and bowed his head in reverence for the first time in his life"

"Tell me the rest of the story, pappou"

"Yes, tall Theseus went…he surely went. It was a summer day. The sun was hot even in the mid- morning hour. The air was filled with the smell of flowers from the people's yards, flower pots with basil and carnations and the most fragrant flower gardenias which were abundant in Crete those days. Lots of people had gathered from all the surrounding villages and the small chapel was full with many worshipers who stood outside in the courtyard. Of course, there were a lot of donkeys which the older people rode to the chapel and these animals always talkative when you don't want them they made all kinds of noise with their calls. There were plenty of sheep and goats that people had vowed to slaughter that day creating a lot of commotion around the chapel so it was impossible for the church-goers outside in the courtyard to hear any of the liturgy. Children were running and playing, young men gazed the girls and sent signals from one to the other: a touch of the hair, a signal with the lips to the ones who were close enough to see it, winking, everything young men did when they wanted to get the girls' attention. Earlier in the day Theseus' wife had informed the priest and a few of the people of what was about to happen. The men smiled under their moustaches while the women were anxious to see the body of that giant of a man. Finally when Theseus came, he went to a side room and got undressed then walked to the chapel.

He lit his candle before the icon of Saint Irene, kneeled and crossed himself and kissed the icon as he was supposed to do. Then he kissed the hand of the priest and went out to go and get dressed. Soon after he came back and stayed inside the church for the whole liturgy. This was my good friend's deed of that day and since that day he was a different man. Every Sunday he would go to church often the first before of all of the others he would come dressed in his traditional breeches with his boots polished and his kerchief tied onto his forehead, like mine, you know, he would enter the church, light his candle and stand by his pew before any other man came."

With those words the old man finished his story. He got up, went to the fridge and filled his glass with wine, fixed his kerchief over his eyebrows and gazed at Pericles who along with his mother eyed each other in silence.

"Well?" the old man said. "Do you understand what happened to my friend?"

"Yes pappou."

"Very well."

It wasn't much later when his father came home from work. After he greeted everyone and went to clean up a little Pericles' mother put together the table and they sat to have their supper. Just before they started eating Pericles said to his father.

"I talked to Mr. Aristides about our trip to Hellas."

His father frown as if he expected something else and not as positive to come out of this conversation while his mother stopped serving the food and came to sit next to her son.

"And what your teacher said?" She asked.

"He confirmed what dad said the other day that sometimes the applications for travelling take too long and sometimes they refuge to allow people to go out of the country."

The old man put his hand on Pericles' shoulder and added.

"Then your father was right. And you have to understand that you have to be patient."

The young man turned and looked deep in his grandfather's eyes before he said.

"I know, as I also know that soon as I become of age, I'll leave and travel to the motherland on my own, even if I do this against the law." His voice sounded firm and cold, the voice of a decided man who plans to just wait patiently until the right time.

His parents didn't say a word but they exchanged glances and the concern was spread on their faces.

Leaving Romania

Five years went by since the night Pericles announced to his parents and grandfather that he wanted to leave Romania for good when the proper opportunity came. During those five years and after he graduated from high school he started working first with his father and for the last three years for a factory. But all along he had begun organizing his voyage. He gathered all necessities, back pack, compass, maps onto which he spent a lot of time drawing a route across the mountains and along the roads he thought would be his fastest way of crossing two countries and two borders until he would get to Hellas.

One night Pericles woke up disturbed by the fierce storm. The wind was blowing from every direction hitting the house with continuous gusts, shaking it to its foundations. He could feel the house fighting to stay put while the wind wished it to just fly away like a bird. Pericles couldn't remember any other night with such strong winds that the window shutters banged so noisily as if ready to dislodge from the wall and fly as far as the wind would take them. Earlier in the day it had rained a heavy, quick torrent but soon after the sun came up and now it seemed as if Aeolus had released all his winds that fought amongst themselves. And to think of even earlier in the morning, when Pericles went to his job at the factory, the sun was up and the day had looked as promising as any other day but this destructive tempest that had commenced by the evening had sent all the citizens of Craiova indoors while all doors and windows had been locked and secured.

Pericles had come back from work around five that day. Since his work place was only two kilometers away he walked to and from work daily which gave him his daily exercise. He had been working in the factory for almost three years. Although his parents thought he could find something better Pericles saw it as a temporary employment since his mind was made up that at some future day he would leave to go back to Hellas to trace his roots. He remembers a few years back he had been encouraged by his parents to apply for a visa but after months of battling with the bureaucrats he gave up. Shortly after that his grandfather died, but before he left his last breath, he asked Pericles, who was alone with him to swear that one day he'd make the trip to Crete. Soon after his grandfather's passing, and since the school teacher Mr. Aristides had retired and lived alone, his parents at Pericles' request had asked the old teacher to move in with them. They put him in the grandfather's room next to Pericles' and the old teacher not only appreciated their gesture but also kept on urging Pericles to carry on his reading and his writing as if he was an in house tutor. And besides he helped Pericles draw a plan of action for his future voyage across the Balkans in order to reach Hellas.

Today, upon his return from work, Pericles said a few words to his mother and went to his room. He lied down onto the bed, closed his eyes, and let his imagination take him where he truly wanted to be: Crete. He remembered the times his grandfather had told him story after story about anything and everything that came to mind. It was a period of his life that he would never forget. Since Pericles' very early years his grandfather had been his tutor and confidant, his teacher and his best friend. Of course Pericles had gone to school and yes of course, he listened to what his dad told him too, but what he had learned from his grandfather was meant the most to him. He remembered the time he had organized a gang with his school chums to fight against the Romanian boys. He smiled at the thought. A few days ago he met with Demetrius, his good school buddy and discovered he was a member of the ruling communist party. He also worked in a factory that made farm equipment, primarily tractors. What surprised Pericles the most was his friend's comments, that he was a married man, he had a woman any time he wanted, and he had a steady job for life. He had said he felt very well looked after. Pericles couldn't believe his ears as Demetrius kept bragging about the Communist Party, what they were doing, and how they were arresting people anytime they had some word against them from someone else. How they would quickly go and arrest the suspect and put him in jail and how they would torture him to get whatever info they were after. Demetrius had told him endless stories and scenarios in the maze of politics, about organizing, espionage, garbage upon garbage that made Pericles' mind spin.

"Poor Demetrius, where you have ended"

His thoughts were interrupted by the appearance of Mr. Aristides by his door.

"Do you want something to eat?"

"No, later on, when dad comes home."

"Alright" Mr. Aristides said, and disappeared as quickly as he had appeared.

Pericles remained in bed and he was dreaming of Crete. He had decided to make the trip and now that he was almost twenty three he believed he was ready to set off on his own, just as a young chick taking its first flight out of the nest. Yes, he was ready. His mind was set, his decision was taken and his goal was to reach the sunbathed island that floated over the serene and calm waters of the south Aegean Sea. He recalled his grandfather's words about freedom and struggle and fighting and beautiful women and he knew that couldn't put up with his factory job any longer. Sometimes he had felt almost happy, as if he had already reached the Cretan beaches, and other times his sky was black and covered by leaden clouds and the tempest in his heart and mind created havoc.

It was during these times, when he thought of the central committee of the ruling party and the provisional authorities and their informers, like Demetrius, he realized that he couldn't trust his friend anymore. In those moments he tried to imagine the warmth of Crete and Minos and his palace, images that gave him a reason to smile.

His thoughts drifted to the kitchen where he knew that his

mother waited for his dad to come home while she prepared their evening meal, and to his teacher in the next room. Mr. Aristides had lived in this country for almost fifty years, alone, retired, never married. He never went back home. The only joy left to him was his life here with Pericles' family. Who else could he associate with? Who else could he become friends with at his age? His only joy were his talks with Pericles, talks which graced both of them with a relief and sweet emotion as if soothing a never- healing wound of life in a foreign land. The pain of every émigré, looked down by the locals, the subject of ridicule for the way they spoke the local tongue. This was the pain one feels away from the patriot lands and all this in exchange for some money they might make and some financial reward they somehow might manage to achieve. Pericles knew that these talks gave Mr. Aristides the strength to carry on and for Pericles, the patience until the time of his voyage.

As he was laid in bed quite unintentionally his eyes searched the ceiling and focused on a specific spot. Perhaps it was meant for him to look at that spot at this particular second, something he anticipated, a premonition, an inexplicable feeling of expectation. Yet nothing materialized and he heard the teacher in the other room stoking the fireplace with wood as it was still very cold even toward the end of this month of April. Pericles eyes could almost see the face of the retired teacher gleaming from the heat coming from the fireplace. After he finished the stoking of the wood he sat at the table and while Pericles' mother kept busy cutting their salad the old teacher's mind flew back.

"Oh, God!" he thought, *"Why old age has come so fast? I still remember my years as a child in the village where I played football with my friends. We played football barefoot and many a time when I would miss the ball and kicked some stone with my bare toes, man how painful that was…but it never stopped me from keep on playing"* he smiled at the thought. He recalled the year he finished the Academy and was ready to start teaching. He had a girlfriend back then, one of his colleagues, Amalthea. They had graduated together. She was deeply in love with him, the skinny Aristides, the best student in his class, the one who read the document of the graduation oath before

the dean of studies wearing his checkered jacket, the most handsome student in class. He was the first one to wear a checkered jacket in Athens and she was so much in love with him; once he had read every word of the document, the dean shook his hand, and she fell in his arms. Right there before all the students, the dean and other members of the faculty she kissed him, a deep erotic kiss that made him blush. He loved her very much too and they talked of being together for life, although fate had its own volition. The position in the Hellenic Community of Craiova appeared and Aristides, the forever romantic and idealist, decided it in a heartbeat to accept. They planned that a year later Amalthea would follow him and they would get married and live together. But Amalthea couldn't wait for him. When he contacted her he received the bitter word: she was pregnant, ready to marry another man twenty years older than her. Aristides cried, alone, for a long time and for the long time since then he would cry every time his thoughts made him remember Amalthea, he cried again and again in loneliness. He never got over it and he lost his trust in women. From then on he stayed alone. All his energy was focused on his carrier: to teach children, born to Hellene parents in a foreign land, what it meant to be a Hellene. He had tried his best to place deep in their hearts and minds that important foundation and cornerstone: the word 'homeland' not only as a concept but as a living entity, an essence that would guide them for the rest of their lives. That was his duty and he never strayed from it.

As the years went by Aristides' back turned arthritic and stooped. His eyes couldn't see clearly and his body ached with the simplest movements. He was tired most of the time, however he didn't regret anything. He considered everything he lived as examples and results of his decisions. This was his destiny and it unfolded everyday as he opened his eyes to face the world and other times he felt like a soldier on the front line, holding onto his space, a soldier taking care of what was allotted to him. He knew that soldiers never give up, soldiers stand tall and take what their fate brings. His war was against the hidden enemy of brutality, uneducated men, and the central committee of the communist party, traitors, informers, and all other negative elements in today's society.

He was glad Pericles wanted to make the trip of his life to go to Crete and trace his roots, Aristides was proud of the young man. He wished he could have done the same, back when he was young. But it wasn't meant to be and now... Now he got up slowly, his movements that of a tired body, he added a couple more pieces of wood in the fireplace and walked to Pericles' room where he found Pericles still in his bed staring at the ceiling.

"How are you, Pericles?"

"I'm fine...I'm just thinking, making plans, remembering things"

"What plans, Pericles?"

Pericles didn't answer but he got up and put his arm over his old teacher's shoulders, turned him around and walked with him back to the sitting area by the kitchen where Pericles' mother was preparing their food although her ears were tuned to every word spoken between her son and his old teacher. They sat at the table next to each other close to the fireplace. Pericles brought the map out of his bookcase and spread it out on the table.

"You don't know my plan, you of all people? I only have one plan: to get to Crete, have you forgotten?"

"Yes, yes, I know. I haven't forgotten and you know it," Mr. Aristides said.

Pericles pointed with his finger the route he had drawn up to the Bulgarian border, a route that would lead him across the Danube River in the vicinity of the last town of Bechet before the border with Bulgaria just across the big River. Although he didn't have a clue of how he'd manage to cross the big river, he was optimistic that he'd find the way once he got there. Pericles finger kept along the route he had on his map, the route along Bulgaria which looked simple. He mentioned he could follow the main road that goes southwards until he would get to the River Struma: that would be his landmark the big river that runs into Hellas and it would be his best place to cross over the final borders.

His mother was listening silently and tears were flowing down her cheeks. Her face showed her concern and worry about her son's decision. She didn't like it from the beginning but she knew how much he wanted to do this and she wouldn't try to stop him. She didn't want to make him feel worse than he already felt by leaving them behind. He promised them, one day when he would reach his roots, he would make the proper papers so they could return to their homeland. A faint smile was spread over her face at the thought of someday going to Hellas and she wished that with all her heart. A sigh left her chest, a sigh so strong her son heard it from the other side of the room.

"Don't forget to avoid the populated areas. Go through the odd town or village or city only when you need. You never know. Sometimes people get suspicious and react in a strange way. The River Struma will be your guide once you come across it" Pericles' old teacher said.

"Don't worry I'll find it. It won't be so hard. And soon after I cross over the Balkan Mountains I'll get directions to find the Struma River."

Aristides sighed the same way Pericles' mother had a few moments earlier. Then he got up to help her do the last preparations for dinner because when Pericles' father would come home from work they liked to enjoy their supper — four people together sharing their food but not their thoughts, sharing their space but not their plans; four people with a lot of common thoughts and ideas yet governed by the all-powerful silence that spread around them.

Two weeks went by. It was beginning May when Pericles decided that was the night he would commence his quest. Aristides organized Pericles' backpack with some food: cans of corn beef, nuts, raisins, fresh fruit, the compass, the map, the Cretan knife with the black handle his grandfather had given to him, a few tee — shirts, underwear, matches, and whatever Aristides thought would be useful for his trek. He finally tied at the bottom of the backpack Pericles' sleeping bag. Pericles was cautious about the weight of the sack; which he would have to carry over mountains and valleys, through towns and villages, along forests and across rivers on his long, arduous journey.

At this time Pericles was in his room and his mind wandered to thoughts of the old man and the night they had spent alone, that night before his grandfather passed. He recalled how his grandfather had requested to be left alone with his grandson and Pericles remembered the old man, who was very weak and had asked him to come closer. Pericles had noticed that despite the condition of his health his grandfather's eyes were full of fire. He went closer and took the old man's hand. His grandfather had showed him where to find his Cretan knife, the one with the black handle, and when Pericles brought it to him his grandfather took it and placed in his grandson's hand.

"You promise. Promise me you will make this trip one day. Promise me!" he said. "My blessing will guide you, and the unspent blood of our ancestors will never rest until you reach our roots. Promise me!"

Pericles nodded his agreement and the old man's soul was ready to be released.

"You go look for my nephew Aristarchus, your uncle. He'll be your guide in Crete, *entaxi?*" His grandfather had said and Pericles nodded again in agreement. The old man died with those last words and with his hand in his grandson's. When Pericles' father and mother came into the room and discovered that the old man was gone, no word was ever spoken between Pericles and his parents as to what transpired those last minutes of his grandfather's life. It was a secret that Pericles kept to himself.

Pericles roused from his reveries and noticed that it was getting late. He went to the kitchen where his parents were sitting. Silence reigned over everything. Words were impossible and emotions raw. The moments seemed to drip silvery tears of agony. No one spoke, no one sang, there was no embracing, just total isolation of four souls ready to become three. Their youngest would go to the south where a lonely island lay on the waves of the bark blue sea. He was leaving them to go and search for his identity.

Aristides brought him the backpack.

"Come, let's put it on your shoulders, feel how heavy it is. Perhaps we should lighten it up a little."

Pericles grabbed the backpack and put it on. It wasn't as heavy as he thought it might be. He didn't bother opening it to see what was in there because he knew Aristides had taken care when he packed it.

Aristides took off his glasses and after he blew on each lens he wiped thoroughly with his kerchief. Seeing Pericles observing every move he made, he smiled and grasping at the young man's hand he squeezed it as if this was the last farewell, his way of saying goodbye.

"Let us not despair. This is not the end of a life rather it is the beginning of a new one," Aristides said. "And yes, I admire you, Pericles, I do. I wish I were in your shoes. However everything has its time and chance. For me the end will come here in this foreign land. You, on the other hand" he said, and he turned to Pericles' parents, "You have a chance to go and meet him in the homeland someday. So don't despair. Let us feel optimistic and as happy as one can be."

They all laughed. A laugh that turned the atmosphere lighter than before until time came to say the last goodbye.

Around two after midnight, while the city was completely in the arms of slumber Pericles and his parents along with his old teacher were still sitting at the kitchen table. During those tedious hours from their supper until now time went by slowly and sometimes his father coughed and his mother wiped a tear off her eyes or Aristides blew his nose, but time went by and Pericles got up to start his quest. Time had passed as it always did, and when the fire was out and the sighs became a lot to bear, when his parents' eyes started to fill with tears, Pericles got up, put on the backpack and hugged Mr. Aristides. His old teacher held him tight for a long time. There were no more words to say. His father held him as well but he knew his son was about to do what he has dreamt all his life and his father had accepted it.

His mother held him tight and didn't want to let him go. Pericles let her enjoy her long hug then he pulled away. "I expect to see you in a year or so." He said, "I'll contact you, first opportunity, I promise. Don't worry. I know what I'm doing."

Pericles walked out into the night which was as cold as he felt at leaving his family behind. The wind was blowing as if it wanted to lift him up and bring him to his beloved Crete the fastest possible way. He cautiously made his way through the narrow streets of Craiova. It took him a good hour and a half to criss-cross the city from the north west side where their house was to the south east side where the national road to the south was. He avoided all major streets and tried to stay away from the light flooded areas. When he passed his friend Demetrius' house he thought of his old buddy. What would he think when he found out Pericles had gone and was on his way to Hellas? Strange thought that was but he kept on going. The night resembled a thick black shroud covering the city and the stars were nowhere to be seen. He passed by the big Nicolae Romanescu Park where the trees stood as lonely as him walking carefully by them. All people were in their houses and mostly asleep this time in the night and Pericles managed to get out of the city and upon reaching its outskirts he wished he would distance himself from it without any unexpected entanglements. Just before four in the morning he noticed the sign Dobresti and he knew he was on the proper national road. His mind ran to the beautiful island that lay over the smooth waves of the Aegean Sea, and with that image guiding his steps he distanced himself from Craiova.

The night went by with Pericles being careful every time during the night he came across a vehicle he made sure not to be visible, people feel strange seeing someone walking alone in the night. However he followed the road to the south and enjoyed the first light of the day that appeared from his left side as he kept on walking all morning without any stop. He passed different locales and different images: a lonely road with hardly any vehicles except sometimes a farm vehicle hauling things from the fields to the house of the owner. His first day of travel went by and soon evening came as the shadows grew longer and the sun declared it was time to rest from the day's struggle. Pericles had been walking since two in the morning and he felt exhausted. A bunch of houses appeared right in front of him as if perched on the edge of nowhere and from the time he had walked he estimated he was in the vicinity of Dobresti. Before he got close to the town he took off the road and climbed about one hundred meters up a small hill away from the road and his glance spread over the horizon below him: the green cultivated land separated in parcels each belonging to a different owner, lots of trees on the edges of the properties and farm houses with hedging trees and shrubbery around them. He located an open area where he decided to take a rest. He stood awhile and observed downwards to the flat land the odd person walking along the country pathways. His eyes caught a man on a tractor hauling a flat-bed filled to the top with four layers of bales of hay. *Animal feed*, Pericles thought.

After resting awhile by the trunk of a huge oak tree, he opened his bag and took out a slice of cheese and a piece of bread. His mind ran to his family, this is his mother's bread he was about to eat. His eyes got teary as his mind brought to him memories of sweet family images. He smiled and started chewing with good appetite. After he had his meal he got up and walked along the road for another two hours. Then feeling tired he decided to locate an appropriate place where he would spend his night. Walking around the forested area he discovered a small creek where he filled his canister with fresh water. First time he will use natural and he remembered his old teacher's words, "be careful with water; although it's healthier to drink natural water, be careful what you use, sometimes bacteria may create adverse reaction in your stomach. Be extra careful." He had a couple good gulps of water and then he looked around until he located two fallen trees. The space between them was the most suitable place to be his bed for the night. He arranged the shrubbery and cut a few dry branches with his Cretan knife to make a natural mattress, placing his sleeping bag on top. He sat down, felt the makeshift bed, felt good about it. It wasn't bad but since it was cool evening, he wondered if it would be better to sleep a little higher up on the hill, away from the moistness of the creek but since he was so tired he lied down and tried to sleep. Yet the creaking of the trees swaying against the light breeze kept him alert and unable to fall asleep. This was his first night in the nature and his mind wasn't totally relaxed. Yet his tiredness was stronger and soon sleep took control of his eyes but not for too long. He woke up his body stiff and aching. He pondered what to do. Then he stood up, gathered a few more of the branches that had fallen from the trees and made a bonfire. Soon the heat warmed him and he felt better. He kept adding pieces of wood to the fire creating a good reserve of burning coals. With that positive image before his eyes his mind relaxed and he lied down again and managed to fall asleep.

He dreamed he was in Crete lying on a hot sandy beach where the heat of the sun and sand burned his body and the dark blue sea reflected the brightness of the day. He imagined the whisper of the motionless sea being in rhythm with his heartbeats, soothing his emotional rollercoaster of feeling happy and at the same time unhappy. Yet he was in his Crete, the place of his dream and the sounds of the sea echoed like heartbeats. Suddenly he felt melancholy and great loneliness and his heart tightened. His thought grew dark, like clouds travelling across the sky covering the whole area like a dark dome above him, an angry dome hanging low and heavy over his chest, forcing him down; a heavy dome that almost touched him. His dream came back as he was laid on the Cretan beach he saw the figure of a man walking toward him. Pericles felt glued to the ground unable to move. The man approached, step by step, nearer to him and as the person came close enough Pericles could see his attire, traditional Cretan outfit with black breeches and black shirt with a heavy dark blue coat like the angry sea coat over the upper part of his body and a shepherd's stick over his shoulders. He wore black Cretan boots exactly as his grandfather had when they had laid him in the casket, and most definitely that headscarf over his head with the fringes falling on the bright forehead from which all the thunder and lightning of the sky emanated.

The apparition was close to Pericles now and he could see his black eyes with a bright flame lit in them, as if he was ready to conflagrate the whole island. Pericles' heart felt peaceful when he realized that this man was his grandfather and he was smiling at him to which Pericles smiled back and extended his arm is if to embrace him. The old man in his dream put his finger over his lips showing to him to remain silent but with his arm he called Pericles to follow him toward the rocky side of the shore. Then suddenly the roof of the world opened and a torrential rain began to fall on them and thunderbolts roared as if they sprang out from the subterranean depths of the earth: thunderbolts that seemed like flaming tongues striking the face

of the earth from unreachable heights. Pericles followed his grandfather who jumped from rock to rock toward the edge of the precip-
itous peninsula where they were headed. Suddenly the old man
stopped before a gigantic rock. It was impossible to climb over it as
on both of its sides the thunderous sea roared ready to gulp everything with its waves. Pericles wondered where they were and the
man in his dream, as if he understood, put his finger over his lips
telling him to remain silent. Then, with a movement of his arm, a
huge hole opened on the side of the gigantic rock. His grandfather
waved to Pericles to come close and look. And in the cavern he saw
bodies, innumerable bodies laid there, corpses decaying as if in their
graves, skeletons, half decayed bodies, bodies of people of every color
and creed withered in there like flowers in the fields come winter
time. Some almost alive wandering as if they were zombies: an unearthly sight. Pericles shivered in fear at the horrible sight of the bodies and he bit his lips as the old man shook his head as if to say: 'This
is the fate of man. Who dares change it?' Suddenly the apparition of
his grandfather laughed a sardonic laugh which shook Pericles' heart,
a laugh that made the sea even angrier than before and the sky even
darker and at that moment the old man jumped into the hole and
vanished. Just as suddenly, a huge wave came over Pericles and took
him to the depths of the sea, and then he woke up.

His eyes searched the area around him trying to discern if there
was someone, something around him, but nothing was there except
the trees with their peaceful quietness and their quiet sighs. Pericles
brought his hand to his forehead and felt his sweat. He noticed the
fire had gone out. It was almost daybreak. He slipped out of his sleeping bag, stood up and gazed the surroundings. Light was coming
through the tree leaves and the sounds of the forest were subdued almost muffled he could say, nothing disturbing except of his horrible
dream which upon recalling it gave him goosebumps. He walked
about, gathered a few leaves and small branches which he broke into
little pieces, and he tried to start the fire again. He added a few bigger
pieces of wood, and soon he felt warm and cozy. He sat beside the
fire, his head resting on his arms and his mind drifted back to the
dream…the strange images, strange emotions, his grandfather, the

hole, the fiery below. His grandfather was like everyone else, then. He died and decayed like all others: food for the earth. "No, it can't be", he thought, "my grandfather wasn't the same as everyone else."

"Impossible" he uttered out loud. But no one answered him, not even the little indifferent creek that kept on running. No words were spoken, no emotions shown, no sweat or tears flowing, just water running silently toward the big river, the one that would end up in the sea.

Time passed, and when the last flame was out Pericles got up as it was time to start his journey. Before starting he consulted his map and he realized he was in the vicinity of Dobresti which he confirmed a little later when on the road he passed the sign pointing towards the houses he had left behind him: the houses that looked as perched at the edge of nowhere which was Dobresti. His next town should be Sadova and then the last big town Bechet just a couple of kilometers before the big river Danube, which he had to find a way to cross, the big river separating Romania and Bulgaria. He grabbed a piece of bread and a piece of cheese and after he ate his breakfast he commenced this day. Hardly any vehicles were passing, allowing him the comfort of isolation, away from any unexpected entanglements, and with a light tune in his lips he looked before him the winding road and carried on walking.

His way took him along fertile cultivated land with fields of grains almost a meter high, next month of June would be the harvest and plenty of mustard fields with their yellow flowers like yellow carpets covering the earth. He came across a man on his tractor going south who stopped and asked whether Pericles needed a ride. The young man smiled and accepting the man's offer he climbed on the side of the driver and rode for 4 kilometers. He thanked the man who smiled without saying a single word as he drove his tractor into his field and Pericles carried on with his voyage southwards. He felt good with his interaction with the villager and he also felt better realizing his stomach didn't give him any problem since he started drinking natural water.

He passed some remote areas with hardly anybody going about which he also enjoyed smelling the fragrances of thyme and oregano and plenty of cypresses on both sides of the highway. Later that evening he decided to look around to find a proper spot to shelter for the night. He left the road and again climbed a hundred meters to the right of the road and his eyes searched the area for the appropriate spot. On the other side of the road to the flat lands he noticed a farm house and he thought it would be a good idea to spend a night on a bed, however at that thought the sky above him turned ugly. Dark stormy clouds were travelling fast from south to north and the wind had perked up forcing him to keep sheltered under the trees. Big raindrops splattered the ground around him and a torrential rain started. He sheltered himself under the thick trees and gave time to the weather system to pass by him.

Time lapsed and finally the rain stopped. He felt cold and his clothes were soaked and splattered with mud. The sky had turned blue and sunny as if it hadn't rained at all when Pericles walked out of the forest and directed himself toward the farm house.

From afar the main building and the barn didn't look much different than the ones back home in Craiova. The house was situated at the northern side of the land, having the north wind on its back. It was shaped almost the same as his house back home. There was also a smaller dwelling beside it. The walls were built of rock and clay. There was one door and one window to the right of the door. The roof was made of wood and covered with a layer of mud that kept the water from dripping inside. The only thing protruding on top of the roof was the chimney declaring when the inhabitants had their fire on. Between the two houses one could see a bunch of small trees and a big bushy osier which dominated the rest of the land around the two buildings. Farther away from the two, and to the back of the area, was the barn: a wooden building with red colored sheet metal roof, two exhaust pipes and a big door almost ready to fall off its hinges. Next to the barn, and of the same height, was a circular structure, a storage bin made of brick also with a red colored sheet metal roof.

Before Pericles reached the farm house he saw a hawk take flight from the roof of the barn. It made a few circles around Pericles then flew away toward the forest.

"A very good omen", Pericles thought. He was near the front door of the farm house when a dog started barking to let know the inhabitants someone was near. Pericles decided it was better if he yelled.

"Hello, anybody there?"

"Hello, stranger," the voice of a man answered.

"I don't mean any harm, I'm passing through," he called out.

An old man opened the door. He stood staring at Pericles while he held the leash of the dog in his other hand. The dog kept growling despite the urging of his owner to stop. The man examined Pericles' face and feeling satisfied he asked him to come inside. As Pericles stepped in the man closed the door and taking a lamp from the wall where it was hanging he placed it on a table. It flooded the room with light and Pericles noticed an old woman sitting by the stove.

Besides the stove and the table there were a dozen kitchen pots, saucepans and other things hanging from nails on the wall. There was a double bed on the left side of the room in front of which the dog sat and surprisingly enough he kept quiet. The smell of cooked food flooded the area. The lamp gave light to the small room which served as a kitchen, living room and bedroom, obviously enough space for the two old inhabitants. The man walked toward the stove and said to the woman: "Come now, come now, we have a visitor," then turning to Pericles he looked at him with questionable eyes.

"I'm Pericles," he said to both of them, "I'm travelling south."

The woman stirred and turned her face toward Pericles.

"Welcome, my boy, welcome," she said and showed him a chair close to the stove.

Pericles sat still looking around the room. The man added another piece of wood into the fire then sat next to Pericles. His wife got up and busied herself putting food on the table: bread, olives, cheese, a piece of dry meat, smoked pork, three wine glasses and a small flask with water. Pericles took a little pork and chewed it while the old couple was staring at him with a wide smile spread on their wrinkled faces.

All three drank some wine and they cheered to good health. They laughed as the food and the heat from the stove and the wine made everyone feel relaxed.

Pericles asked how they managed with their farm and things of the house alone in this wilderness and how they got around doing things at their age. They both answered with laughter and the man of the house said:

"We do what we can and we don't do what we can't."

"You have no children?" Pericles asked them.

They exchanged glances and remained silent. Pericles realized his question had struck the wrong chord and apologized.

The man interrupted him. "Yes we had two sons. The older of the two Demetrius fell in love with a pretty young woman from a very rich family. But we are poor people, son. Her parents simply said 'no'. We understood. My Demetrius and the girl, Persephone, didn't. They hatched it up and they left together and found a small place to live in the city, not far from here. Her parents and her brother didn't take it well. One night her brother and a couple of his friends went to the city, and took his sister back after they killed our sons, Demetrius and our younger son Odysseus." The face of the old man turned saddened as he narrated his story but Pericles felt curious and asked.

"What did the police do?"

"The police…ha ha ha ha…the police are only good for the parties, the food and the wine… ha ha ha ha…the police." His face got lit by the laughter of pain, the sad laughter of irony.

Pericles felt as if the ceiling of the house was sitting heavy onto his chest. He didn't know what to say to the old man who had the weight of the whole universe on his shoulders. As if he felt the pain in the heart of the young visitor, the old man poured some more wine in all three glasses and they cheered to their good health. Then the old man got up and added more wood into the fire while the woman made a bed for Pericles on the floor at the end of the room.

"You can go and rest anytime you like." The old man said, "You probably will start early tomorrow, eh?"

"Yes, I would like to do that" Pericles said and got up. As he walked to the other side of the room the old woman had finished her preparations and seeing him getting ready to go to bed she smiled and went back to her chair by the fireplace.

Early in the morning after Pericles had his share of the food which they offered him, he thanked them and started his journey southward.

Crossing the Border

His next day on the road was almost as nice as the one before. He walked steady for three hours from seven thirty in the morning to ten thirty when he decided to stop and rest. Got off the road and after he climbed twenty meters up the bank he sat on a rock and gazed the vicinity down below. He enjoyed the view of the green country-side along the winding road passing between two small hills to the left and right with a light forest of conifers on both sides. Lots of cypresses and pines where the buzz of bees was heard in every direction and the aroma of thyme visited his nostrils making him smile at the peace and beauty of nature. He took his canister and drank some water, noticed he needed to refill it first opportunity. He ate a few bites of lunch and his mind travelled back to his base. His father must be at the grocery store now, probably weighing an item for a customer with his mind not on the scale but on his son travelling in foreign lands. His mother probably was preparing their noon meal with her mind not on her preparations but on her son travelling on foreign lands and on what danger he might be. His old teacher was probably alone in his room reading a book with his mind not in the plot but on his student travelling on foreign lands and living his dream. A tear slowly filled Pericles' eyes and with no restriction slowly rolled down his cheek.

An hour later he got up and carried on with his quest. His walk was easier as he came across a few cars and farm vehicles; most people waived to him and he responded exactly the same way as he kept walking, a tune in his tongue reminding him to be focused and have his mind on his task. He passed the town of Sadova exactly the same way he did with Dobresti: he took off the road about a kilometer before the town, he climbed a couple of hundred meters on the right bank of the road and watching the town and the road below him he went down to the national road only after he had passed the town and he was about two kilometers to the south of it.

Without any unforeseen incident he finished his day half way between Sadova and Bechet, the last major town before the border with Bulgaria. He took off the road again and found his proper spot where he made his rough bed and placing his sleeping bag on it he spent his night. The next morning he woke up from the chirps of the myriad birds flying around and doing what birds do best: sing and laugh and play and sing again. This morning he came across a little creek and he replenish the water in his canister. The images of today weren't much different from yesterday and he managed to spend his day covering the approximate 30 kilometers he had put as the minimum distance he had in his mind. Early in the afternoon he arrived in Bechet, the town only two kilometers from the Danube River. He walked to the center of the town and stopped at the first café he found. He ordered a souvlaki which he discovered they had in the menu, a glass of beer, and he enjoyed his late lunch. The rest of the patrons looked at him but in general they were indifferent to his presence. When the server took his money Pericles asked him in a very low tone how one goes to the other side of the river.

"There is a boat service" the man said and pointed with his hand the direction.

Pericles gave him a good tip and added.

"Wish to travel on my own." He winked to the man who responded with a smile and getting closer to Pericles ha added, "I know someone who has a boat"

Pericles added a little more money to the tip and the man promised to find the boat man for him. Pericles followed him as the cafe man went behind the counter and dialed the phone. He spoke in a low tone voice and when he finished he winked at Pericles who smiled and gestured his approval. Ten minutes later an old man walked in the café and after he talked to the café man he came and sat at the table Pericles was sitting. They shook hands. It was agreed.

"Tonight" the man said. "But for now let's go. I want to show you where we start and where we cross the river." Pericles got up and followed the man who walked to the south towards the river. They followed a narrow path along the fields and sometimes they were invisible due to the height of the vegetation and other times they could see quite some distance around them. Birds and bees flew around them, sounds of nature and smells of wild flowers, multitude of colors anywhere Pericles' eyes could turn. Half an hour later they were almost at the river when the path turned westward and they walked along the river for a kilometer when the man stopped. He led Pericles to a spot where he had his boat, a four meters craft with a small motor. He pointed his gray colored boat and said.

"This will do it. Ten minutes to go across with the motor or three quarters of an hour with the oars. You owe me one thousand leu."

Pericles asked him if he could give him some Bulgarian money and after they calculated the difference Pericles gave him two thousand leu and got back from the boatman almost five hundred of liev, the Bulgarian currency. They sealed the deal with a handshake and agreed that depending on the weather and the conditions of the night they should start around midnight.

They went back to town and spent their evening and night together at the house of the boat man who led him again on foot to the boat and they started under the moonlight of the night. Since the sky was decorated with stars and the night was quite lit the boat man preferred to use his oars just to make sure they didn't make any sound to be heard by the people in Oryahovo, the town on the Bulgarian side.

The oars touched the water of the great river like a soft hand. The strokes of the oarsman were steady, as if he was making love to a tender virgin. Pericles wished the voyage would soon end so that he could reach the opposite shore without any entanglements with the border people.

A little later shrubbery and trees of the shore drew nearer and the boatman slowed down his oar strokes and extended his arm to show Pericles where to jump out of the boat. It was only a few more minutes before he would be on foreign soil for the first time. Instinctively his hand clasped the edge of the boat tightly as if he didn't want to let it go, then he heard the sound of the keel touching a sandbar and the oarsman stopped rowing. He showed Pericles where to step into the waters and walk the last few meters to the trees. Pericles thanked the man and put his leg over the edge of the boat. The water reached half way to his knees. In early May the waters of the great Danube were icy cold. Yet this cold, which he felt all the way to his heart, didn't deter him.

He walked slowly and as noiselessly as he could toward the bushes while the oarsman started his way back to the Romanian side of the great Danube. With his bag on his shoulder he started walking through the thick bushes and trees and within minutes he was far from the river.

He must have walked for almost an hour when he decided to sit down and rest. It was still dark although the moonlight flooded the area yet Pericles felt a bright sun shining in his heart as he had passed his first test, one of the two borders he had to cross. After catching his breath he started walking again in a southern direction leaving the Danube behind him and passing field after field his mind ran to the fact that soon when the first light would appear he would be able to find his bearings easier under the sunlight. He knew the road was to his left and perhaps only a kilometer or two. He stretched his legs. The wet lower part of his pants bothered him but he had to keep them on knowing it would dry up soon.

An hour or so later and as he was well away from the river he stopped and took a piece of bread and a bunch of olives from his bag and sat down to under the trees to rest. He was in Bulgaria now, which he estimated would take him two weeks to cross if he kept up with his goal of about thirty kilometers per day. The only big obstacle in front of him was the Balkan Mountains which he guessed would take him three days to go over. And of course the capital city, Sophia, which he wanted to avoid. He had decided to circumvent the big cities just to make sure he wouldn't come under the scrutiny of the police. His ability to speak a bit of Bulgarian was an asset, although he didn't want to put himself to any test by being around people for a long time. He kept thinking of his beloved Crete, especially the hot sandy shores and the image made him feel optimistic.

After eating his humble breakfast, he got up and seeing the reflection of the river water in the glare of the dawn he calculated which direction to take. He started to walk into the forest. The forest floor was green because spring was in full bloom a thought that made him feel feel good. Even his wet pants didn't bother him anymore. He walked among the trees until he was face to face with an upright rock formation, like a wall. He was forced to stop and felt the rock wall with his palm. It was cold and moist, covered by moss but full of sharp edges. Ferns grew on every side of the rocks. He sat down to rest and decided to wait until the daylight became stronger.

His mind ran top his parents who would be still in bed. Would they be asleep or awake worrying for him, concerned where he would be at this time and night? He got up again and looked around; it seemed he could easily make his way around the rocks so he carried on walking in the direction he knew it would take him out of the forest.

A Cretan song came to his mind and he hummed it to himself as he trudged with steady footing over the various forest obstacles, shrubs and small rocks and fallen tree trunks. At one time he noticed he was walking on a narrow path, a path made by people and he wondered where it might lead to.

He kept on going with his mind filled with images of sunny seashores until he heard the slow trickle of water. Ahead of him was a babbling creek the water fresh and talkative, a rushing little creek a couple of meters wide. It was too wide for him to jump over so he had to walk through it unless he could find another way. He made his way toward a tree fallen over the creek like a bridge onto which he walked and crossed the talkative creek. By that time the sun shone over the lands and turning to an eastern direction he decided to find the main road which he would follow southwards. It took him a good half an hour until he reached it. He turned to his right and having the sun on his left he knew he was heading to the right direction.

Nothing unusual happened and one hour later on his way he read the big sign Vratsa 51 kilometers. This was his way, the right way. An euphoric emotion overtook him and without any effort a song materialized which without any formality became vocal. It was his company for a while, then another one and another as his day took the positive shape he wanted it to take. And the moments became hours and the fourth day of his quest neared its end when early in the evening he found a dark opening of a cave and he decided to spend the night there.

The sky had darkened, inviting thoughts of rest and sleep. His body ached from the soles of his feet to the top of his head and he went inside the cave where he laid a few dry shrubs onto the floor which he had gathered from outside. He made a pillow of his back-sack, spread his sleeping bag and lay down.

Through the opening of the cave he could see the moonlit shapes of things. Outside there was serenity, quietness, and Pericles' mind was calm. He heard the sound of a cricket, a tree branch creak, a rustle of leaves. Pericles readied himself to spend the dark hours until the first hue of light in the eastern horizon would give him the sign it was time to get up and start his quest again.

As he drifted off to sleep, his dream came again and he saw himself in Crete. Deep in his heart he knew he was there, he knew that around him was his homeland and the sea he gazed as he sat on the sand was the Cretan Sea with its majestic sound of the pebbles rolling behind each receding wave like unearthly music the sea's eternal motion, like an endless song as wave after wave roiled onto the beach. The Aegean Sea was before him, dark blue, sweet, open, inviting.

In his dream, he sat with his toes hidden in the warm sand, his fingers playing with the granules, letting it flow through his fingers. His eyes observed the sights around him, the village, a ship far out at sea, a slender ship running on top of the sea line, no weight pulling her down, no attachment to anything, totally free of bonds, on a voyage that promised its passengers new virgin lands where man's feet have never made footprints, seas never before ploughed.

Then he heard screams and he saw three women wailing as they pointed toward a man who was running down the narrow path. The women were chasing the man as if he had committed a horrible crime. Pericles saw the man get behind some big rocks of the seashore to hide from his pursuers who after they lost track of the man they chased and upon seeing Pericles on the shore they ran to his direction. They yelled and they gesticulated and screamed and by now Pericles saw that the ship had changed direction and turned, coming toward the land. When it was close Pericles saw people going down the stairs to board a small boat which would take them to the shore. The other man's pursuers also got closer to him and the more they came nearer, the angrier they seemed. Pericles saw their faces and when they reached him they yelled: "It's him! It's him!"

He just looked toward the ship and beyond it the open sea. He jumped up and started running toward the boat that had reached the shore and as he struggled to get onto it he felt the cold water and yelled a wild "NO!" Then he woke up.

Pericles opened his eyes. He sensed a strange emotion building up from within, a sense of fear, a certain loneliness and uncertainty, as if he was headed in the wrong direction. This strange emotion overwhelmed him. He felt heat all over his body. His mind ran to his folks at home. They must be asleep. It had been a sad day when he left them. He remembered how they had said "take care of yourself" when he had started his journey. He had covered a good distance in these first days away from home. He was in Bulgaria and he had managed to stay away from the main towns. Yet he felt it was time for him to get to a town and bathe himself and all that without falling into the hands of the police. After walking at a good pace all day since he crossed into Bulgaria he estimated he was close to Vratsa, which he should reach midday tomorrow. He decided to go through this town and find a place where he'd clean up a little. With that homey thought in his mind he looked around him. Quietness. He felt a presence, a strange feeling that he was watched, but he couldn't see anybody as the cave was well lit by the moonlight. Dawn was near although even now in the darkness of the cave he could discern the spirits of the alive from the dead, the real from the imaginary and as far as he could see there wasn't anyone around.

He sat up. Soon it would be daylight. He needed to stretch and mentally prepare himself for what the day may bring. He stood up. He stepped toward the opening of the cave, ten steps or eleven. The sky was still ablaze with flickering stars and the horizon was dressed in a light rosy hue which lifted his spirits. He smiled. Yes, it was crazy, simply crazy to start on this journey. What else would a sane man think?

He sat on a rock. His glance captured the images around him as the morning twilight made some patches of the earth look different in color from the darker secretive patches of trees and shrubbery and their secret pathways and complex entwining. Pericles' dream was still very vivid in his mind. He remembered his grandfather who always insisted that dreams had a meaning and they came from another dimension of a person's being beyond the sensory. His grandfather used to tell him that dreams showed us ways we can't see when the senses are alert. Pericles got up and began to pace around the opening of the cave. He didn't know what he wanted. Perhaps it was time for him to start his journey. The day looked promising, late spring, almost summer. The trees, shrubs and rocks were sunlit, and slowly all the creatures of the forest would start moving, the odd beetle, the earth crawlers took their first steps, birds appeared in the sky. Farther away, in the sea, the fish, the urchins, the abalone, all stretched to wake up from the night's slumber and Pericles imagined them as his mind travelled to the sea, the blue sea of his Crete, the sea of his dreams which was waiting for him, still far away but closer than when he started his quest.

He admired the nature around him and smiled. Time passed, and the sun was almost up on the horizon when he decided it was time to start. He went inside the cave, gathered his sleeping bag tied it to his backpack, placed his bag on his shoulders and turned his direction southward.

The main road he reached yesterday was to his left, and according to the map this road would take him to the next stop the city of Vratsa. Vratsa was a center of this province with almost forty thousand people. But for now Pericles decided to walk along the road except when he could save time by climbing a hill.

It was middle May and the temperature was a comfortable heat. He checked his water canister which was half full. He would have to look for fresh water to replenish it. He noticed that around him every little earth dweller was busy doing what nature had provided for them: the ants were gathering, birds mating, going back and forth to their nests feeding chicks or sitting over their eggs. He saw the occasional snake here and there and plenty of lizards crossing the road. Each creature was pairing with its mate. Swallows sliced the sky creating unimaginable shapes, entangled algorithms like human thoughts, indecipherable.

> *"a solitary swallow to find the value of spring*
> *it takes a lot of effort to make the sun turn around"*

He thought of a folk song he remembered, lyrics from a well-known poem. His lips slowly repeated the verse and a wide smile spread upon his face. He had rediscovered himself. Crete waited for him at the end of this journey. His smile grew wider his sunlit face reflected his enthusiasm and courage. He thought he was almost there, in Crete, his Crete, and that was the most important moment of his life.

Time passed and almost midday he climbed the side of a hill where he decided to catch his breath and eat his lunch. From where he stood he could see the city of Vratsa. It looked as any other city on earth. The streets were narrow, the houses small, the stores on the main road about the same shape and size except for a place in the middle which must be the center of the city. Pericles thought he would find a place where he could clean himself. He started going down the hill keeping extra careful to avoid any unpleasant encounters with authorities who might stop him.

When he reached the first house he smelled a light fragrance in the air, probably the flowers in the people's yards and the orchards close to the town along the roads. He hesitantly walked toward the center of the city. A car went by him, then another one and soon after a bus full of people. Yet oddly, there were not too many people in the streets. Perhaps most were attending to their daily affairs.

He came across a general store with a big sign and observed the other buildings around him. He walked into the general store and bought three cans of corn beef, a package of raisins, since he had almost eaten all he carried from his house, a new lighter, two apples and half a loaf of bread. He paid the man and took the bag with his shopping which he would put in their proper place in his backpack. Nothing around him seemed different than any Romanian city, not much different than Craiova, although a lot smaller and he observed three and four storey buildings with stores on the main floor and apartments above.

He passed a small park with a fountain in the middle and noticed a few café bars where people were enjoying the warm day of May. He kept on walking and watching carefully when he noticed the sign of public bathrooms and he went towards it. He opened the door and behind sat a middle-aged blond woman who extended her arm to give him a roll of toilet paper. He took it in exchange for a few Bulgarian coins and smiling, he told her he wanted a towel, to which the woman smiled back and gave him a small towel and showed him the direction of the showers.

He finished his bath, changed into clean clothes and put the dirty into his bag. He smiled at the blonde woman on his way out and began walking toward the city centre. People were going about their daily affairs. A young mother was pushing a baby carriage and her son or daughter in it was very upset since his or her voice was heard from every direction of this city. A mailman delivered his mail to the business of the block and smiling he passed by Pericles who reciprocated the smile. There was a policeman in the middle of the intersection controlling the traffic and when Pericles stood at the edge of the sidewalk the man in the middle seeing him raised his arm and stopped the traffic enough to give him the time needed to cross the street. Then the traffic resumed its flow and Pericles walked away. Slowly and carefully he passed through an old part of the city and crossed a back lane when he came across two youths who confronted him. They stood in the middle of the lane to block his way, showing him that they wouldn't let him pass. Pericles observed them carefully. The one, who looked like the leader of the two fashioned his uncombed blond hair and was dressed in jeans with a tee shirt and a light jacket with its zipper undone. The other boy with dishevelled hair as well and black trousers gazed Pericles and readied himself to throw the first punch.

"Where are you going asshole?" he said in his language which Pericles understood.

"None of your business butthead…" Pericles answered and the youth with the black trousers taking an offence in that walked a little to the side signaling to hid buddy to take the other side enclosing the passer by.

Pericles wouldn't have any of that. Instead he stepped towards the leader of the couple who also moved to his direction. The other Bulgarian youth in black tight trousers and a black hoodie, as if he followed orders of the first one, also moved toward Pericles. Pericles had never been in a fight since his school days and he tried to avoid the confrontation, but the two young men blocked him from passing and the blond leader kept repeating the word asshole. Suddenly Pericles responded by turning back at the same time when the leader of the two jumped toward him. Before the fair-haired hoodlum reached him, Pericles made a sudden turn and gave him a powerful punch in the gut. The youth folded and Pericles added another strong hit on the side of his head which forced the youth to fall while he let a painful grunt out of his mouth. In that moment Pericles grabbed his knife from the side pocket of his bag and showed it to the other youth. He froze at the sight of the knife and at the swiftness with which the Pericles had hit his buddy. Pericles walked slowly away with steady, direct steps. The second youth didn't do anything but instead attended to his injured friend and Pericles got the time he needed to walk away. The bones of his fist hurt but Pericles ignored the pain and while he put his knife away in his backpack he distanced himself from the two Bulgarian youths.

With no other incidents Pericles distanced himself from the neighborhood and soon he was far away out of the city. His mind struggled to bring him back to think of Crete and her beautiful sandy beaches where beautiful women waited for him. The Crete his grandfather described to him, his Crete where the sun shines every day and the country side smells with the aroma of oregano and thyme; his Crete where the people sing and celebrate their name days and they dance the *pidihtos*, like the old days.

The Wolf

Pericles left Vratsa behind him and after he walked for three hours he came before the Balkan Mountain range. He kept on going, knowing that with every step he was coming closer to his destination. This was a thought that truly calmed him and without any unexpected incident his day went by as he covered the distance he believed he had to cover every day. He followed Highway 15, which tomorrow evening would bring him around the next big city of Botevgrad 55 kilometers south of Vratsa. But for now he was walking an uphill and soon he had to go off the road to find a place to spend the night.

Upon leaving the road he climbed 100 meters, while thinking that it would take him another full day of walk to pass the mountains. He also knew that once he passed the mountain range he would follow the valley southward until he came to the Struma River, called the Strimonas River in Hellas. Struma River would be his landmark.

He noticed around him the trees weren't too high nor too dense. He stopped at a little plateau and gazed around the surrounding area. The open area gave him a good view of everything.

He walked a little further and found a spot between two trees and a big boulder on the far side. That spot welcomed him as his place for the night. He put his back-sack against the boulder and after he gathered a bunch of leaves from a tree which he used to make a ·makeshift bed onto which he laid his sleeping bag. He gathered a few pieces of wood and made a circle of a fire pit with a few rocks. He arranged the firewood and lit it with the help of some toilet paper. In a minute his fire was ablaze.

He felt content, and smiled. He had promised his parents that he would be extra careful and avoid the big places, and he had kept his promise by following sometimes the road and other times keeping away from cars and from the eyes of curious people. He had not have any bad encounter up to now, other than his fight with the two youths in Vratsa and as the fire warmed him, thoughts flooded his mind. The only sound was the crackling of the wood so loud he could almost hear every single piece of wood being consumed by the hungry fire.

He opened his bag, took out a can of corned beef, one of the three he bought earlier today. He was about to open it when the sudden sound of a howl abruptly stopped him. He looked around. Where was it coming from? Were there coyotes around here or wolves? His spine shivered. He put another big piece of wood in the fire and got up. He looked around again. His eyes searched for a suitable piece of wood in case he had to use it to defend himself. He chose one broken tree branch. He grabbed it and taking his knife from his bag he cleaned it off its bark twigs and even made a handle where he could hold it. He was ready. He heard the howl once again, a strange lone howl. Was the animal close or far away?

Pericles lied down with his back against the boulder while his eyes kept on searching the surrounding ground but there wasn't anyone he could see. He was alone. Above him the endless sky. Around him quietness, forlornness, abandonment. In his heart he felt benevolence. In his mind, fear. Adrenaline flooded his arteries and veins. His pulse accelerated. Internally his fiery spirit sang a vibrant rhapsody. He was alert and ready. He grabbed the Cretan knife in his hand. He placed it next to him. Grabbed the club and waited. Yet, even that didn't make him feel any better. He sat up, with his back against the big boulder, and tossed more wood in the fire. Minutes passed, although they felt like hours, when his attention was caught by the sound of a low howl very close to him. He listened, and heard the howl again, this time definitely closer. He got up and looked around. It was coming from his west side. He couldn't discern any movement in the twilight. Nothing was there so he sat again feeding the fire with wood and keeping a wary eye on the area when suddenly he caught a movement. An animal was moving slowly toward him. He grabbed the club. He picked up his knife with his other hand ready to use it. His heart felt ready to explode. It was a wolf, a lone wolf. Strange, he knew they usually travel in packs but he couldn't see any others. The lone wolf slowly was coming closer. Then he noticed that the wolf was limping. The right hind leg of the animal was lame and the animal hopped with each step like a man who couldn't use one of his legs. The injured wolf kept coming closer to him. The lone, wounded wolf, a wolf discarded by its pack, a lone wolf traveling in the forest just like Pericles. Perhaps because it was lame, it was useless to its pack, a wolf left to fetch its own food alone, abandoned, left to die alone: a hungry wolf looking for food, but what food? Pericles stayed vigilant counting every step the wolf made as it limped towards him. He stood motionless. He held the club in one hand and the Cretan knife in his other and he waited. The wolf kept coming closer to him. Pericles stepped toward the animal and waved his arms holding the club in one hand. They were like two animals ready to charge each other, to rip each other's flesh. Then suddenly the wolf howled, a strange howl, a howl of recognition, a begging howl as if it needed something. Pericles realized that the wolf was definitely hungry. They eyed each other for moments that felt forever. Pericles stepped back, retreating closer to his fire and the injured wolf, only six meters away, sat on his rear legs eyeing him. Pericles took the corn beef can from his backpack he opened it slowly and carefully and when finished, he grabbed the meat out of the can and threw it to the wolf. The animal limped backwards startled but when it smelled the meat it came closer and after sniffing it, his tongue licked the meat. In a few seconds the corned beef was consumed. Then strangely enough the hungry animal raised its head as if asking whether there was more. Pericles looked at the wolf in amazement. Then he took another can of corn beef out of his bag and opened it, dug out all the food and threw it toward the hungry animal. This time the wolf didn't move backward but instead it almost run, a limping run, toward the food which it consumed in the same eagerness as before.

All was well, one of the two animals was satiated the other was certain that the injured one posed no threat to him. Indeed the wolf laid down and placed his head on top of his front paws staring toward the young man. Moments passed, the wolf's eyes closed, and Pericles felt his own eyes closing as sleep overtook him.

Soon after the cold woke him up and he realised the fire was almost out. He rekindled it and when the fire was strong enough he realized the animal that was laid on its side was probably asleep.

The morning star rose in the eastern horizon prodding Pericles to start his day. When he got up, the wolf was still in the same place as he was last night. Pericles took a small pebble and threw it toward the wolf but it didn't rouse. Then he threw another pebble but still the wolf didn't budge. Pericles walked toward it slowly and touched the animal's fur. But there was no reaction. The wolf laid motionlessness, quiet, breathless. Dead! The wolf died during the night. Pericles stayed for a few moments contemplating what to do. He realized now why the animal was alone. An injured wolf is always abandoned by the pack. These were the rules of animal life. And perhaps that was why, because it was incapable to find nourishment, weak, old, injured and hungry, the wolf had died in his company. Even though Pericles didn't notice the wolf's last breath, the animal died in his presence. He remembered that it was exactly as his grandfather had requested: that Pericles would stay by his bed the night his grandfather took his last breath.

He inspected the fire pit and felt the warmth coming from the ashes. He took some wood and restarted the fire then took his small saucepan from his back-sack, filled it half way with water and half a handful of sage tea and set it over the fire to boil. He wondered what to do with the carcass of the wolf. He ate a piece of his bread along with a cup of the hot boiling tea.

The sun had climbed to its height on the eastern horizon. Pericles decided to bury the wolf and took his club and a piece of wood and placed them on each side of the dead animal. He covered the wolf's body with stones and rocks which he placed on top of the wolf's grave making a small mound to completely cover the dead animal. Upon finishing his rite he stood for a moment looking at the grave mount. His mind ran to the time when he let a handful of dirt fall over the casket of his grandfather. It was his farewell. And today he said farewell to the dead wolf by placing the last stone over the burial site. He felt good. He smiled.

Before leaving, he put out the fire then gathered his things, put the back-sack on his shoulders and walked away with his smile still lighting his face.

The Trapper

The following day Pericles reached a beautiful valley. As he gazed across it from the side of the mountain where he was and where the forest was very thin he observed the road he was following going in twists and turns along the mountains. For this reason Pericles decided to walk off the road for a while to shorten the distance between where he was and the far side of the mountain where the road was visible again. He whistled a Cretan tune as he walked and kept his pace among the tall trees and the dry forest floor.

Soon after, he came to a small moss-covered log cabin surrounded by trees. The cabin was built half a meter above ground steadying itself on a rocky base onto which the base beams of the floor rested. It had one door and one window and two big logs positioned against each side of the door as if supporting it from falling outward. The moss on the roof was brown and dry. Beside the door there was a fenced area where one could keep a dog or other animals.

Pericles walked toward it hesitantly. Something inside him warned him of possible danger. Suddenly as he came close to it, a man in black clothes appeared by the door brandishing a hunting rifle. He gestured to Pericles to stop. The man was about the same age as Pericles, but much bigger in size, a giant of a man and with rough features, dark face, mustache and beard. On his head he wore a hunter's hat. Pericles saw that the man's finger was lodged on the trigger of the rifle.

Pericles stepped back.

"I don't mean any harm." He said to the rough guy who signalled to Pericles to come closer.

"I'm passing through." Pericles added.

"Where are you headed?" the man asked.

"South" Pericles answered.

"Very well, then, come inside." The man said and Pericles followed him into the log cabin.

"What's your name?" The trapper asked.

"Pericles, and yours?"

"Ivan."

"You live here?"

"Yes, Pericles, but I was about to go and check my traps just before you came, so…"

"I won't hold you up. In fact I would like to see how you do your trapping. Can I come with you, Ivan?"

Ivan realized that Pericles had neither hand-gun nor rifle he invited Pericles to go along with him. Before going, however, the man explained he must organize his equipment.

Soon after they walked together and after a few minutes they reached a spot where the man uncovered a small leg-hold trap he had hidden under a few small branches of spruce, but the trap was empty. The trapper placed it back where it was before and they walked a little further. Suddenly the man stopped. His expert eyes had seen from a distance that his next trap had an animal in its claws. He walked slowly toward it and Pericles followed not far behind.

They reached the spot and saw that a fox was caught and it was still alive. Ivan pulled the chain and the animal growled. He took his rifle and shot it right on the spot. Pericles was astonished at the quickness of action and sudden response of the hunter. Ivan freed the leg of the animal and after putting the dead fox aside he reset the trap and hid it under the pieces of tree branches. Then he tied together the paws of the animal and placed it onto his shoulders.

They carried on and soon they reached a small pond where a couple of beavers were busy in their annual ritual of building their den. Pericles could see the chopped trees in the area surrounding the pond. Ivan signaled to Pericles to keep quiet and sit to watch the animals doing what nature has guided them to do. A few minutes later they left the beavers do their work and the two men carried on with the trap inspection; at the end of their round Ivan had in his hands a fox, two minks and one beaver.

Back in the cabin Ivan skinned the animals, hung the pelts from the central beam of the cabin. Then he cleaned his hands and sat down with Pericles who was observing the space inside the cabin. There was a bed made of wood planks, a table, two chairs, and toward the window a small sink. One could see that almost all things were made by the man himself. A kerosene lamp was lit and its pin was placed between two logs flooding the cabin with ample light.

"What made you come and live here?" Pericles asked Ivan.

"I didn't like the life in the city. Here I live in the clean air. I only go down to the city to sell my catch and buy the necessities from the general store."

He also mentioned that in the city he only had to deal with one person — the general store man who was his uncle. Pericles told him he was headed south and that his roots were Hellenic. The man smiled, said no word, but extended his hand in a firm grip as if to congratulate Pericles. They both laughed.

Soon after the trapper offered Pericles a piece of dry meat and a small piece of cheese; they ate together and drank fresh water from Ivan's pitcher. Then they shook hands once more and Pericles got up to leave.

At the door the giant of a man showed him the direction to the south and Pericles walked away from the log cabin. The forest welcomed him again in its arms as if it was promising to protect and take care of him.

After he had walked for a several hours he stopped on a mountainside overlooking a small valley. He sat to rest on a big rock while his eyes explored the valley below. A few trees were scattered here and there, and green fields with crops spread out in an array of colors. He recognized a big mustard field in full bloom resembling a beautiful yellow carpet. In the middle of the field a stand of trees were enclosed by a fence, trees, and farther away, toward the top of a little hill he could see more trees and a farm house. Beyond the farmhouse a group of houses indicated a small village. Pericles sat awhile enjoying the perfect picture below him, fascinated with the view of the yellow mustard field and the rest of the green valley. He had already spent a week on his trip and now he had reached the middle part of Bulgaria, which meant that soon after he would pass the next big place, Botevgrad and soon after the capital Sophia he would be able to locate the river Struma which would lead him to the border between Bulgaria and Hellas.

Days of Relaxation

One week passed almost the same as the days up to Botevgrad. When he reached it the sign Blagoevgrad proved to him that he was on the right road. It took him three days to reach Blagoevgrad a city of seventy thousand people. Further south from Botevgrad Pericles reached Sophia which he also passed in the same way. Since the capital was a city of over a million inhabitants he spent six hours going around it. He walked west of it for quite a distance and then he veered south and again he turned eastward to find the main road going south. Here again he veered west, then south, then east until he came back to the main road which would lead him to his next big town Sandanski. Soon as he passed Sophia he discovered the River Struma to the right of the highway going south and although he travelled east of it he often gazed the river from afar when the terrain allowed it.

He usually walked for nine to ten hours each day. At times he laughed at the sights he encountered other times he was somber, sad, disheartened. Often his mind ran to the house and to his family, what they were doing at that hour, how they felt for his departure, he had to phone them first opportunity. But when and which phone could he use?

Sometimes he would sing himself a folk Cretan song, other times he silently observed the various sights and taking in the impressions like the lens of a camera, impressions that would be photographs he would keep in his mind forever. During these times his face reflected the brightness of the sun and his thoughts soothed his aching body.

He knew that Crete was at the end of his trip and it would be his reward. Other times his journey seemed to him long and difficult, and he thought probably he might never make it to Crete. But even during those times, when a negative thought would pass through his mind, he tried to focus on his goal and he would think of something different; something positive like the beauty of a Cretan beach where he was sunbathing, with the light breeze playing a soft tune in his ears. He imagined being with his family members under the grapevine with a glass of fresh water or a shot of *tsikoudia* along with almonds and walnuts that they usually offered it.

Content of seeing the valley down below him he got up and walked down the mountain side until he reached an area full of blackberry bushes which created an obstacle as they entangled onto his clothes, making it very difficult to pass. He found a way around them and went down the hill until he reached a village: a sign just before the first houses read Strumyani, population 438 souls.

Perhaps it was time to become human again.

He smiled at the thought of the simple people who live away from the populated cities, sweet people who worked for their daily bread not concerned nor being much influenced by the consumerism, people who worked hard for their fresh fruit, the home cooked meals, things a villager usually offered to the passersby.

The sun was almost up to the middle of the sky. It was hot so he took off his jacket and placed it on his shoulders. He kept on going until he neared the first houses. The village dogs smelled his presence and started barking. A window opened and shut as quickly before he could say good morning. A couple of people glanced toward him then disappeared behind the closed shutters. Pericles pretended he didn't notice as he walked slowly toward the center of the village. On one side of the square was a cafe where a dozen villagers sat enjoying the sunshine. Some of them seemed lethargic, almost asleep from the bright glare of the sun, others had their backs against the wall and he could smell sweat and strong body odors as if these brutes didn't know of soap or bathing.

The men noticed him and got up, obviously surprised at a stranger coming to their village. Pericles thought that probably not too many visitors frequented the place. The village men seemed uneasy when he walked toward them. A few pulled their chairs aside to make room for him to pass. Pericles smiled as he walked toward them. He took his backpack off his shoulders he grabbed a chair and sat at an empty table. One of the old fellows greeted him.

"Welcome to our village, young man. What good wind has brought here? Where you come from and where are you headed?"

He understood a little Bulgarian and his mind quickly measured all answers.

"I'm passing through. I'll stay long enough to rest, and then I'll make my way to the south."

He mentioned the names of the two villages north from this one and one to the south, and this seemed to please all the men. They offered him a drink which the café owner rushed to bring on a serving platter. He stretched his legs and had a couple of gulps of the orange juice. Everyone was watching him and he wondered what they were thinking.

Then their conversation turned to their well-known subjects: their fields and the crops and the co-op that provided the various annual fertilisers. They talked to him about their olive trees and the grapevines and how good the crops were last year and how optimistic they were about this year's crops, all the everyday concerns and worries farmers have in every corner of this earth: the weather, fertilisers, seed, harvesting, and the pain and reward of their fulfillments. They talked to him about the animal thieves: their worst enemy who even the police couldn't handle to their satisfaction. Pericles paid attention to everything they said, so much so that he didn't notice the signal one of the older men gave to another one, who got up and left, only to soon after return with a big fellow of a man, a giant almost, and a priest with his outfit fluttering in the wind making him visible from afar.

The heads of the village; are they here to welcome me or to interrogate? Pericles wondered. He wasn't wrong. The leaders came and sat close to him. First they welcomed him and slowly they asked questions about him and his plans. It was nothing short of an interrogation. Pericles informed the priest that he was headed south.

Knowing that Hellas wasn't too far to the south, the priest spoke to him in the language of the Hellenes and Pericles answered all the questions clearly and with no hesitation. He also mentioned he wanted to leave as soon as possible, to which the priest insisted that he better sleep there overnight and rest before he resumed his way to the south.

Pericles evaluated the situation and decided it was good to stay overnight. The priest invited him to stay at his place. He hadn't slept on a bed for a while and it would be good to stretch his body and relax for a night. So Pericles decided to go with him to have a good meal and rest before he started again his quest to the south. The priest got up, straightened his cassock and motioned for Pericles to follow him.

They walked along the narrow pathways of the village until they reached the priest's house. From outside it looked large and imposing. It was newly built with stones in neoclassic style and newly painted walls and cement walkways. The priest opened the gate and they both walked inside the yard. A young woman appeared and greeted them.

"My daughter Penelope," the priest said.

Pericles smiled at the girl. She lowered her eyes and said, "Welcome to our house."

Pericles noticed the clean walk ways and abundance of flower pots with geraniums, basil plants, hibiscuses and gardenias. There was a beautiful light fragrance all around the yard as beautiful and fragrant as the young woman who escorted them inside the house. The young's eyes were fixated on Pericles. She gazed at him and a hidden yearning woke up inside her. As she followed them inside the house her father ordered:

"Penelope, set the table."

She didn't answer, but rushed away to do what was necessary while Pericles and the priest settled in the sitting area.

Penelope spread a new tablecloth with cloth napkins and set the table with silverware, plates and glasses. All the while, at every opportunity, she eyed Pericles. Their glances met numerous times and the young woman didn't try to hide the sweetness of her glance. On the contrary she smiled at him every single time. In a while, as her father and Pericles exchanged views about things with common interest, the food was prepared and placed in their plates. The priest said a quick prayer they started eating. Not a single word was said until they had consumed the content of their plates and once that was done the priest sat with Pericles on the sofa to enjoy a coffee. Pericles kept quiet to give the priest the opportunity to start the conversation.

"Let the name of the Lord be blessed, my son, everything is in its proper place. You feel hungry, God provides you with food to enjoy. You're cold he sends you the fire to warm you up. When you get hot He sends the wind to cool you down. He sends the rain to grow the crops and the cold of the winter to kill the bugs, the heat to ripen the fruits and grow vegetables. Everything is put in its proper place, my son, Pericles. Although people are greedy and never satisfied with everything they have and always complain and stray away from God's path."

Pericles looked toward the wall where he noticed a picture of the priest with a woman, perhaps his wife, a woman missing from tonight's gathering. The priest caught his glance and sighed.

"God bless her soul, my wife. The good Lord took her from us two years ago." Tears welled in his eyes, "But now I have to leave you for a while since I have to go to the orchard to do some work with the grape vines. You stay and rest. I'll be back in a couple of hours." Then he turned to his daughter and added, "Get the bed for Pericles to rest."

"Yes father," she said, and returned to what she was doing.

The priest left, Pericles stood up and walked around the house looking at the pictures on the walls and all the other things displayed. He noticed Penelope's beautiful stature, her dark complexion, her black shoulder- length hair flowing on her shoulders, her black eyes, light chin and rich lips. Her white neck was like a swan's, her body calligraphic and naturally flowing, good hips, legs.

She caught his eyes and smiled at him.

"You're going south?"

"Yes, south."

"How far is where you are headed?"

"Very far."

She laughed and her eyes seemed to indicate that she understood more than what he might think.

"You'd rather keep that to yourself, eh?"

"No, not really. I'm going south. Isn't that enough?"

"Yes of course, more than enough. I'm going to prepare your bed."

She walked to the room next to the kitchen and Pericles heard the echo of her steps and the bed-sheets spread on a bed. In a couple of minutes she reappeared.

"Ready for you" she said. She pointed to the room and then carried on with the dishes.

Pericles went to the room, undressed and lay down. He noticed from that position the mirror on the opposite wall gave him the view of the room next to his but his attention was interrupted by Penelope who appeared at his door.

"I'll go lay down too. If you need something please don't hesitate to call me."

He nodded and she walked to the adjacent room. From where Pericles lay, he could see her undressing and for a fraction of a second he thought their eyes met and she smiled at him. Her body shone, half naked and beautiful as she covered herself with a light bed sheet. He couldn't see her face, but he could see every move she made as she lay in bed and a strong desire overpowered him to get up and go join her. Instead he turned toward the wall so he wasn't able to see her. Then suddenly he thought he heard her calling him and with no other hesitation he walked to her room and slipped under her bed covers.

When the priest returned home later in the afternoon he found Pericles sitting outside and looking toward the southern horizon while Penelope was in the kitchen preparing their evening meal. She sang as she walked around the small room.

"How are you, son?" the priest asked Pericles to which Pericles said, "I'm good, father."

After remaining silent for a few seconds the priest said, "You'll go tomorrow morning or do you prefer to stay for a few days?

"If you need a hand with the orchards father, I could stay for a few days and then carry on with my trip," Pericles offered.

"Ah, yes indeed son. I could use a strong hand with my grapevines. We usually apply the fertilizer these days and clean the soil off the weeds. It would be nice if you could help me for a couple of days. You know, the work is easier when two men share the load. Two days are enough, I think."

"Are your grapevines around here, father?"

"Yes, I have a couple of pieces of land on that hillside." He pointed to the right side of the horizon.

Pericles said "Alright then, I'll stay to give you a hand."

When he said that, a joyous singing voice was heard from the kitchen a singing voice noticed by the priest who sighed and in a low tone said to Pericles.

"I can't tell her not to sing, my son, since her heart is so young and full of life. How can I tell her not to sing? To tell you the truth we're still mourning the death of my sister, her Auntie Erato, who left us a week ago. But how can I say this to her at her age, so beautiful and full of life?"

Pericles agreed, adding: "No problem father, no problem at all. In fact in the ancient days when one died people used to celebrate the person's life and enjoyed the occasion knowing that the soul of the dead was free to go to where it belonged."

It was the priest's time to be surprised.

"Imagine that! The soul is free to go to where it belongs. What a great idea!" He thought a moment and then he added: "Is it so? I didn't know that."

"Yes it is so, father. I read it in the books" Pericles added.

"Then it must be so."

"There isn't any need to worry, father."

"No, as you say, there isn't." Then he yelled toward the kitchen "Penelope, is the food ready?"

"Yes father, I'm setting the table." Penelope replied.

The priest and Pericles went in and took their places at the table. As the priest had his habit, he said a quick prayer and with a good appetite he started to eat his food and Pericles followed him as he also was hungry. Penelope, smiling, looked at him and filled her plate with food as well. She often raised her eyes and met his and Pericles noticed in her eyes certain sweetness and her wonder of who was this man who travelled to the south. He sensed her wonder, but he pretended he didn't notice although a little devil in him prompted him to move his legs toward hers to which she responded by turning and giving him her sweetest smile.

After they ate, the priest asked whether Pericles wished to go to the café for an evening drink. Pericles said he preferred to stay at home since he was tired, so they went out to the courtyard where the fragrance from the flowerpots perfumed the evening air.

The priest and Pericles sat to enjoy the quietness of the evening. Pericles was absorbing the peaceful and relaxing smells of the yard enjoying every single moment when Penelope appeared with a tray containing their evening coffee and a glass of cool water. She placed it down close to them then she sat next to them browsing through her magazine under the faint evening light.

"You have to do some digging tomorrow father?" Pericles started.

"Yes, and to tell you the truth, it is too much for me at my age."

"You aren't that old, father." Pericles laughed.

"Well, I wouldn't say that. But it isn't as much the old age as it's very hard to find help, even workers you pay. You see, everyone has their own fields to work and no time for me."

"But this time you found me, father. Or better, I found you and we'll take care of your grapevine. Then who knows, perhaps next year I may pass by again and help you."

Penelope raised her head from the magazine and saw the smile on his face.

The priest laughed. "Truly Pericles, God always finds a way. But we still have to do our part and better when we plan on our own and don't wait for God to save us every time. On the other hand, how can He take care of every one of us?"

"Father...no," Penelope interrupted.

"You stay out of it. You couldn't understand" the priest said to his daughter and turning to Pericles he added "Listen to me, son, I'll tell you a story the leader of the monastery told me once. You know

93

the story of Jesus, when he walked on water, don't you? Well, the leader of the monastery says the story this way. When Jesus walked on water and Peter saw him walking on the waves, he asked that Jesus make him do the same and Jesus told Peter 'Come Peter, come, believe and walk on the water' to which Peter got the courage, and walked toward Jesus. However at one point he felt scared and suddenly the fear made him sink and as a result he cried out to Jesus to help him. This happened again when the third time as Peter asked for Jesus' help Jesus turned and said to him in a stern voice: 'Believe in me, Peter. Come, walk onto the sea. Believe in me and come, but step on a rock here and there.'

Pericles' mind ran to the priest of the Hellenic Community back home and his teachings, not much different than his host's views. But he couldn't stop himself from laughing at the last sentence and Penelope did the same. However her father said in a very serious voice: "Yes, it may sound funny, and it may be laughable, but there is some truth to it. There is another meaning hidden in it."

"What meaning father?" Pericles asked.

"It means that, yes, we believe in God and we feel protected and safe under Him but we also have the responsibility to take care of ourselves on our own. Don't we all have a part of the same God inside us? I mean our soul, isn't it part of God?"

"Your words speak the truth, father, and I wish all people saw things the same way," Pericles agreed. "At times such as this when I feel relaxed I sit in the yard with good company and the fragrance of the flowers all around us and talk of these things: the where we come from and where we are headed and about the everyday things; we have to be concerned with the digging of your vineyards, father, and the removal of the weeds, and all these other things that make us as human as we can be. At times the demon inside me tells me not to be concerned with such things and to only be aware of the body, the five senses that help us perceive things and forget about everything else."

Both Penelope and her father listened to him and smiled, although for different reasons. They both thought they had a very wise man with them and he was a very good company and each for a different reason they wished he could stay with them for a while.

"Listen to me Pericles; it's not the priest who's talking right now but an older man, a widower with a young daughter. What would be the meaning of our lives if we didn't strive to reach higher? Why are we here? Who knows to state the reason clearly? This is another meaning the story of Jesus and Peter has. First it is the disciple who wants to reach and do as the teacher does, but it is also the miracle of Peter's effort and every other human being's for that matter to raise himself to reach higher. Peter wanted to reach the level of God, to be like his teacher, Jesus. This is the duty and purpose of everyone on earth to make one step higher than the parents, a step higher than the one before. And many people say we are what we do every day in our lives. The farmers, for example, say, 'Our God is full of rain and when we need it for our fields He rains and the crops grow' while others have given up and have walked away from the church and from God. But what I believe is to keep on trying and to keep on climbing up a step at a time, because this is our duty and purpose on this earth." He took a deep breath and leaned his head on one side as if he was feeling nostalgic.

"You, father, did you ever feel you had your own God?" Pericles asked.

"Yes, there was time that I felt that way. I imagined my God an old man with gray hair and eyes full of love and I felt close enough to Him and free to ask Him everything that came to mind. Then my wife got sick and I begged Him day in and day out to help her heal. But no, in two months and after a long struggle and pain, she died and I couldn't take it anymore. I remember I told Him a few choice words back then and after that I walked away from Him and truly Pericles, to tell you, I feel a lot freer now, I feel I have discarded some heavy weight I had carried all along."

He raised his eyes toward the sky as if to question: "Am I really free?"

They sat in silence for a while. Time went by peacefully. The odd cricket was heard around the flowerpots. Penelope couldn't take her eyes off Pericles and every time their eyes met full of promises and desire. She smiled at him and her white teeth shone in the evening light.

Finally, the priest got up and said good night because it was time for him to rest and go to sleep.

When he disappeared behind the door Penelope sat closer to Pericles and took his hand in hers.

"Have you ever had your God, Pericles?"

He didn't expect such a question and laughed with surprise "A God? Yes, I have a God."

"And how does He look? What does He ask of you? What does He give you?"

Pericles remained silent for a while, pondering the question.

"My God is a warrior. He's in full armor and he's a sea-farer. He travels all over the world. He can't stay in one place for too long and I, to pay tribute to Him, I have to never stay in one place for too long. I'm destined to travel and meet new lands and people all the time, because my God says 'You've reached here, now it is time to move to the next place.'"

"For this reason you like to travel Pericles? For this reason you are headed to the south?" Penelope's voice almost choked as she uttered the last words.

"No, that's not the reason" Pericles said.

"Then why don't you stay here with us?"

He looked into her eyes. "Perhaps I'll stay, yes, Penelope, perhaps I'll stay for a little longer than what I had in mind."

"Stay, yes, stay" she repeated.

"We'll see, we'll see. But you didn't tell me anything about your God."

"My God is young and strong and full of love. I imagine him exactly like you, a true man who makes me happy, in every respect." She leaned closer to him and her lips searched for his. He said in a tender tone. "What about your father?"

"He's asleep Pericles." She kissed him. "Come, let's go to bed"

Pericles hesitated. He held her hand but didn't get up to follow her. He forced her to sit with him a little longer. But Penelope wanted him more now than earlier in the day and her insistence made the best of Pericles who finally followed her to her room.

The Grapevines

The roosters heralded the day for the second time yet, and the morning star was still hanging up on the horizon, when all the animals started calling for their morning food. The village sounded like a war zone with every front covered by voices and noise of every kind. The donkeys, the most patient and obedient soldiers, were waiting to get loaded with today's ammunition – spades, shovels, and picks, food for the workers, and water, and wine for their masters' lunch. People finished their morning drinks, with the traditional cigarette for the smokers. Some crossed themselves before heading out, others cursed the sun for waking them up, and others just didn't care to look up onto the sky, but put their day in front and started following their fate with no comment.

The priest, smiling and full of eagerness, had prepared two spades and a flask filled with water and waited for Pericles to get up. Penelope prepared their coffee and toast with some marmalade. Then she pulled up a couple of buckets of water from the well to water the flowers of the yard.

"Penelope, get Pericles up; it's time to start going," the priest said. "Let us go early to manage most of our work before the sun rises too high and the day gets too hot."

Penelope went to Pericles room and found him almost ready. She gave him a quick kiss and left.

"Penelope," her father said, "go and find my old boots. I hope they fit Pericles" then, turning to the young man who had just come out of his room, he added, "I don't want you to use your boots in the fields."

Penelope brought her father's old boots and luckily they fit Pericles almost as if they were made for him. Pericles laughed when he saw how they fit him but he laughed even more later on when they were in the field and the priest lifted his cassock and arranged his clothes to make sure he was ready for the digging.

The priest raised his spade up high and then it fell on the soil with force enough to go all the way in the earth thus softening it up and separating of the weeds off their roots. Soon the lines of grapes were clean and fresher than before. About two hours later they stopped for their first break. They went to sit under the shade of a pear tree by the edge of the field and the priest took the water flask, poured some and offered it to Pericles.

"Come now, Pericles, tell me the truth. Where is your destination? You said to the south, but where to the south?"

"I didn't lie, father," Pericles said thinking whether he could talk to this priest of his life's quest.

"Going south means nothing. South is the South Pole. Is that where you are going?"

Pericles felt he couldn't hide the truth much longer. But what could he tell the priest?

"I know what you mean, father. It's simple. I have relatives I'm looking up. They live in Crete, the island my grandfather came from. That's where I'm headed."

The next question surprised Pericles even more than the first one.

"Are you married, Pericles?"

"No."

They remained silent for a while.

"You don't ask me why?" The priest asked.

"Ask you what, father?"

"Why I asked whether you were married."

Before Pericles could answer they heard Penelope's voice greeting them as she brought them their lunch. Pericles was relieved for the abrupt end of the inquisition while the priest took the bag from Penelope's hand and looked in it.

"Good to see you Penelope; what goodies did you bring us?" he asked.

"Tasty food" she answered laconically.

The priest arranged the contents of the bag on a piece of cloth he spread over the soil: two apples, two forks and two plates carefully wrapped and tied with a cloth napkin. He undid the wrapping and discovered a plateful of stewed meat and potatoes.

Penelope looked around at the field. "I see you're doing well with your work."

"Blessed be His name and with the help of Pericles, yes, we are doing very well," her father answered.

"You don't have to praise me, father. I'm just trying to help" Pericles added.

They said no more as they finished their lunch and Penelope gathered her things and left to go home. Pericles got up, took his spade and went back to where they had stopped and the priest followed him. They worked without saying anything until late afternoon when the priest suggested they stop for the day.

"Time to stop, son; tomorrow we will finish."

He hid their spades under some shrubbery at the edge of the field, took the water flask and they started their way home along a wild terrain that led toward the village. There were bulrushes and other vegetation, occasionally a wild pear or almond tree and nothing else. They passed a river bed and came across blackberry bushes that wrapped themselves around tree trunks and tugged on their clothes as they walked by.

"Wild nature, son, eh?" the priest commented.

"Yes; I'm surprised your grapevines grew around here."

"True, but it shows us how powerful nature is. Where you don't expect it something grows."

"Father, who helps you take care of your fields? You said it is almost impossible to get help from the villagers as everyone is concerned with their own."

"In the old days I used to do it myself but last year my nephew, Hercules, was around and helped me; the year before that another passerby, like you. God is great, He always finds someone for me"

"No one from the villagers ever finds time for you? I mean besides their own properties, isn't anyone ever available to help you for a good pay?"

The priest laughed at his comment. "Aha, the villagers, they're always willing but only when it comes to a game of cards, to which they are experts. They play card games in the café, day in and day out. You find them there playing cards. They have no time for the priest, no time for anything else, even when it comes to their own fields to be taken care of. You hear them talking about it for days on before they decide to leave the card game for a day and go do their work."

"But then how do they manage? How they find money to buy what they need? Food for their animals, things they need in their houses?" Pericles asked.

"Well God has provided even for that Pericles. You see in every village there is a general store and here we have the one run by Hermes, son of that old man in the café. His son runs the general store of the village where one can find almost everything from food items to clothing to supplies for the fields and the houses: almost everything."

"Yes father, but how do they buy what they need? How they earn money to buy things?"

"It's simple son. Hermes keeps a good book of sales and every time the villagers produce something he receives the value of what they owe him in kind, which means he takes part of their produce, at a huge discount from the market price, and sells it. He makes money left right and middle as the saying goes. The villagers don't mind, he becomes richer and they settle in their card games all year around. It is simple, really. God has found a solution, short of."

"I understand. A good solution, of course; everyone is happy as it seems."

They had almost reached the village and from the turn of the path they were passing the village came into view. On the western horizon the sun hid behind the high mountain tops as it was time for it to set. It was time for them to relax from the days digging of grapevines and weeding the fields. The village had come alive with children playing their games and parents were preparing the evening meals.

When they got home Penelope greeted them. Everything was in order, the table set and a bottle of wine in the middle. They cleaned up and sat to eat. Penelope had cooked artichokes with potatoes in the casserole with plenty of dill weed and onion and garlic. Pericles loved it as he remembered his mother cooked that same dish for them at home. For a second his mind brought to him images of their dinners and his eyes got teary to the point that Penelope noticed it and with her eyes she question what was the reason for it. Pericles nodded to her not to worry.

"Very tasty artichokes, Penelope," he said, "thank you. It reminded me of my mother's cooking," he added.

They each had a glass of wine and after they had finished the two men walked to the yard. Pericles felt relaxed, and smiled a smile which the priest noticed. After he took a sip of his coffee, he turned toward Pericles.

"It is good. Truly, the lord's miracle: you feel hungry He gives you food, you feel tired from digging the grapevines all day long He gives you this quiet serene evening in the yard: enough to relax you and make your heart feel full of love and compassion for everything alive, man or beast." He sighed and took another sip of his coffee.

From inside the house Pericles could hear Penelope singing. The priest had also noticed since Pericles' arrival, how his daughter seemed different, happier, more joyous than before He leaned closer to Pericles and said, "Hear her, son. She's singing like a nightingale and I have to add, this young woman, my daughter, is my only concern on this earth. I just want to take care of her, get her married and then if the good lord wants to take me I'll be more than ready. I have so far given her everything I could. She went to the city, passed all six grades of high school, now the only thing left is to find a good man for her. Then my life's circle will be complete. Then I can say, come Hades, I'm ready for you."

Pericles understood what the priest meant. Ever since their lunch when the priest had asked whether he was married, the thought had been in his mind. He smiled at the idea of settling down and take

Penelope as his wife, but at the same moment the image of his gray haired grandfather appeared and he remembered his quest – to go to Crete.

He turned to the priest. "Father, I like the straight forward talk and I understand what you're trying to tell me. I thank you for your care and respect and I thank you for opening your door to me and offering me a few days of relaxation before I recommence my way to the south. This is my goal. I can't stop and settle down. My goal, my commitment to my family, my grandfather and myself leads me to Crete. I'm sure you and Penelope understand."

At that moment Penelope joined them outside. She looked at her father who was ready to tell her to leave them alone.

Pericles stopped him with a gesture "No need for privacy father. What I have to say is not a secret. Penelope can hear too."

He told them where he had come from and where he was headed. He told them about his family in Craiova, his father working at the shop and his mother and his grandfather, the old man who had raised him in his own way. He told them about the old man's words and what it meant to him to get to Crete. He made sure they understood how impossible it was for him to let go of this goal and settle down here at the border of Bulgaria and Hellas. He was so close to achieving this goal. He told them how his grandfather had him swear that one day he would make this trip, and that he must see it all the way to its end. He also told them how there were times when he felt the soul of his grandfather was inside him, deciding, guiding him in what to do and where to go. He told them everything he had in his mind and both the priest and Penelope understood, since they knew they had with them a good man who was committed to a goal and nothing would stop him from achieving it.

As they listened to him tears rolled down the Penelope's cheeks and her father touched her hand and turned to Pericles.

"We understand, Pericles. It's good to have a purpose and a charted path. It's admirable that you wish to reach the land of your forefathers and it's also admirable to seek to know their homeland better by living there the rest of your life. But be open-minded. Things are usually quite different in reality from the images and imagination we have of them. What do you think that you will find in Crete? People and things change everywhere. Why do you think they haven't changed there? Do you know what you'll find when you get to Crete?"

"I'll find what my grandfather described to me in his stories, father. I know it deep in my heart. I'll find that."

"I wish you to do that son. I truly wish you will find the peace and love and acceptance you expect to find there. But what happens if you don't? Have you thought of the disappointment you might experience come the time you arrive and you encounter something totally unheard of, something completely opposite of what you have in your mind?"

Pericles rebelled at this and in a stern voice he said.

"I know what to expect father. But if my expectation proves to be wrong I won't stay there."

"How many years have passed since your grandfather left Hellas for Romania?" the priest asked him.

"At least thirty."

"And you have never been there?"

"No."

"I'm sure you'll find it different from what you've imagined. Everything changes over the years. What your parents and grandfather told you have changed like everything else. I'm sure you'll find it different, but I understand you have to go and discover that on your own."

"Yes, this I must do and if someday my way brings me back, I know where to find you."

"Where will you go then son?"

"I don't know. But I know that I'll leave."

"Then, let me tell you this. If you face that situation, come back this way. This house will be open for you, I promise"

"Yes father, I promise that if it comes to that, I'll come back to you and Penelope."

The priest reached out and hugged him.

"Thank you, son" he said, "You're always welcome here. Now, I'd better go to bed. Tomorrow is another day of work, hard work." He got up and left Pericles and Penelope in the yard.

They were alone under the starry sky and the fragrance of the flowers and she sat close to him. With her trembling hand, warm and inviting, she took his and she leaned close to him, her lips almost touching his.

"You'll leave? You won't stay?"

"I have to Penelope, I have to."

Tears flowed freely down her cheeks. "Yes I know. I also know I'll be here when you come back, because somehow I feel you'll come back. Yes, one day you'll come back."

He kissed her, a soft kiss and tasted her tears, salty and warm.

Early the next day Pericles went to the orchard and worked diligently with the priest. Later, in the evening, when they went back to the house, Pericles told them he wanted to leave the next morning.

Penelope prepared the table and they ate the last supper together. It felt as though a shadow hung over them. In his mind, Pericles thought how nice it is when one arrives and how hard when one leaves.

After they finished their supper and spent some time outside in the fresh air of the courtyard the priest went to bed and Penelope went and sat close to Pericles. Her lips searched for his, a deep erotic kiss that woke up his sexual desire. He wanted her and knew she wanted him as much as he did. They went to her room where they undressed quickly. It was their last night together.

The next morning it was time for him to leave and recommence his adventure.

He put his backpack on his shoulders, opened the door walked out.

As he said his goodbyes, Penelope was sobbing while her dad tried to comfort her.

"He'll come back, Penelope. Wait and see. He'll come back."

Antigone

Later on that same day Pericles passed another small village but he didn't stay for too long because he noticed that people looked at him with suspicion with the exception of an old man who provided him with a piece of bread and some boiled goat meat. But now it was time for Pericles to stop for a while. He walked off the road and when he found a good spot he sat down. He took a piece of that meat and a piece of bread from his back-sack and ate a little before he would start his trek again. He felt refreshed and getting up he walked back to the road which ran between two hills. There was a small creek to his left. Perhaps it would lead him to the Struma River.

Along the road the fields were in full bloom with wildflowers and shrubbery. Bees hummed among the colorful flowers. The wheat and barley fields were already high enough to form the seeds and if this month passed peacefully the upcoming June would be the month of harvest.

Pericles' eyes attention was on the road which took a sharp turn changing its direction. He noticed at the far side the gleam of water. The Struma River! *Yes, this must be it,* he thought. The river was quite some distance from where he was but he would be able to reach it be evening, he was certain of it. Feeling euphoric, he started humming his favorite Cretan *mandinada*.

A strange shiver ran down his spine. Was he really so close to the Hellenic border? With the sight of the river in his view he directed himself toward its gleam.

Late in the afternoon he had almost reach his destination: the last big town of his route, Sandanski. Then suddenly he heard sound of bells from a flock of sheep grazing the green tapestry of the fields and a voice addressed him, a boy's voice: a boy no older than twelve.

"Hello to you too" Pericles answered to the young shepherd's call.

"How are you? Where are you headed?" the shepherd boy asked.

Pericles pointed to the river without saying a word.

"Ah you're going to the village?" the boy asked.

"Where is the village?" Pericles asked.

"That way" the boy pointed him in the direction behind the turn of the hill.

"Yes, that's where I'm headed."

"Who do you know there?" the young shepherd asked.

"Are there any boats in the village?" Pericles asked instead of answering the boy's question.

"Yes, of course, a few. Who are you looking for?"

"I'm looking for work. I'm a fisherman" Pericles lied.

"Then go find my uncle, Hercules. He works alone and he may need help," the boy said.

"And who's your uncle? How do I find him?"

"You ask for Hercules. Everybody knows him. Perhaps you'll find him in his boat, *Antigone*" he added.

"Thank you"

Pericles turned in the direction the boy showed him. It wasn't late in the day when he reached the village. There were about twenty houses and a good size dock where four boats were tied. Soon after as he got closer he discovered *Antigone* and walked close to it, but nobody was on the boat. There were two cafes across the road and a few men having their daily discussions and Pericles walked over to them.

"I'm looking for Hercules" he said. The men eyed each other; then a short blonde man answered.

"I'm Hercules. Come, sit," the man showed him a chair.

Hercules called the café owner to bring a drink to the visitor. Pericles sat with him, introduced himself to the man, and said that he was travelling south and was looking for some work, enough to give him some money to buy necessities for his journey.

Hercules laughed, "And what do you know about fishing?"

"I have worked on boats." Pericles hoped the man would believe him.

"How long you plan to stay here?"

"A few days."

"Okay then, enjoy your coffee and when you're done we'll go ask *Antigone* whether she likes you, and if she does we'll talk about work."

When Pericles finished his coffee they walked across the road to *Antigone*. As Hercules started showing him the boat Pericles was feeling guilty for lying to Hercules a little earlier, so he grabbed his arm he said, "I'm sorry I lied to you about being a fisherman. Sorry, I'm not a fisherman, I just need some work for a couple days to get a few supplies and carry on with my journey. However, if you hire me, believe me I'll do my best, and whatever you may ask me to do, it will be done."

"I know Pericles, I somehow sensed it earlier. But if you need some work, I don't mind a helper for a few days. I hope you don't expect too much money." Hercules laughed good-naturedly.

"Whatever you think is good Hercules, whatever you think is fair."

"Okay then, it's settled." Hercules shook Pericles' hand to seal the agreement.

They walked around the boat while Hercules showed him the ropes, anchor, the cabin where he slept when he was away from home. He told Pericles that *Antigone* liked him, so the deal was sealed. He also told Pericles how he does the merchant's work along the river by buying and selling things from one village to the other. "I know almost everybody in the area," he said.

After Pericles' introduction to *Antigone* they went to Hercules' house where Pericles met Hercules' wife Athena, a short dark haired woman with a stocky build and strong arms. One could see in Athena's features and body the strength of a woman who in her youth would compete with the men in digging and shoveling and doing every possible work of a man. She had small piercing eyes, a round head, a nose like a hawk, fat lips and her hands were fatty and big.

Nonetheless Pericles recognized her good heart with the first look and her way of welcoming him into her small house.

Pericles' eyes ran around the space and got caught onto the hanging batch of garlic and onion, a bunch of tomatoes dried like prunes, dry herbs, oregano and thyme and on the opposite wall a shot gun and the bandolier.

At that moment a young boy ran into the house.

"Here is my son, Achilles" Hercules said and his eyes sparkled.

"I wish the best to all of you." Pericles said.

"Tell me Pericles where are you headed? Earlier at the cafe you talked of a journey."

"Yes, I'm going south,"

"You mean to Hellas, because we're only a few kilometers from the border. I've seen people who have done the same and, truly, I admire them. At least there's more freedom in Hellas even with the dictatorship that runs things there these days."

Pericles didn't make any comment.

"I don't blame them for going south," Hercules said "I don't blame you either; it's better there than here."

"How do you know these things Hercules?"

"I know people. I travel, I talk to people, I learn, it's simple. But don't be concerned with us, you have no fear, after all I'm a Hellene too,"

"Really..." It was Pericles' time to be surprised.

"Yes and *Antigone*, my boat originally belonged to my father. He and I travelled up and down the river year after year and made good money trading and bartering and bringing things to some who never had a chance of getting it without us merchants. I remember when my father grew old I had *Antigone* to myself and although my father's advice was to always stay on the side of Hellas I travelled not only to the Hellenic side of the river, but to the Bulgarian, and I did a thriving business. The guards on the border gave me trouble in the beginning but after a while they knew me and didn't even bother to check out what I carried in and out of Bulgaria. I was making so much money I calculated that in a few more years I would had saved enough to buy a big piece of land and build my own house. But my bad luck hit me the year this country turned into communism and the borders were shut. I was forced to stay here. In fact they confiscated my boat and they put me in jail for a couple of months. You wouldn't believe it, interrogations, physical abuse, torture, until finally they couldn't pin anything on me and they let me go. But I couldn't go back to my homeland. They wouldn't give me the permission to go and soon after I got married and here I am now with a wife and a son. Hope someday he may have the courage to do what you have in your mind."

"You never know, perhaps he may" Pericles smiled at Hercules and showed him Achilles.

"I hope so and I'll help him anyway I can. But tell me, Pericles, where you come from?"

"From Craiova, in Romania," Pericles answered hesitantly.

"You weren't born in Hellas, am I right?" asked Hercules.

"No, my father and grandfather were born in Crete."

"Aha, Crete, the most beautiful of all the islands. But please tell me all about it, how you started and your way up to here?"

Pericles told him about all his days and nights on the road, the difficulties, the pleasant moments and the unpleasant ones, his fight with nature and his interactions with people. Hercules listened to him and admiration gleamed on his face.

"Trust me, and don't be concerned, we'll find the way for you to cross the border. I know every single turn and current of this river. Past the border this river becomes the Strymonas River in the Hellenic language, here we call it Struma."

"Thank you Hercules," Pericles said. "I trust you. We will do what you think and when you think the right time comes."

"Yes, in a couple days, but for now you need to rest and tomorrow we will go together to do the business of the day. The last village before the border is about two hours away and the border from there only three to four hundred meters. You can almost swim down the river. The current will help you even if you don't try much on your own. For all the people we meet we tell them you're my future nephew-in-law, my niece's fiancé. Don't worry it'll all go well, you'll see."

Hercules' wife Athena put the food on the table and all four ate their meal; they clink their glasses to health and good luck. After dinner, Hercules asked his son to run and get his aunt, Anna so he could introduce her to Pericles and explain to her the scheme he had in his mind. While they waited for Anna, Pericles and Hercules sat alone and talked.

For Pericles this man proved to be an endless source of information and also a great source of funny stories about his younger age when he chased girls along his travels up and down the river Struma. He reminisced with a gleam on his face his adventures as a young man. He laughed a lot and Pericles laughed with him since as they drank two more glasses of wine.

"I was the best dancer in the area," Hercules bragged. "All the young women had their eyes on me, and I had a girlfriend in every village along the river."

Hercules stretched his legs, one boot on top of the other and his eyes flashed as he recalled the joys of his youth when he went about with his boat and had his affairs in every stop he made. His face took that euphoric expression of the man who has seen, tasted and enjoyed everything life could give to man.

"Come now Hercules, don't overstate things, don't exaggerate," Pericles laughed, "I know we all have a story to tell, and I like your narratives, they bring me to Crete with the most beautiful women and the dark blue sea, with the sandy shores and the whitewashed houses and it makes me feel nostalgic and heartbroken. Now you know why I've started my quest, why I want to go and find my family. Now you know why I've travelled all this distance and why I can't stop until I get there."

It was as if this was the kindling in the fire and it rekindled in Hercules' mind more memories about when he was a single man. "I remember, Pericles, I was in one small village outside Serres where a wedding was taking place. I wasn't a church goer, perhaps this was the reason the Almighty condemned me to spend my years in a foreign country." He said and got up. He went to the sink, took a glass and poured some water. Walked back to the table as Pericles waited to hear the rest of the story. Hercules drank some of the water and turning to Pericles he carried on.

"I knew the family of the bride. Her father was a grocery store owner I remember I sold some supplies to him from time to time. I also knew the young woman because her uncle caught us one time in their orchard behind their house and for this they were much surprised that I was at the wedding. The groom, a mountain man, a shepherd, but he had a good name in the village and the people said he had a good bank account too. So the parents of the girl agreed to the wedding. The bride wasn't much enamoured with him but she couldn't disagree with her parents' decision. It was settled. I went to the wedding and also took part in the big feast. We ate and drank and danced more than any other time. I had a couple of my buddies with me."

He stopped. He looked at Pericles to make sure the young man had his attention tuned. Satisfied he carried on his story.

"It was a beautiful summer night, as soft as the bride's breasts and my mind was working overtime how to get the woman on the side and away from all this activity. The music was in full blast and it was tradition to get every man from around the tables to dance with the bride. Each man took the front spot and took the bride by the hand and he would dance a few steps following the song played by the musicians and then the other and the other. My turn came at some point and I grabbed the soft hand of the woman I had in their orchard some time ago. We both felt as if we were losing each other. I also felt angry because that beautiful young woman was about to sleep with that big animal and also sorry because the mountain man would have her take care of his animals and make his cheeses. I felt so angry I wanted to have this bride this same night before him. I turned my head to her, and squeezed her fingers and winked at her. She knew what I wanted and with her imperceptible agreement I felt I was flying in the clouds and started dancing like no other time."

He stopped again and turned to look at his wife working away at the sink, cleaning their dishes and his face got lit as if by a sudden sunlight that came into the room from an unknown source.

"I felt I could fly" he carried on, "I felt I could jump over all these people who were sitting around the tables drinking and eating and laughing and having a good tome; I felt I could jump over all of them with my beautiful bride in my arms and I would take her to my house, to my room, to my bed. This was crazy but I felt right in wanting to have this woman once more just before the animal would put her under him and violate her beauty."

He stopped again, took a deep breath, looked toward his wife, as if he wanted to conceal the rest of the story, as if he felt it was only for Pericles' ears and for this he lowered his voice when he continued.

"She knew what I wanted and she wanted it as much as I did. After the dance finished I went and sat next to my two buddies who knew something was going on after seeing me and her. They tried to cover for me so I could get my chance, which came not too long after when the bride got up to go and change. On her way, she gave me a glance and I knew what to do."

Hercules stopped and his imagination was reliving that image of the bride when she got up to go and change. The he remained quiet, deep in thought for a while. Then he began to speak again.

"Around daybreak the feast was over, the people dispersed and we had to leave as well. The groom took his new bride to the house of a relative. My two buddies and I took the narrow paths of the village until we reached the house where the groom and the bride went. Indeed I felt right, Pericles, and once she knew I was outside, she came down and I don't know on what excuse. I didn't ask, but I enjoyed that flaming body once more, in the barn, with my buddies keeping an eye on the surrounding paths and houses. And when we had enough, she left to go to her new husband. I've never regretted that, I don't think she ever regretted it herself: our secret, before she became the wife of that animal. A little later when I went to my *Antigone*, my boat, and saw the sun rising on the other side of the river, it seemed to me red as blood and the river like throbbing arteries of a gigantic man who wanted to penetrate every woman possible and the horizon looked to me as if crowned with a beautiful wedding crown. I couldn't help myself, and I raised my arms toward the sky and yelled with all the might of my lungs 'God almighty please bless me one more time with this beautiful view of your sun and your river and your horizon.'"

He stopped and looked at Pericles with teary eyes.

"It never happened to me again." he said. This was his pain, his unfulfilled wish.

At that moment his wife turned her face from the sink towards them and seeing Hercules' poetic expression she laughed and she said to Pericles.

"He narrated his adventures to you? I'm not surprised. He does that often."

Pericles let his mind travel. He felt warm and comfortable with Hercules just as he used to feel with his grandfather. He wished he lived in a place where men like Hercules and his grandfather lived: Hellenes, only Hellenes who feel and speak and react like in such a way.

Stefanos, the boatman's son who had gone to get Anna, Hercules' sister in law, came back home with his untie Anna, a woman with black hair flowing to her shoulders. Her warm, friendly eyes made Pericles feel a strange attraction to her.

Hercules had told him that although her parents had done every possible effort to educate her and prepare her for life, and although she was a very attractive young woman, she was still single. Hercules had said that she preferred to be alone than to marry someone she wouldn't like to be with.

"Come in, Anna," Hercules said, "I want you to meet my friend."

Anna hugged Athena, then Hercules.

"This is Pericles, my good friend," Hercules said. "He'll work with me for a while. He's going south. I'm going to help him get past the guards. You keep all this to yourself, no word, not even to your parents. They don't need to know. I want your help, I want you to help me, help him go to his homeland."

"Yes uncle" she glanced at Pericles who smiled at her.

"Well, this is why I called you here this time in the night. If anyone asks me who he is and what he's doing here I'll say that you two plan to get married"

"*Imagine that,*" Anna thought as a smile lit her beautiful face "*Me, married to this handsome young man. Surely he's younger than me, and so handsome!*"

"Yes, Hercules, I know what you want. I'm good with that."

"Thank you Anna, I knew I could count on you. No word to anybody, promise?"

Anna agreed with a nod of her head. Her mind went to the suggestion, *what a thought, imagine if that was possible,* she thought, *to get married to this Hellene.*

Pericles's eyes met with Anna's and for an inexplicable reason he winked. Anna laughed a light laughter and her cheeks got blushed. Touched Pericles hand and said in a funny way.

"Yes, my future husband, I won't say anything to anyone."

Hercules and his wife Athena even young Stefanos joined them in a good felt laughter.

Early in the morning Hercules took Pericles for a stroll to the boat.

Hercules wanted to sail down to the next village and such an excursion was an opportunity for Pericles to learn the tricks of the fisherman's work and how he deals with the villagers. It was also time for him to learn how they would undock *Antigone* and get her ready to sail.

Hercules told him the people in the villages around this part of Bulgaria lived mostly from their own produce, their fishing and the little commerce which took place between the villages. Some even had a few flocks of goats and sheep which they herded up and down the slopes of the surrounding hills. There were three other boats besides *Antigone* doing exactly what Hercules did.

"So you have some competition!" Pericles remarked.

"We all have to survive, Pericles. They aren't in it for the competition, they're just good friends who do what I do, and the river provides for all of us."

They found *Antigone* waiting for them like a good wife and Pericles wasn't surprised at all when they stepped on deck and he heard Hercules say "Hello beautiful!" He wasn't even surprised when Hercules tuned his ear for the expected answer and he kept a few moments of silence to make sure he didn't miss it.

They untied the rope and collected it in a big spool, the engine was fired and the boat left her mooring. The shrubs on the shore became smaller as they headed southward to the following village.

Hercules held the steering column and Pericles stood beside him marvelling at the sights, the trees and smaller vegetation on the river banks, farther away the mountain peaks, the flat areas with the odd houses, the orchards along the river banks, the fields, the animals grazing here and there and a small flock of sheep with the bell of the lead ram clearly heard from the boat. The aroma of wild flowers floated in the atmosphere and Pericles took it all inside with pleasure. The water also not only sparkled and reflected the sunshine but also revealed its moist fragrance as if it was welcoming the new comer.

Soon after they were on their way Hercules asked Pericles to take the steering wheel in his hands and showed him a landmark far away down the river. He told Pericles to keep a steady route towards it, since this was where they were headed. It wasn't difficult at all, Pericles discovered to steer the boat to their destination.

The water flowed smoothly toward the Hellenic border which would be his destination. They passed a few houses along their course, smoke rising from the chimneys. To the starboard of *Antigone* the houses were laid as if in layers upwards on the side as comfortable as children in the arms of their mother. Below the houses the mighty Struma River flowed without any hesitation.

Hercules explained to Pericles that these houses were built mostly by Hellenes and although this mountain on top of the village had fallen down twice over the centuries and destroyed them, the inhabitants insisted on rebuilding. It was inexplicable, he said, why they kept on doing this, but there was also another reason. It was three centuries ago when a few families, wanting to escape the wrath of the Turks, travelled up the river from their homeland and settled here where they found refuge and protection under the mountain and after they went through hell to reach this point they pledged never to leave their mother-mountain, no matter what.

"This was the reason this community was built" Hercules said, " but I also give them credit for being so stubborn like mules and have remained here despite the unfortunate landslides that occurred a couple of times over the years."

Pericles pointed toward the slope of the mountain.

"I see a cave up there." He pointed at the dark spot in the face of the mountain.

"Yes and even that has its story." Hercules said. "A lot of years ago after they had rebuilt the village for the third time a young man from the village decided to explore and find out why the mountain gave way and rolled down over them, he climbed up to the '*hole*' as they called it, searched around, came back down, studied for it for days, a very smart man he was. He couldn't trace anything. He even went to the holy land where he stayed for a year, studying, inquiring, learning, and finally he came back a year later with a title, he was a *hatzi*, a wise man. He climbed up to the cave again, and remained there for days on end. The villagers used a basket to send food up to him. He meditated, prayed, he did whatever a *hatzi* knows to do. Then one good bright morning they saw him standing on the edge of the cave's mouth gesticulating and crying out words the people below couldn't understand. The villagers asked him what was going on. He said he had discovered the reason for the mountains habit of sliding down. However when they asked him to define what he meant, he jumped over the edge and fell to his death and no one learned what he the *hatzi* had learned. Some didn't even care, they buried the man. They went on with their lives as if nothing had happened. Some believed their *hatzi* was crazy, and since then when one says something totally unacceptable, or something totally unbelievable, they usually say 'You too belong in the hole.'"

Hercules slowed down the boat as they had almost reached the dock. They moored and jumped out. They headed toward the first café in the little square of the village. A dozen villagers were sitting around drinking their coffees.

When the two boat-men entered the café the man behind the counter, a chubby man greeted them. He laughed with joy upon seeing Hercules and his inquiring eyes fixed on Pericles. He winked at Hercules, curious to know more about the young man. Hercules leaned to his ear and said "He's my nephew in law to be."

"Where did you meet this fellow?" the proprietor asked, pointing his eyes toward Pericles.

Hercules told him that Pericles was the son of a good friend, and pointed out to the café owner that he had a lot of friends along the river. He said that Anna would be a very happy woman as they would get married, which was to take place sooner rather than later. He also pressed the man to keep everything secret which wouldn't happen as the boat-man knew well the café owner would be the first to blab all this around to everyone who would pass by his spot.

"What you bring us today?" the café owner asked. Hercules laughed and said he always brought good things to the place, but his time he had some extra special items for them. He opened the package he carried and showed it to the cafe proprietor. The other men got up from their chairs and came close to look.

Hercules called one of the boys who were playing soccer in the street, to run and tell the village people that the boat-man had arrived and good things were available at the café. The young lad, upon hearing that he was to get a reward for his effort ran as fast as a goat climbing the side of a hill.

In a short time a group of women arrived at the café. They were all dressed in heavy clothes that reached down to the ground and wore sandals. Their faces and their characteristics were dark and because by that time the heat of the day was at its highest point, the heavily dressed women must have been very hot. Their faces were almost covered by their clothes and only their eyes were clearly visible. They came close to look at the merchandise and picked the various items. One of them bartered for eggs, another for chicken's feet tied with a string another was holding in a bag a bottle filled with olive oil, another useful item. Soon everything Hercules had brought to the village was sold or exchanged for something else.

The job was finished the day was more than half way passed and it was time to feed the little donkey, as Hercules used to refer to his body, "The little donkey that has carried us all along this life and if we don't feed him, he wouldn't be around for too long."

"What can you prepared for us?" He asked the owner.

"I have a kilo of lamb intestines and I would be happy to pan-fry half of it. It wouldn't take too long" he said.

"Cook it all and bring the wine. Let us all have a good lunch."

Hercules shouted to him.

Soon the intestines were cooked and placed on two platters, a flask of wine was brought to the table, two plates of olives, some feta cheese and a sliced garlic coil appeared as if from nowhere while the men gathered close to the visitors and the eating and clinking and good wishing started. It didn't stop until evening came. After they sang a few songs and drank plenty of wine along with the fried intestines it was time for Hercules and Pericles to start their way back home.

Hercules fired up *Antigone's* engine and his hand took the control, the route was already pre-arranged, a route *Antigone* knew too well. The stars gleamed in the heavens and everything was as it should be although the current worked against them on their way back.

"Didn't you tell me most of these people were Hellenes or of Hellenic descent Hercules?" Pericles asked as they sailed along the river.

"But, yes, of course. Why?"

"Their ways looked strange to me, their appearance, but also the way they carried themselves, both men and women, the ones who came to barter, I mean."

"Why did they look strange to you?"

"I imagined Hellenes to be graceful, proud, people," Pericles said. "I remember my grandfather telling me stories of the proud Hellenes, the heroes who resembled the Gods of ancient Hellas. I didn't see or feel those images when I met these villagers. They all behaved like thieves, grabbing, and how quickly they came and sat next to us when you ordered food. Their eyes looked suspicious and they preferred to stay aloof, far from us and the women, like gypsies. None of these people looked like true Hellenes. They seemed to be easterners, afraid of something invisible, yet controlling their reactions, their behavior and their attitude. It was truly strange but I felt they weren't Hellenes at all."

Pericles felt as if he had just confessed his darkest secrets but he felt a lot lighter than before, although a strange fear had dived deep in his essence, an imperceptible agony, a strange premonition he could say. Was he to experience the same disappointing emotion

when he'd meet his compatriots in Crete? Suddenly his optimistic demeanor changed into fear which lurked inside him, a premonition
that things might not be as good as he imagined them when he
planned his quest.

"How many years had your grandfather lived abroad?" Hercules
asked.

"Well, since the early 40s."

"Over thirty years, that's what it is. Things change in such a long
time, Pericles, nothing stays the same. Don't forget that from the time
your grandfather left, a World War took place, the German occupation, the civil war. The time it took to rebuild the country. All these
things have a profound effect on everybody. Whatever the war didn't
destroy the civil war completed."

Hercules' eyes darkened as if covered by an ominous anticipation. His hands held the stirring wheel of *Antigone* but his heart
ached at the disappointment he felt was waiting for Pericles when he
got to his fatherland.

"But let us talk of these people here in this village" he continued,
"their story started long ago when they travelled northward. Think
of the difficulties they dealt with, and what they went through over
the years to establish themselves. Don't forget they also had to deal
with thieves and pirates who somehow find everybody, no matter
where they might live; pirates who sometimes came from the river,
other times they walked over the mountains. And the end result was
always the same. After the gang of thieves walked away the villagers
had to rebuild and start all over; years later communism came, another curse that we dealt with and still do these days. Yes, the situation is a little more secure now. But we also have the committees and
the party authorities, them being the central and the local. They
come, they search, they arrest, they take away people they put them
in jails. There is no end to it. Just four years ago they came and arrested the café owner's son. They took him away, interrogations, pun-
ishments, you name it, and finally they executed him as he was an
enemy of the state, they said. His body was discovered thrown down
a cliff, a bullet in his chest. Who did it? Why? Nobody ever found
out. People suspected there was a traitor amongst them in the village

and nothing went unnoticed."

Hercules looked at Pericles to make sure everything he said fell into the proper ears and all along his hands moved in every direction to emphasize the meaning of his words. His face expressed each emotion with the appropriate grimace as if expertly painted by a magnificent painter.

Pericles shook his head. He understood all he had heard, but this wasn't what he had meant. His problem was with the general attitude of the people, the way they carried themselves, their untrustworthiness, their constant fear and suspicion, their servitude after they realized that the food was ordered for all of them. They had started licking Hercules ass, their low down your head attitude as if they had no pride. This wasn't the way he expected to find in the people who originated from Hellas. They weren't the way his grandfather had described them to him. He expected to see proud people with their heads up. He expected to find something totally different. A strange premonition overtook his thoughts and his mind ran to Penelope. Perhaps she was right. Perhaps what he was after didn't exist.

Hercules must had seen that what he had said up to that time wasn't enough so he added that he had heard that Hellas was under a dictatorship government for the past three years and this wasn't much different than the communism they lived under in Romania and Bulgaria. He also added that there wasn't much freedom in Hellas as Pericles probably hoped. With this unexpected information Pericles jumped up. He remembered that while in Romania he heard the word dictatorship and he remembered his grandfather being upset every time they talked of it with his father or other Hellenes who lived in Craiova.

"When did you hear of this Hercules?"

"Some time ago. I heard of instability or government changes every so often, until one morning, April the 21st 1967, four colonels took over the reins of the nation and they've been governing ever since; for three years now and they've arrested thousands and they've taken them to various concentration camps in some islands of the Aegean. They were some killings too, incarcerations and many other ugly things."

Suddenly Pericles thought he smelled a foul odor floating in the air, as if a dead animal was laid on the banks of the river, an imperceptible odor that reached his nostrils which he felt was exhumed by dead flesh as if someone was staring at him, watching every move he made. His senses were altered he wasn't who he was a little while ago. Perhaps it was the news of another snake biting his dream? *Dictatorship, yes,* he thought, *but perhaps things will change someday it shouldn't be as bad as in Romania, no matter what.*

Time passed slowly as the current of the river worked against them and made *Antigone* try her hardest to bring them home to Hercules' village. When they finally arrived at their port, they tied the boat onto the dock and walked straight to the house where Hercules' wife had cooked some stew with potatoes. They both enjoyed the meal and washed it down with wine.

Hercules said that in two days they should make the effort to have him cross the border, while next day he and Pericles would go to catch a few fishes; the day after they should sail down-river to Kulata, the last village before the border, where they would sell whatever they had available. The same night before they would start their way back, Pericles would be free to go, and hopefully with no unexpected surprises.

Pericles smiled upon hearing the plan Hercules had unravelled and agreed that it was doable. He shook Hercules' hand as if sealing the deal and they clinked their glasses and said *stin ugeia mas,** as people cheer in Hellas.

That night Pericles went to bed with his mind jumping from one thought to the other. Nothing was worse than not knowing what he would find when he was in Crete, things he had heard today from Hercules had left him with a void, an emptiness that consumed his mind and wouldn't let him relax. Was it as bad as he had heard back in Romania in the discussions his father and grandfather had? How could it be? Was this a reason for him to give up his trip and turn back or should he go northward to the village where Penelope lived with her father?

To our health

Images of his childhood came to mind, his fight against the Romanian boys, his gang of friends in school, his grandfather's talks about Crete and her people. No it couldn't be as bad as Hercules meant, it couldn't be.

With this decisive thought sleep came. But soon enough he had a dream. His grandfather's face appeared. The old man's black eyes were on fire and his lips tightened as if saying to him 'No you won't stop now, you have to get to the end of this quest. No more hesitation, no change of mind, no change of plans. You won't ever be free until you reach Crete. You belong to your family and your family's wish is that you get to the end of your quest, to find your answers. Your resolve will help you complete your journey. Only when you reach Crete will you discover who you are and where you are headed in life. Don't fill yourself with thoughts of going back. Your goal and purpose in life are to get to Crete and live there as I did back then. Only when you do this you'll truly discover who you are. No turning back, never!" Pericles woke with the image of his grandfather. This was what he had to bring to fruition, come hell or high water. It was his destiny to fulfil his quest.

The next day Pericles and Hercules kept busy fishing and taking turns at the equipment, trying to outdo each other, with Hercules winning almost every challenge. Pericles enjoyed his last day in Bulgaria and he kept on thinking of it all day long. They had started their day early, when a light pink hue painted the horizon. A pleasant smell of jasmine came up from the river as if one had sprinkled perfume into it. Both men noticed and inhaled the heavenly fragrance deep in to their lungs.

They had anchored *Antigone* and placed the net into the river. After they pulled in and put aside the few fishes they had caught they moved *Antigone* to another spot. They threw the net three more times and after they fished for a couple of hours and gathered a good catch, they placed the fish in containers, pulled up the anchor and headed home.

Upon arriving they took care of the fish, putting them in ice to have them ready for the next day. They ate their meal and then Hercules said.

"Tomorrow we will go southward to the last village before the border where we'll sell our catch and whatever other merchandize he have available. We'll spend the whole day there, and only late in the night we'll start coming back home. I'll get you close to the border which you can cross by swimming down the river. The current will help you and if everything goes as planned, you'll be in Hellas in no more than half an hour."

"Would it be better to swim down the river or try to cross on land?" Pericles asked and added, "I'm afraid the border would be lit by strong spot lights so it would be easy for the guards to spot me in the water."

"I have devised a device" Hercules said, "that you can use to cover your head and your backpack. I have constructed a box which you can place over your head while swimming toward Hellas. I have also built a small shelf onto which you can place the backpack. That way you can swim noiselessly down the river and no one will see you in the water as the only thing visible will be the box, and usually there are boxes and things that the river takes along in its current" Hercules assured him, "it will be a perfect hiding place for you."

They got up and Hercules took him to his storage room where he had all his fishing gear where among all things. He showed Pericles a big wooden box full of flasks, nets, and all kinds of things he used. Next to it he had a smaller but new box which was the box Pericles would use as his cover. Pericles admired Hercules' ingenuity to come up with such an idea. Hercules explained not to worry about anything, because although the box would cover him well, it had gaps between the planks so air could circulate easily and he wouldn't have any problem breathing.

Hercules turned it upside down and showed Pericles a shelf, roomy enough for Pericles' backpack.

"Imagine it in the water in front of you. The only thing you have to do is dive and put your head under it. Then you hold it by this ledge and you swim slowly down the river. No one will see you until you reach the other side, and when you're far enough from the Bulgarian border you can get out of it, since you'll be in Hellas by then. The Bulgarian outpost is on the right side as the river flows south and the Hellenic outpost on the left a hundred meters further south. You'll try to stay on the left side of the river you'll end up close to the guards at the Hellenic outpost."

"You've thought of everything, Hercules, thank you." Pericles said and shook the man's hand.

"I have calculated the distance, no more than four hundred meters from where I'll drop you off the boat. It will be easy to cross with hardly any effort. The river will do it for you."

Pericles agreed. "Very good Hercules, I'm amazed with your plan."

"When you reach the Hellenic side, you know what to do from there on."

Hercules took his hand-drill and in the most perfect spots he drilled two holes as large as they should be for Pericles' glance to peak through in order to tune his attention to the river banks as the current pulled him downriver to Hellas. He hung the drill on a nail on the wall and smiled. And Pericles who was observing every move the boat-man made smiled back at him.

"You'll do just fine, you'll see," Hercules said. "Don't be concerned with anything. This is your last obstacle. Everything will turn out alright."

"Even if I had to face a lot more difficulties I would fight to get through, Hercules, you know it," Pericles said, and thanked him.

The boat-man looked at Pericles and in the flash of time their eyes met Hercules' glance sensed that the young man who had travelled for so long and from so far wouldn't be stopped by anything.

Suddenly Pericles' eyes turned teary as emotion overtook him. He thought of how lucky he was to meet this man who had done so much to help him. There must be a higher power that had orchestrated all this and has brought in front of him people like Hercules and the priest with Penelope and the bush man. They all meant something to him, they all contributed in their own way to make his long journey a bit easier, even that lone injured wolf in his hunger taught Pericles a valuable lesson, one that is learned in life, in nature's university. He felt happy for everything he had met and experienced.

"I've pondered how lucky I have been all along this trip, how many good people I have come across, and how you have made this last piece of the trip easier. I have no words that can express this emotion…Thank you, is all I can say." He shook Hercules hand again and almost in tears he felt in the other man's squeeze his warmth and good heartedness. He also knew if he were in Hercules' place he would do exactly the same for the passer by who was searching for his roots as he was at this time.

"You don't need to thank me for anything. I don't help to get a 'thank you', that's not my goal." Hercules answered and one could see his eyes full of tears, "It's what I wished I could do myself, not now of course, but when I was a lot younger and more courageous. Life has taken me as it takes everyone to its path, and one has to keep afloat, like you, Pericles will have to, when you swim down this mighty Struma River which will take you to the motherland of your parents."

Hercules' words touched the young man's heart. They both understood what it meant to escape from tyranny, what this voyage meant to the birthplace of civilization.

Before night came they carried what equipment they would need to *Antigone*. The next day they placed the various items in their appropriate spots and secured them. Upon finishing the task they returned to the house to relax for Pericles' last night in Bulgaria. Tomorrow night would be the night of the crossing the second and last border to Hellas.

Pericles' thought about border and how the guards there would see him when he would walk to them and talk to them. What would they think of him, coming from such a faraway place? What would they do when they hear him say he had been travelling for all this time? But why was he worrying about of all these things now? He was an Hellene and he would be talking to Hellenes. What was there to worry about?

Anna visited them on this last night. They all sat at the table together, even Stefanos, Hercules' son sat at the table but the words were hard to be spoken. It was as if a heavy shroud was over them, a heavy blanket over their hearts that kept them quiet. They would separate with one of their own; a member of their family, a good friend,

ᴧ no one could speak of it, although their minds were fixated on
ᴧ. Even Athena, the boat-man's wife, as hard to bend as she always
seemed, from time to time would take her kerchief and wipe her eyes.
Pericles tried to start a conversation and Hercules asked him to narrate some of the events that had taken place along his voyage, who
he met and how they reacted to him, in which villages or towns he
stayed, how he spent his nights, what he ate, where he slept. He
wanted to know everything that transpired from the day Pericles left
Romania until he reached their village.

Pericles narrated to them, in as much detail as he could master,
the experiences he had with Penelope and her father, the fight with
the two youngsters, the bushman he found up on the mountains, his
unforgettable experience with the lone wolf. Everyone listened quite
attentively and gasped with joy at the end of the narrative when he
told them how he had buried the dead wolf before he re-commenced
his quest. He related his experience digging and cleaning the grape
vine field of the priest of the weeds, his good rapport with the bushman, and how he worked his traps with the utmost respect for nature.
He told them how he had crossed the great Danube River, the first
border, and how lucky he was to find that boat man who, for a good
pay, took him across the water. He described his time in various caves
and natural hideouts where he had spent his nights when he couldn't
be close to a town or village. They all listened to him and there was
admiration in the eyes of everybody, especially the young Stefanos
whose eyes gleamed in awe. One day, like Pericles, perhaps he might
start his own quest southward to the country his grandfather and father had come from. One day he might go and find Pericles in Crete:
if Pericles can accomplish it why not him?

"Even if I had to face three times worst situations, I would have
still tried to travel to my Crete" Pericles told them and all four understood. Nothing other than death could stop him, from accom-
plishing what he had dreamed off for all his life.

There wasn't anything the others could say but listen and occasionally nod to show their understanding. After all they were listening to a Cretan who, only in the name of his island found comfort
and refuge, even if the island was only in his imagination.

Anna was silent but from time to time she would raise her eyes and stare at him as if she was seeing the man to whom she was truly married, and her mind played with her and suggested how nice that would be, to have a man such as this one as her husband. Pericles was a man with such fire in his soul and such determination in his life, a man who could turn the earth upside down in order to achieve his dream, his ideal, a man who would do anything and everything to accomplish his goal irrespective of what that goal was.

Pericles caught her eyes and smiled at her, an imperceptible signal to her to which her response was a light blushing of her cheeks a reaction that didn't go unnoticed by her brother in law Hercules.

However time came for the young woman to go home. She got up and after she kissed her sister and said good night to Hercules she extended her hand toward Pericles who didn't take it, but instead opened his arms and gave her a warm embrace.

"Thank you" was the only words she said before she walked out of the door along with Stefanos, who would keep her company along the way to her house.

In Hellas

With the first rosy hue on the eastern horizon the boat-man and Pericles got up. The water at first glance looked inviting, its ripples
smooth and continuous, its depth clear and reflective as if responding
to the virginal prodding of the light.

The boat's ropes were untied and secured on the deck and the
land slowly distanced itself once *Antigone's* engine started and the
propeller began its revolutions as the strong hand of Hercules guided
the controls and Pericles helped the best he could. Tomorrow by this
time he would be on the soil of the motherland. Hercules blew the
horn of *Antigone* twice and it filled the air with its sweet reverbera-
tions.

Pericles gazed at the endlessness of the horizon toward the point
where earth and sky touched and the sun winked his eye behind the
small cloud, a puffy cotton ball, trying to play hide and seek with Pericles' patience. So strong was Pericles' anticipation and anxiety for the
day to pass that he felt as if he was held captive in a deep prison cell,
a thought that prompted him to stand up, open his arms to the horizon, and cry out in Cretan a verse he had just composed at that moment

> *"Oh sun you great master*
> *a day's play and a victor*
> *come pass as fast you can*
> *wish to see the moon arrive"*

The boat-man was left with a gaping mouth at Pericles' sudden outburst of poetry, which was the reaction of a man committed to a goal and ready to summon it, as ready as a bullfighter grabs the bull's horns and somersaults over it to the expecting arms of the Kore, like those in the fresco he had seen in books, an image that had remained intact in the mirror of his soul.

Hercules answered him with a verse of his own

> *"The sun has always turned*
> *the earth's fine-tuned wheel*
> *don't think of it as idle*
> *as the ass of the milkman's wife"*

They both responded with a loud and free spirited laughter that even the trees on the river banks heard and rustled as if agreeing with the boat-man's song. The little birds perched on the tree limbs also let a joyous chirp fly over the fragrant air to reach their ears so they understood even they had a good laugh out of this poetry.

Hercules told Pericles to be patient, the day would go by slowly and the night would come when he would have his turn to act as he has planned. Pericles responded with a deep and long sigh. Sometimes words couldn't express the emotions and this was one of those times. The boat-man captured the meaning of that long sigh and said nothing further leaving the smooth water of the Struma and the slow swaying of the trees on the riverbanks and the ethereal discussions of the birds and the soft humming of *Antigone* sailing along the shallow water to do the talking.

"You're right, it'll go by," Pericles said, "Tell me, though, you think we may run in trouble?"

"No, I'm sure everything will go according to our plans, rest assured!"

"I mean since we came this way south a couple of days ago, does anyone keep an eye on when and how often you come here?"

"Not really," Hercules said. "I come to this southern village often, and no one will ever see or do anything, or notice anything unusual. Relax, and we'll have a good time in the village."

"How are the people?" Pericles asked

"What do you mean?"

"You said most of them are Hellenes or of Hellenic descent. Is there something special about them? Is there any story about them like the other village we went two days ago? I remember you mentioned their story, do these people have some story that you know?"

"No, nothing in particular," Hercules replied. "They're as they are supposed to be. But be a bit cautious because they look at everyone new they meet carefully, since they know that not far to the south is the border."

Pericles didn't say anything but Hercules' last words dived deep inside him and he promised to be vigilant.

Nothing else was said, and their day went by smoothly and indeed Pericles did notice the glances of the villagers fixed on him, on what he said, when he laughed, when he was serious about something. It was a nervous reaction to Hercules' warning, but Pericles dealt with it as best as he could.

He and Hercules spent most of their time with the merchandise trading and selling, buying and bartering.

"We do our best', Hercules told Pericles, "it wouldn't matter whether we made some profit or not what was important was to keep busy with the villagers, make them feel comfortable and insure that what they were doing was good and fair."

Pericles looked at him with questioning eyes.

"What do you mean Hercules?"

"Let the profits be for the more greedy people." Hercules said, "I'm not in this world for the profits nor a big bank account, or pressuring the villagers to buy an item at whatever price just for the sake of the gain."

Pericles listened to him and tuned his actions according to Hercules.

By sundown the two boat-men had finished their daily affairs and after they organized things on the deck and in the hold of *Antigone* they went to the only café in the village to have a bite to eat and to spend some time with the villagers.

There were a few men of various ages at the café, having coffees or drinks and their usual card games. Two older men were alone at a table when Hercules pointed to Pericles to sit with them. One of the two old men, who Hercules introduced as a good friend, had hardly any teeth. His breathing was fast as if he was running but his voice was firm. He spoke like a man who knew only truth and spoke only truth, who understood the world as it was supposed to be understood, and dealt with it as one should deal with such matters, with simplicity — no fanfares, no extras, only what was necessary, only what was applied, only what mattered to be said or shown. Hercules whispered to Pericles that the man was a Hellene who had lived there for a long time, who travelled to Hellas quite often and came back with Hellenic goods and news. This made Pericles pay more attention to what the old man narrated to them.

"Every time I came to this village" Hercules said, "the old man would invite me to his humble dwelling and we would share a glass of wine. However today since we found him here he prefers to stay put. He lives alone, with no problems, no heirs, no wife, not any relative, since his wife had left him for the long voyage to the unknown."

And today the old fellow was cheerful and talkative, as if something special had occurred and turned his day into a spectacular affair, one that one seeks to have from time to time. Another reason, of course, was the few glasses of wine he had enjoyed. He had a peculiar way of drinking his wine in one big gulp and once the contents of the glass would reach his stomach he would bring his hand in front of his mouth and like a child he would let a tiny burp that sounded like the chirp of a bird. He had dark eyes into which one could see a visible gleam as if they had caught fire, as if he wanted to light the whole universe with them, as if he wanted to be forever lit by its invincible power, a power Pericles knew lived only in his Crete, a power that was the characteristic of a Cretan. The old man's face was full of wrinkles as if eons had ploughed over it, as if the abating time had clawed on it and had left deep scars the results of joys and aches he had lived through. It was as if the only witness of his livelihood was that face and everything that had happened to him for a good eighty years were deeply incised in his face. His teeth, if the last three broken roots were called teeth, were dark in color and full of cavities, like tired tree trunks standing without knowing what their purpose of being there was. They were reminiscent of the experiences of hard meat he had eaten. His lips were discolored by the persistence of the years yet they were soft like the lips he had kissed back before the decay of the years had carved onto them. He had wrinkled and rough hands, scarred and full of trouble as if he had wrestled an invincible giant from morning to evening for many days on end, hands that fought against the blackberry bushes that were abundant in his land, as if they had fought against enemies visible and invisible, yet they were hands that provided him with the hard earned daily bread. His ears were thin and almost transparent while his wispy hair was scantily spread over his dark scalp, snowy hair, a witness of the years that had gone by. And the clothes he wore were torn, with patches sewn over rips and holes.

Pericles savoured the images of the old Hellene as he fought against the finger food the café owner, had brought to them at Hercules' request. The old man placed a piece of meat into his mouth and it was truly hilarious to see how he managed to chew it with his half decayed teeth. Yet it was done and the food was gulped with a light burp that followed. The old man looked straight, Pericles thought, one of those who 'called the figs figs' as the Hellenic saying goes, one who didn't know the word lie, one who only spoke when he was asked or his opinion was expected. His essence was fiery and sunlit, always ready to spark at the first strike of injustice he saw, and though he rarely said much, one could understand this man had no enemies, no concerns. He had no fears or wonder of where he was destined to go as he had already reached it. He had no questions of where he may go after his passing as if he already knew there was no need for such a concern since when Hades would come, the old man would leave him a free hand to search into his soul with his own eyes.

Pericles felt awed by the simple yet meaningful gestures and words of the old Hellene. He smiled at the old man's wondering eyes and the answer was written on the man's smile.

"As one grows, my dear boy" the old man said looking at Pericles, "one learns to savor the simple things in life. This piece of tender meat that I have difficulty chewing, this glass of wine which is of the few

I'll enjoy for the rest of my life, these things, one learns to savor better when one grows to my age."

Pericles's face turned lighted as if the sun flooded the café and everything became shiny. He nodded his agreement with the old man's comment and added.

"Even if one isn't old, one can still appreciate these same things, provided he sees them through the same lens." My grandfather used to tell me this.

"He was a wise man," the old man added and kept on turning the tender meat in his mouth hoping to soften it enough to swallow it.

"Yes, I know," Pericles answered and a soft ache took control of his heart at the memory of his grandfather. His image at his death bed came to Pericles' mind and his last words: "swear to me you'll go to Crete." The pleasant thought that he has followed what he promised his grandfather made Pericles feel better and looking at the old man he added.

"He was not only wise, but also my grandfather."

The old man grabbed Pericles' hand and squeezed it as if saying, 'good, very good, young man, you know where you're headed.'

Slowly time passed and when after sundown the tender night arrived he and Hercules got up to leave, but not before they had their last clink of the glasses and after emptying them they cheered once more. The old man got up, almost staggering, shook their hands in an official way.

Hercules and Pericles walked to where *Antigone* was moored. They untied the ropes, coiled them on the deck and fired the engine. As they were distancing themselves from the village the young man walked nervously on the deck. Sensing Pericles' nervousness Hercules tried to remind him things he had said before.

"Remember after you pass the Bulgarian guards to your right as the river flows south not more than a hundred meters you'll see the light from the Hellenic outpost to your left."

"I remember," Pericles said.

"The Bulgarian guards may use their big spotlight, but don't be concerned, they can't see you. Keep moving slowly, not much splash-ing, keep slowly moving, you'll do just fine."

"*Entaxi*, Hercules." Pericles said.

"Now it would be better to relax until the right time came when you'll jump into the water."

He advised Pericles to take off his shoes and when he would be in the water to place them within his backpack on the little ledge he had built in the box.

Time passed slowly and Pericles' heart started beating in a fast rhythm, sending him goosebumps. When *Antigone* was far enough from the village, and no one could see what they were about to do, Hercules helped him lower the box with its open side in the water and, holding it with a rope, he helped Pericles over the deck.

"Good bye Hercules. Thank you for everything," were Pericles' last words as he shook Hercules' hand.

"Good luck," the boat-man answered as he helped him dive into the water.

Once Pericles' was under the water and placed himself inside the box; it wasn't as difficult as he thought it would be. He put his back-pack, along with his shoes, on the little ledge. The two handles on each side gave him a good grip. From the boat's side he started swim-ming southward and in a few minutes he was quite a long way from the vessel which had started to sail northward toward Hercules' vil-lage.

The water was cold, and in order to retain his warmth Pericles stopped swimming and he let the current take him slowly on its course toward the border not more than a hundred meters away. Time passed.

Outside the box the night was quiet, smooth like the water of the mighty Struma which was taking Pericles to his destination. As if the night was his co-conspirator working to his favor, it seemed to stand still and noiseless shielding him from the danger of suspicious eyes. It was a night when even the wind worked on his side refusing to blow, keeping sounds to the minimum. Pericles' mind ran to what would come next and he tried to answer to every question that came to his mind. He knew that soon he would go across the border and would locate the Hellenic outpost and report to the soldiers there who he hoped would help him find his way south to Crete.

He felt cold, so cold that his body had difficulty responding to the orders of his brain. He let the current take him, when suddenly he noticed the strong beam of a spot-light reflecting on the water. This must be the border and the light of the Bulgarian border guards.

He took a deep breath. His heart started beating as if ready to explode. He heard some words between Bulgarian and Hellenic, words such as 'box', 'current', and others he didn't understand.

He heard one soldier calling to the other to shut the spot light off and go draw a card. He heard him say "It's your turn" and understood that the guards were playing cards.

Suddenly the spot light was on him, on the box covering him, then it disappeared only to come back on the box and he heard one of the soldiers tell the others about the box that was going down the river. A voice from the other direction told the first man to shut the spot light off and come to draw his card before they took his bet away. Pericles' mind ran crazy with ideas and fear overtook him.

Then, as suddenly as the spot light had appeared it was gone. The darkness of the night engulfed the river again. Pericles gave a sigh of relief and hoped that soon he would be close to the Hellene guards.

A few more meters, Pericles thought.

Soon he would be on the Hellenic side. He decided to swim slowly toward the shore. It took a little effort to beat the current. But in a few minutes his felt his feet touch bottom. The river floor felt soft and sandy. His soles were caressed by the river sand. This first touch that he felt on Hellenic soil was cold, but gentle and appealing.

He pulled the box out of the water, grabbed his backpack and put his shoes on. Although his body was cold he began to walk toward the dim light he saw coming from the Hellenic outpost only a short distance from the riverbank. When he was close enough he yelled to the soldiers inside and a soldier appeared by the door of the outpost fully armed.

Pericles called to him, "Hey, compatriot."

"Who is it?" questioned the guard.

"I'm a Hellene. Can I come closer?"

"Damn you. Come closer, so I can see you," the guard commanded.

Pericles made a few steps toward the soldier who was pointing a rifle at him. Pericles saw that he was panicking and ready to fire at the first second of doubt. By then two more soldiers stood by the door of the outpost and they also had their rifles ready for action.

"Who are you? What are you doing here this time in the night?" They demanded.

Pericles answered that he was a Hellene from Romania and he had travelled quite some distance to come to his motherland. The soldiers exchanged glances as if they had to deal with a crazy man who had travelled all this distance to cross into Hellas on the mighty Struma River.

"My name is Pericles," he told them, shivering from the cold.

"You swam to get here?" a guard asked incredulously.

"Yes."

"How did you manage to pass across the Bulgarian guards?"

"They didn't see me."

They signalled to him to come inside the little guard room. They offered to him two blankets and told him to change his wet clothes with a set of army garments they provided him. Soon after he was in dry clothes and they showed him where to sit by the portable heater.

The outpost room was small but cozy and soon with the help of the blankets and the dry clothes he felt warm. There were two cots one on top of the other against the wall a third one on the other side of the room and a small table behind the door where they placed his backpack. All three soldiers eyed him as they stood around him as if they had never seen a man like this coming to them in the darkness of the night out of the river. Of course they had a protocol to follow. One of them went to the phone and dialled Fort Roupel, one kilometer east of the outpost, to inform the official who he talked to about what had happened and to receive instructions as to what to do.

Pericles noticed that one of the soldiers was a sergeant and was in command of this outpost. He eyed Pericles as if trying to size his stature, his attitude, his demeanor, to sense whether they still had to point their rifles against this man who came out of nowhere. He asked Pericles to empty the contents of the backpack on the bed next to the table. The sergeant grabbed the knife and showed it to Pericles. He asked whether he was born in Crete.

Pericles answered, "No, but my parents and my grandfather were, and you too?" The sergeant shook his head but pointed to one of the soldiers who he said was a Cretan.

The man, the Cretan, extended his hand toward Pericles and said "Welcome to our motherland"

The sergeant asked, "You said you have come from Romania? Why? Are you visiting someone?"

"I'm headed south to Crete to find my relatives," Pericles said. He also told the sergeant that his roots were from Kolibari, a small village west of Chania. That was where he was headed.

The sergeant shook his head and continued questioning him. "From Romania? All the way here?"

Pericles told him the whole story, from where he had started, how long ago, where he had passed and how he managed to be where he was this night. The three soldiers seemed to believe him. The orders from the base were to accommodate him for the night until the next day when they would take him to the base and leave to the officers the responsibility of what to do with him.

They set a portable cot in the middle of the room for him to lie down and the sergeant asked him a final question: "Why you have come all this way to Hellas?"

Pericles answered that from a very young age he had a dream of coming to his fatherland to find his roots. He wanted to relive all the stories he had heard from his grandfather, to re-connect with his family.

"My uncle lives in Kolibari", he said, and it was his plan to look him up and to meet all the other relatives he had on the island.

"Bravo" the sergeant said and proudly extended his hand to shake Pericles'. The other guards agreed that it was crazy plan but they were glad it had come to fruition. They showed him where to sleep, on the cot in the middle of the room next to the heater, which had warmed up the small room.

First Impression

The first impression of his homeland was as perfect as he had dreamed of it. An ambient horizon to the east was dressed in pink garments and the breeze was soft and full of lullabies while the sun climbed slowly the steps to heaven, a celebration for Pericles' arrival to the holy grounds of his dreams. The greenery insisted on being playful, as if wanting him to dance around the shrubs and grass and further to his left the mighty Struma River, like a throbbing artery in the earth's body, unceasingly kept on rolling slowly toward the Aegean Sea. He felt as if everything welcomed him home, everything and everyone did their best to underscore their joy at seeing him in his patriot land. And then he noticed the soldiers who got up with eyes half open to start their daily duty.

The sergeant had informed the base about the arrival of the night visitor and Pericles was anxious for the officials to come and get him for the regular protocol affair. He ate the breakfast they offered him and waited for the car to arrive, without any suspicion of what the protocol demanded of a man who came into the country with none of the required papers. He had only his word of who he was and where he came from, at a time when Hellas was under the strong hand of the military government. He could have chosen a different time for his visit, but luck and circumstance, ambitious dreams, and the unyielding desire to come to his homeland had guided him to be there, this morning, only to be looked at under the suspicious eyes of the military protocol.

In no more than an hour a jeep arrived with a lieutenant and his driver. He stayed awhile, he had a coffee with the other soldiers, got a good verbal report as to how Pericles came to them: the time of night, his condition, the weather, the wind speed and all other details he needed to gather in a situation like this one.

"He came around midnight, sir" the sergeant, "he claimed he has come from Craiova, in Romania, and he's Hellene."

Pericles was listening to the report which was as detailed as it should be. He felt the palms of his hands sweaty. He didn't know what to expect. He wasn't sure he liked the turn of events. He felt uneasy on his chair, but of course he couldn't go anywhere.

"Who you know here and who you seek?" the lieutenant asked him.

"I come from a big family, most of who live in Crete, uncles and cousins. I look forward to meeting them." Pericles answered.

The lieutenant was still looking at him with a suspicious eye but eventually all the talk and reporting ended, although the lieutenant, upon hearing the sergeant's report and Pericles' descriptions and details, didn't seem any happier than earlier when he had first arrived. Nevertheless, he had his orders to drive Pericles as fast as possible to the base where the higher officers would carry on with the rest of the required questioning. Pericles thanked the three guards for taking care of him, but when he went toward them with an extended hand the lieutenant responded with a sharp "Never mind that now. Let's us go."

The lieutenant made a gesture, showing him to enter the jeep and sit on the front seat, while he sat in the back and they started the short ride to the base along a narrow rough dirt road.

Pericles passed the time on the bumpy ride preoccupied with the scenery, enjoying the images that went through his mind and were enclosed deep in his heart, images sweet and tender, images of his motherland, images of Hellas and everything he saw was his country. Everything around him was what he had always yearned to find, longed to meet, imagined to touch and feel. Even the brusk attitude of the angry lieutenant couldn't make him feel bad. On the contrary, his mind ran to the sweet image of a beach in Crete, in

Kolibari, where he fantasized he was and there she was, the dark skinned young woman he had in his dreams all his life. Yes, it was her, the woman he would meet in Crete, the woman he would fall in love with, a Cretan woman who he would marry and stay with for the rest of his life. Yes, everything was coming together as he had imagined and the unfriendly behavior of the lieutenant wouldn't alter it, no matter what.

Soon they reached the military base where he could see a few buildings and huts. Pericles observed everything, these images of Hellas, his country. The driver parked the jeep on the side of the big gate and they started walking toward the main building in the center of the base. A soldier who was close by called to the lieutenant, "Are we having a new class of soldiers coming in, sir?" He laughed while the lieutenant looked at him with an angry glance.

The lieutenant and Pericles walked to the main building. Upon reaching there he was led to a room, asked to sit down and the lieutenant left him there with the driver of the jeep. Not a single word was spoken until the door opened again and the lieutenant with two different officers came in. The jeep driver stood to attention, saluted the two officers, and addressed them as "colonels." At their order the lieutenant and the driver walked out of the room leaving the two officers with Pericles.

They asked Pericles his name, where he lived, who were his parents, his grandfather, where he was born, how old he was, how long he had been travelling to reach Hellas. They asked him why he had come, who gave him the idea of taking this voyage, why he had no proper papers and visa, why he had decided to come to Hellas after all these years? Where was he going in particular? Did he have any relatives where he was headed? Who and what were their names, their age, their family status, their property, did they have any political affiliations? Did he have any of that? Questions, a lot of questions and he answered them all.

"Although it sounds so strange to you," Pericles told them, "I've come to my motherland for two reasons: first because I wish to find my roots, where my family originated, and second because I promised this to my grandfather just before he died."

"Yes, but still it seems so hard to understand it" one of the officers said. "Are you sure this is the reason you have come? What will you do in Crete? How long do you plan to stay?"

"I want to find my family relatives and live with them for a while. I don't know for how long. That will depend."

"What happens if you don't find your uncle? Are you certain that your uncle is alive?"

"If my uncle isn't alive, his children and their children are and I'll find them and live with them."

"Are you a spy?" The sudden question startled him.

"Spy? No, why?" he answered.

"Why do you wish to come here?"

"From a young age I heard from my parents and my grandfather about our homeland. All my life I've dreamed of starting this trip. All my life I've waited for the opportunity, the chance to leave, and of course this was something I promised my grandfather, and I would never revise my plans."

"You covered all this distance on foot?"

"Sometimes I hitched a ride, a short ride from a village to the next but most of it I walked," Pericles explained.

He added that he crossed over two rivers, one with the help of a boat-man who he paid, and the other under the cover of a wooden box.

Both colonels laughed and one turned to the other and whispered something in his ear. They both agreed with a nod of their heads and one turned to Pericles and said,

"We have orders to send you to Athens. The lieutenant will escort you. You'll arrive in Athens tomorrow night."

"Why I'm escorted to Athens? I wish to go to Crete" Pericles said and his eyes were on fire. He stood up and if he would have flown out of this building, free like a bird.

"We have our orders and we follow them. Don't be concerned with anything. From Athens it only takes an overnight boat trip and you'll reach Crete."

Pericles felt glad hearing that comment. He would be in Crete after his arrival to Athens. He counted in his mind the days between now and then and said:

"Then it will take just three days until I get to Crete. Could I make a phone call to my parents to let them know I'm okay?"

The two officers exchanged glances and, in their secret military way, they had agreed.

"Yes. Before you leave the lieutenant will take you to the telephone center to make the call. Then you will come back here and, after the lieutenant gets his papers, off you go to Athens."

Just as the officer said, he was taken to the telephone center where the lieutenant ordered the soldier to open a line for him. Once he gave them the phone number of their house in Craiova, the soldier passed a phone to him. He put it to his ear.

"Hello." His face felt suddenly lit, knowing that his mother and father were on the other side of the line.

His father came to the phone.

"Hello, son, how are you?" was his first question his voice obviously confused.

Pericles felt his eyes filling with tears. His legs trembled as he said.

"I'm *entaxi*, I've made it to Hellas. How're you both, how's my mother?"

"We're good, considering. I'll put your mother on the line. Take care of yourself and talk to us soon." His father's voice choked.

Pericles was trembling in a big way now as his mother's voice echoed in his ear, choked voice, low tone almost difficult to discern what she said.

"*Ti kanis poulaki mou?**" she could only utter.

"I'm *entaxi* mom, don't worry. I'm in our homeland. In a few days I'll be in Crete."

"Be careful, my little bird, be careful."

"*Entaxi*, mom…bye for now, I have to close the line. Love you."

He didn't even hear his mother's answer… "I love you too, son."

During the short conversation the lieutenant, with a different phone in his ear was listening in to what they. Nevertheless every-

---

**how are you my little bird?*

thing went alright, and after he shut the phone he followed the lieutenant as they walked back to the office and Pericles was handed a document which one of the colonels signed and gave to the lieutenant.

"Don't take a week to come back. We need you here as soon as possible," he ordered.

The lieutenant took the paper, folded it in four, placed it in his shirt pocket and after he saluted the two superior officers he took Pericles and guided him toward the big gate where they jumped into a jeep and drove off.

The trip to the Sidirokastro train station, the closest city from the border, only took half an hour along a narrow and winding country road pitted with potholes. Flowers were blooming everywhere the eye could gaze and the smells of nature were abundant while small birds were responsible for the musical side of the remote country they were travelling. Finally they reached Sidirokastron where the train would take them first to Serres and then to Thessaloniki.

Pericles felt full of enthusiasm as he boarded the train. A sweet shiver went through his body as he sensed the pleasant event. He was finally seeing the end of his quest; he was so close he could almost smell the smell of sweet fragrance of being in patriot grounds, as if smelling the aroma of a beautiful flower that had just bloomed for him.

"What is your name?" Pericles asked the lieutenant.

"Homer...Ambetis" the lieutenant answered.

They shook hands. They knew each other and felt familiar with each other. They belonged together as long as this trip would last, until the lieutenant reached the military compound in Athens and released him to the higher officials of that camp.

As they walked side by side the lieutenant guided him to one of the coaches and they found two seats where they sat. A young boy no more than fourteen years old was walking in the train station selling his most tasty circle shaped bread sprinkled with sesame seeds. The lieutenant opened the window, leaned over and bought two of which he gave one to Pericles who thanked him. After he had his first bite Pericles realized this bread was truly delicious. He was hungry and the fresh baked sesame *koulouri** was as good as heaven. When lieutenant saw him devouring the *koulouri*, he leaned out the window and called the seller to get a couple more of which he gave one more to Pericles.

"You don't have any money, do you?" the lieutenant asked him.

"I have some Romanian money, but no *drachmas*."

"No worries, I'll treat you until we get to Athens."

It was the first time the lieutenant said in a clear way something positive to him. Pericles felt warm and his words came out softly.

"Thank you, thank you so much."

They ate two sesame breads each when the whistle of the train was heard and the train started moving. Their trip would take almost an hour to Serres and then two more hours to Thessaloniki. Passing a small village the train slowed down to stop at the station of the town and Pericles noticed a bunch of children in a field playing soccer. Their voices could be heard all over the area. In the village the people were going for their daily tasks, heads down as if they were sad about something, as if they were looking for something they had lost. He also noticed a foul smell in the atmosphere, as if the sewage of the whole world was emptied in this little town. He saw a man carrying a big bundle of clothes on his back, another carrying a heavy sack full of something, perhaps fertilizer or manure. The foul smell all around this town was very strong. There were a few cars and most of them were parked in the small square near the train station. Some people sat at the sidewalk tables of the three cafes. Pericles noticed they weren't much different than the villagers in Bulgaria and Romania, only the place and country were different.

After a short stop of about fifteen minutes the engine started again. The car where Pericles and the lieutenant sat was almost empty. Just four men and five women occupied the space along with two young children who were yelling and arguing. The train official went by and reprimanded them.

"Rough people, no different than animals" the lieutenant said

---

**circular shaped piece of bread with lots of sesame seeds well known to northern Hellas.*

without addressing anyone in particular.

Pericles asked why he spoke about them in such an unfriendly way.

"Don't you see how they behave? Animals do better than that," the lieutenant answered "and to boot, animals may live in a sheepfold but behave better than people." Then the lieutenant continued with a question: "Tell me is it true that you jumped over the fence last night?"

"What do you mean? Which fence?"

"It's an expression: it means that you passed the borders with no proper papers. Did you?"

"Yes."

"How didn't you get caught by the guards?"

"I swam in the river."

"Still I know they have very strong spot lights which we see from our side we know they inspect the water on a regular basis. How did you manage?"

Pericles smiled at the question and explained to him that he was covered by the fishing box his friend Hercules had prepared. The lieutenant laughed and congratulated him for devising such a trick. "And you came all the way from Romania?"

"Yes, from Craiova."

"Good. I admire your courage to travel all this distance on foot. I don't think I would be able to do so, if I were in your shoes."

Silence flooded the space between them and Pericles' mind drifted to the landscape outside the window of their coach. This was Hellas, his motherland. The mountains which they were passing, the valleys, the open fields, the waterways, the small lakes they were all Hellenic lands. He felt an inexplicable sweetness, a strange emotion that made his heart feel content and happy, a feeling one can't explain, a feeling one only lives through once.

It must have been about noon as strong sunshine flooded the space around them which made Pericles feel very warm. The train climbed a little hill and struggled to make it to the top. It whistled almost continuously and its cars tilted from one side to the other trying to keep up with the contours of the rails making up the uphill grade. Quite far and down Pericles could see the open fields with green grass and shrubs scattered across the plain as if the magical hand of a gigantic painter had thrown them in proper order to constitute his new painting. Groves of olive trees covered the sides of the hills. One thing absent was water. Only here and there he spotted the odd sign of moisture and even more scarcely there was a small creek or shallow lake. The scarcity of water made him contemplate on how the farmers in the villages watered their fields and crops which were scattered as if at random.

Suddenly the train entered a tunnel and its whistle echoed loudly. Once out of the tunnel Pericles noticed all around them hills and valleys. He noticed birds, scarce as they were, yet visible, feathered bodies that flew upwards soon as the train came close to their hiding places in the leaves of a tree, or the branch of a shrub strong enough to take the weight of the smaller sized birds or on the rocks where bigger ones perched and perused the surrounding space in search of prey. Pericles was watching out of the train window when the lieutenant sitting next to him disturbed his reverie.

"Tell me, Pericles, how was life in Romania?"

"Life in Romania" said Pericles "yes it is a little different. My father has a grocery store and I work in a factory. I started working there right after high school. I work eight hours six days a week, have one day to relax."

"What do you earn at the factory?"

"It's hard to explain, because it's in Romanian leu and I don't know the equivalent in drachmas. But my wages help our house expenses."

"Your father works eight hours daily as well?"

"No, my father's hours are longer than mine since he has to have the store open for about twelve hours daily. Seven days a week. Only that I help him a little on Sundays so he can come home earlier than regular weekdays."

"Ah, I see." The lieutenant said and then asked, "How was the political situation?"

"The most difficult thing of life in Romania is the communist regime. They spy on every one of the citizens. They arrest for no real reason most of the times. People aren't as free as here."

The lieutenant listened quietly as if his imagination was trying to capture the images and events.

"How were the jobs, your father's work at the grocery store and your job at the factory? How do people behave in Romania? Would you say that here is better than there?"

"We never had problem finding work," Pericles replied. "My father has been working on the same place all his life. From what I heard and experienced personally there was plenty of work but very limited wages. One would work eight hours per day and take home just what we called beer money. It's the system that controlled everything including the wages."

He carried on saying that he couldn't compare the two places since the political systems were different and consequently not comparable, but the whole difference as he saw it was on the concept of freedom which they never had in Romania.

To that the lieutenant added, "Even in Hellas these days the system isn't a hundred per cent free since the 21st of April 1967."

But of course it wasn't the way Romanians lived. Pericles noticed his exactness when he mentioned the day when the dictators took control of Hellas, being an officer of the army he knew every little detail regarding that and Pericles understood it clearly.

"Well, if there were plenty of jobs in a country that all people are treated equally in a communist political system" the lieutenant said "everyone should be happy and go about their days without any concerns, right?"

"Yes, they find jobs and they have the necessities but they aren't treated equally, as you said. There are always the few who being connected with the system have their privileges and their rights considerably different than the rest of the people. Yes, there isn't any equality as you said it. People always take advantage of a situation if they have the chance. And yes, they would behave like anybody else in any place of the world. There were a lot of traitors and police informants there too, and quite often one could be taken away falsely accused by one who didn't like him; the one who had a good connection with the committee's members and that would be enough for the man to lose his freedom and often his life. Military courts, false statements, words put in the mouths of witnesses, events that occurred again and again in Romania especially the early days of communism. Things like that don't exist here."

"We have our problems here too" the lieutenant added.

"Yes I understand, but no matter how bad if may be now, it's still my homeland where my roots are. This is where I thought I would find my purpose in life, my path on the right direction if I could state it this way. And for this reason I decided to come here and there isn't a word as sweet as the word homeland, believe me, I know." Pericles said.

"That may be so, but here isn't as rosy as you imagine," the lieutenant said.

Pericles was surprised at the lieutenant's comment. To make sure the conversation wouldn't lead them to unpleasant territory the lieutenant added, "We won't dig into this. We should leave this subject alone. Sometimes digging into the mud brings up unwelcomed odors and unpleasant stinking things."

Pericles didn't insist and turned the conversation to another subject.

"How long you still have to serve?" he asked.

"Sixty seven and one left. I mean in a two and a half months I go home."

"You've served for two years?"

"A little longer, twenty seven months to be exact."

"You have family?"

"In Athens, for this reason my superiors told me to come back as soon as possible. Usually when I go to Athens on a certain mission I spend a few days at home. However this time I won't do so."

The train carried on and before long they reached Paleokastro where they would stop for half an hour. The lieutenant proposed to Pericles to step out of the train to stretch their legs for a few minutes and also to find some food. They walked together toward the small plaza with its commotion of many people coming and going, its small vendors calling out for their merchandise and the various smells of people, animals, car exhausts and home cooked meals. People greeted each other and shook hands. Some pointed to others the proper direction and advised visitors to be vigilant of the odd thief who would go out of his way to grab a purse or a wallet. They all had a purpose for being in the square this time of the day, when the train passed through bringing new faces and things to disturb the quietness of the town.

The stop only lasted half an hour but this was enough for the Paleokastro citizens to get out of their routines. The smell of cooked potatoes with meat reached Pericles' nostrils, the fragrance of cooked olive oil and herbs reminded him of his return from school to their family home and his mother's kitchen that smelled exactly like this moment, here in Paleokastro in Hellas. Upon that aroma hitting his nose, Pericles stopped as if in reverence, as if he waited for his mother to console him in her tender embrace as any other day after school. So strong was the memory of the smell of cooked food that brought tears to Pericles' eyes.

The lieutenant located a local vendor serving food but he saw that Pericles had stopped as his nose, like a hound's had smelled the air of the little plaza and there were some exquisite food fragrances in the air strong enough to make him stop.

The lieutenant walked over to the food vendor and after he asked Pericles to choose what to eat he paid for two sandwiches which the vendor prepared. They sat on a bench and slowly ate their food. No words were spoken, only Pericles' appreciation that was evident between them bringing the two men closer to each other. They finished, their lunch and headed to the train. After only a few more minutes the train recommenced its voyage taking them slowly toward Serres, their destination.

Pericles let his eyes gaze at the country side that was full life, buzzing with sounds exotic and sweet. The Hellenic country side, his homeland; a tear flooded his eye and, leaning his head back on his seat, he let it flow down his cheek. Pericles hid it from the lieutenant and, letting his eyes close, he tried to sleep for a while as the train unerringly carried them south towards Serres.

From afar Serres looked large enough and with a central area easily recognized. A few tall buildings made up the image of a cosmopolitan skyline, while the rest of the houses were strewn over the large anomalous landscape as if from the amateur hand of a gigantic city planner. High up the clouds circumnavigated the sky as if ambivalent whether to travel eastward toward Drama, or westward toward Thessaloniki and since the decision wasn't as easily fermented they moved back and forth pretending to accomplish something allotted to them while the train slowly passed neighborhood after neighborhood and the narrow streets one after the other and brought them to the shabby station that smelled of unkempt promises and lost souls.

There were flowers in pots and flower beds of the houses they passed that let a light fragrance fill the air, a fragrance reminding everyone that people with soft hearts and tender dreams lived in this city. It was a city of rebels and undoubtedly of lovers according to the rumors among its inhabitants that gathered in small groups and under the umbrellas of the busy cafes. A few trees were strewn in various spots along the streets and in the station area. Everything indicated a lively city of fifty five thousand inhabitants known for their rebellious demeanor and their incessant guerilla attacks against the Turk occupiers, a demeanor unlike any other in Hellas. All these images captivated Pericles' mind when suddenly he was distracted by the voice of a young vendor, no more than twelve years old, selling yogurts which he carried on a tray sitting quite eloquently on top of his young head. Pericles and the lieutenant looked at the boy, and exchange glances and without any effort on their part they both turned teary.

They had a few minutes to spare in the shabby station and decided to step out of the station to stretch their legs. An inexplicable quietness overshadowed the space around them, people walked about to their destinations avoiding to make eye contact. They kept tight in their individual thoughts, overpowered by their own little wants.

The lieutenant an Pericles were walking side by side observing the citizens of Serres going about; everything was indecisive today including the clouds and the light breeze coming from the south bringing news from the Aegean Sea. The birds flew in and out of the small square of the train station.

Yet time flashed by and the train's whistle informed them of their imminent departure. They returned to their seats. Silence occupied the space; only the sound of the wheels turning against the rails was heard. When the wheel hit the gap between the rail pieces a sound echoed at regular intervals, sometimes reminding them that the speed had increased taking them to Thessaloniki even faster than before.

The lieutenant got up and told Pericles that he would be absent for a few minutes. Pericles noticed about a dozen relaxed passengers, some laying back their heads, sound asleep as the doornails of the car. Others were busy with newspapers and a couple of mothers were tending to their children. Then he noticed a young blonde woman who was sitting alone at the far end of the car. Their eyes met. He smiled, she smiled back. She was pretty. When she smiled she showed a line of beautiful teeth and plush lips.

Pericles wondered where she would get off. Perhaps she was headed to Thessaloniki, perhaps even south all the way to Athens. How he wished he knew. He wished he could introduce himself to this young woman and talk to her.

He turned his head and as if waiting for him to do, so the blonde woman smiled at him again as if inviting him to go and sit with her. Pericles thought of various scenarios. Perhaps he didn't understand her properly. Perhaps she wasn't inviting him at all. Perhaps she wanted to be left alone. Yet a strange thought took control of his mind. He was certain the young woman wished him to go and keep her company. It was a thought so strong that he got up and walked over to her. He extended his hand, saying his name, to which the girl responded politely that she was glad to have met him. Her name was Calliope which Pericles thought was beautiful, and he smiled as he shook her soft hand. He sat next to her. The conversation was easy.

"Where are you headed?"

"Athens, and you?"

"Same"

"Are you from Athens?" Pericles asked.

"Yes, and you?"

"No, from Crete."

"Well, then, why are you over on this north side of Hellas?"

He said he was travelling south to Crete. He told her that he had come from Romania and had passed two borders. He had met soldiers in every border guarding invisible lines. He also said he grew up in Craiova, Romania and that he was going to Crete to find his roots, his relatives.

Calliope raised her eyebrows in excitement.

"From Romania? You've come from Romania?"

"Yes. And I'm headed to Crete." Pericles repeated.

A little fire appeared Calliope's eyes but before she said anything the lieutenant showed up.

He said that he didn't want to interrupt them, but he felt responsible for the well-being of Pericles, therefore he asked him to stay put. That ended any conversation between Pericles and Calliope and when the lieutenant went to sit back in his seat she leaned toward Pericles and asked him.

"Has he arrested you?"

"He's taking me to Athens."

"Why is he escorting you to Athens?"

"I don't know."

A strange silence slowly developed with Pericles neither knowing what to say or what to do. But what he knew well was that he was in his homeland and he was headed south where Crete was laid over the dark blue waves of the Cretan Sea. Nothing else mattered at this moment.

Then a couple of other soldiers came into their car and their voices interrupted the quietness of the space which gave Pericles the chance to look at the country side passing by outside the window. Calliope, as if sensing his state of mind, did the same, both ignoring the noisy soldiers.

The sun was high above them and the clouds had gone eastward leaving the sky dressed in its shining light blue.

"You want to go to the bar and have a coffee?" Calliope asked him.

They got up and under the vigilant eyes of the lieutenant they walked to his seat first and after Pericles told him they would go to the bar for a coffee. The lieutenant nodded his agreement and they headed toward the bar. Calliope walked in front of Pericles who had the chance to observe her delicate body, thin and with beautiful lines. Her waving hair flowed over to her shoulders, a light brown hue and shining from the bright sunshine that flooded through the train windows.

The bar was just a small area with a narrow door on one side for the barman to enter, the counter, a few glasses hanging from slots over the counter, bottles of wine and hard alcohol arrayed on shelves behind the bar. The barman was a very tall man who said his name was Odysseus. His thin stature made him look like a branchless tall conifer with a head fitting perfectly his thin composure. He was wiping glasses, at this time and he was placing them in their proper spots on the small shelving behind him. When Pericles and Calliope sat on two stools he looked at them with questioning eyes.

"Coffee please, cream and sugar." Calliope said.

Pericles remained silent and Calliope suggested he should try the coffee too.

"I don't have money at all" he confessed feeling embarrassed.

"I somehow sensed it since you come from that far. No worries, I'll buy us the coffees, ok?" she reassured him.

They sat for a while, the coffee was tasty and the company of a beautiful woman was even better in Pericles' eyes.

"I wanted to take you away from the lieutenant since I've sensed they escort you to Athens for a reason you wouldn't suspect." Calliope told him.

"Why you say this? What do you mean?"

"Coming from Romania the way you did, without the proper papers, made you a suspect and the military government surely would like to ask you a few questions before they let you lose in the country. This meant that most likely the lieutenant is escorting you to a base in Athens where they will interrogate you and when they are satisfied that you pose no danger for anyone they'll let you go."

"How do you know this?" Pericles asked his voice choked in his throat. His face turned red and his breathing echoed fast.

"These days they are extra careful since the logic of the army regulation that controls the country is a lot stricter that the regular laws," she said "and you better be prepared for the unexpected because the simple reality of it is very harsh."

Calliope also told him that she had just graduated from the University of Athens, with a major in Psychology and she was ready to start her practice by opening an office soon.

Pericles listened to her attentively absorbing everything she said. He knew that what he had accomplished up to that time sounded to the average person as if he was crazy to come all the way from Romania on foot. He understood that what she described to him was logical but he felt that he was mentally ready to deal with everything circumstance would bring him as long as the final destination of Crete remained in his mind and as long as he kept focused to achieve it.

Calliope's face had an expression of inexplicable melancholy and tears swelled in her eyes. Her lower lip almost trembled when she informed him that the freedom he had dreamed off all this time didn't exist in Hellas, not at this time in her history.

"Unfortunately you've come at a difficult time." Calliope added, "Yet you never know, one day things may change and if you would stay long enough in Crete perhaps you might be lucky to live in a free Hellas."

He listened to every word she said and felt as if he was in a trap, like an animal caught by the trapper's trap his leg squeezed between the sharp jaws' painful teeth. His mind ran back home to the old man and all the beautiful stories and wondered what happened to all that beauty? Yet his mind remained steadfast in his resolve that he must follow his quest. There was no going back anymore, not until he went to Crete and not before he lived there for a while. Animal caught in a trap or not, painful as it was or not, his goal was still ahead of him in Crete.

Thessaloniki

The commotion and activity of Thessaloniki was much different than the bucolic countryside and the quietness of the smaller towns they had travelled through. Here Pericles could see high-rises one next to the other, lots of cars on the paved streets and crowds of people, walking like toy soldiers. Past the suburbs and before they reached the center where the main train station was located, Pericles noticed the different way of life people had in this big city, opposite to the life in rural areas. When they reached the most central area of the city he saw many stoas connecting one building with the next and a multitude of citizens going about their daily affairs. He hardly saw anyone smiling but above all he noticed the unbearable smell of exhaust from cars and buses. Smoke rose from the streets into the atmosphere creating a little cloud that hung over the center. Although this didn't seem to bother anyone, it came in the car of the train through the open windows choking every passenger. Only the little decorative trees planted here and there along the sidewalks and the open areas didn't seem to mind the smog.

At the train station there were even more people, some saying good bye and hugging their loved ones, others yelling about unfinished business.

The train slowly came to a complete stop. Pericles gazed out of the window observing every possible image his eyes and mind could grasp. Images of Hellas which were interrupted by the lieutenant who came to warned him that they had to change trains before they would take their leave towards Athens.

The lieutenant and Pericles stepped down off the train and Calliope followed them to the open area of the station. They read on a big chalkboard the designated train to Athens and they walked toward it although they had half an hour before the train to Athens would leave.

The lieutenant met the other two soldiers and they talked while Calliope and Pericles stood by the main post and watched the people coming and going. A soldier and a young woman were just behind them on the other side of the post and Pericles heard her say to him, "Remember I love you. Promise to write every day."

Pericles looked at Calliope. Melancholy was spread over her face and he felt uneasy at the intensity of her glance. His fingers touched her cheek and a sweet emotion overtook him. She didn't say anything, but her face leaned toward his hand as if she wanted his fingers to stay on her face longer, as if she wished to make his touch last longer. Pericles smiled and she smiled back to him. Yes, Pericles felt close to Calliope, she was in his mind all the time and he was curious why she had that melancholic expression on her face most of the time.

She made a signal to him with her eyes and he turned to the direction she pointed and noticed the lieutenant and the two soldiers looking their way and laughing.

"Why they laugh?" Calliope asked him.

"I don't know." He answered and felt a tightening in his heart, an unpleasant sensation which he couldn't explain. He took Calliope's hand and held it in his.

Other passengers destined for Athens started boarding the train. Pericles and Calliope did the same. They found two seats in the first car. The lieutenant came in and sat two rows behind them. It was late afternoon when the train started moving and soon they were out of the station and slowly accelerated through the Thessaloniki suburbs heading southward. They would arrive in Athens in about ten hours.

The afternoon shadows slowly became longer and the car where they sat was full of smells, rancid and languid, soft and sharp. A few windows were open but the strong wind due to the speed of the train made it unpleasant to keep them open.

Pericles' eyes were only for Calliope this evening: he observed her and he let the aroma of her body enter him. It made him feel warm and captured by its inexplicable tenderness. Calliope's ways and gestures simple and tender and they brought memories into his mind. He remembered his mother's way of attaching her arms around him. His mother had breast fed him for a long time up his age of three. He even remembered asking his mother to come and feed him by showing her a chair where to sit and he remembered her big breasts in his small baby-hands.

And now Calliope's breasts were next to him, breasts well sized and he imagined feeling their smoothness. Quite unexpectedly his hand rested next to hers on the side of his seat and suddenly with at an abrupt movement of the coach, her hand landed on his. Pericles held her hand in his and the touch of her hand in his gave him a pleasant sensation.

Calliope smiled and Pericles saw the bright straight line of her teeth behind her beautiful lips. He was attracted to her. He wanted to feel her skin, her body. He turned and his lips searched for hers. She turned to him and kissed him, a deep emotional and sensual kiss. His hands almost instinctively ran over her firm body. A sensation overtook him that he hadn't felt for a long time.

Yet nothing could be done in the train with lots of other passengers. He tried to feel content with just holding her hand and gazing out the window at the beautiful Hellenic countryside full of images sweet and tender: a farmer riding his donkey along a narrow path leading to his village on the hillside, two girls playing in the yard of their house, a tall mountain on the far west side of the horizon toward which the sun was headed, images passing by fast thus making them indescribable and other times going by so slow he could see the color of the roofs of the houses.

Pericles took all this with a happy heart while Calliope was silent leaving him in his reverie. The echo of the iron wheels on the rails was constant, and the vibrations and movements of their seats familiar.

"Tell me about your family. Do you have any brothers or sisters?" Pericles asked her.

"No, do you?"

"No" he said nodding his head.

"What does your father do?" Pericles asked.

"He was a surgeon."

"You mean he's dead?"

Calliope turned toward him and looking deep in the eyes she added, "He doesn't practice his profession these days." Seeing his questioning look she said, "He isn't practicing his profession because he's in jail."

"What happened?" Pericles asked.

"They arrested him the first morning this military government took over. They claimed he was a Leftist. He's been in prison for four years."

Shocked, Pericles asked, "Why? Have they imprisoned others too?"

"Lots, they've kept them in various islands of the Aegean Sea. They consider them enemies of the state. They'll keep them in prison for as long as they want or until this savage military government is replaced with a civilian free elected government. This is what we call dictatorship. For the same reason they have you escorted to a military base in Athens. For the same reason they'll interrogate you. Do you know where the lieutenant is taking you?"

"No, they said Athens, but nothing else." He said and his mind ran to an isolated dark prison cell as if he was condemning himself to it a priori. The thought shook him and his body responded with a strange shiver. *Something wasn't going right; something wasn't as it should be.*

"The lieutenant knows I'm sure. So don't expect them to place you in the boat that will take you to Crete." Calliope warned him and her face again took that melancholic expression of fearing for him as she feared for her father.

"I understand. They'll interrogate me and then let me go, since they won't find anything against me." Pericles said.

"Not so fast," she continued, "first they'll investigate to make sure all you say is true, make sure there isn't any file against you, make sure you aren't a spy because don't forget you've come from Romania a country under the influence of the Soviet Union, a communist country. To these military assholes you could be simply a spy."

Her harsh word referring to the government people surprised Pericles and he turned toward her. Her eyes full of tears ready to cascade down her cheeks. He leaned and kissed her lips.

"Oh, don't be so pessimistic...perhaps things aren't as bad as you believe." Pericles said.

"I sure hope so, but I'm not optimistic at all. They could keep you as long as they like. For this reason you've been escorted. What you think? They were afraid you might get lost? As soon as we get to Athens the military police will arrive to take you from this lieutenant and they will take you to the designated base where you'll be kept until they get satisfied that you aren't a problem. And only when they are satisfied that everything seems good they might let you go."

"They'll put me in jail?" Pericles gasped at the thought. The image of a free Hellas where people go and do as they please suddenly didn't make any sense to him.

"How foolish I have been," Pericles continued, "to undertake such a difficult task, my quest, my dream, what a fool could I be in their eyes, in the eyes of everyone. Why did I decide to come to my motherland to face imprisonment and harassment?"

Calliope shook her head as if saying, "How naïve have you been, poor Pericles, to believe in concepts such as motherland, when everyone is for himself, where everyone bows his head to the military rulers, when the masses only care for a loaf of bread and nothing more, where the country may be beautiful but only for the romantics such as yourself."

"But, Calliope, I'm not a criminal." Pericles exclaimed.

"Yes, you're right, you aren't a criminal." Calliope said "Neither was my father. He was a surgeon, a very useful member of our society. Yet they took him just as they'll keep you for a while." She said and her face took the expression of certainty as simple as you say the sun will rise tomorrow. "I wish I'm wrong" she continued "and I wish they let you go fast, but you'd better be prepared for the worse. Since that day, April 21st 1967, when the military pigs took control of this country thousands have been retained in concentration camps, tortured, killed, exiled. They claim this was done for our own good. I can't follow this lunatic claim. Imagine the most stupid argument made once the Prime Minister came on TV and said that Hellas was like a sick person and they had to heal it, to put *a cast on a broken arm*, that's what he called it and to keep the cast on until the arm healed. That was his logical argument."

A wind of despair blew over Pericles' face and suddenly he feared he had made a mistake when he decided to come to Hellas. But why his grandfather was so adamant and made Pericles swear to come here? Thoughts, strange thoughts, unwelcomed thoughts took control of his mind and his face looked as if everything around laughed at him.

"And you thought coming to Hellas you were coming to Paradise," Calliope added, "the country of your parents and grandfather. You've been fooled, my friend. This isn't Paradise. It hasn't been for a long time. It hasn't been for me or for my mother the last four years that my father is been isolated in an island, sleeping in a tent, winter and summer, eating the army foods, he's been idle to death, a man of such usefulness for our country. No, this isn't a Paradise. Hellas, the last four years, has been worse than hell. You'll find that out on your own as the days go by when you'll see a brother shooting his brother, a father violating his own daughter; when you come across the priests who steal on the open with no remorse; when you see whores and pimps, drug addicts and thieves, liars and cheats. You'll see lots of these. I'm afraid, dear Pericles. The country you imagined to find existed only in your imagination. The real world isn't that, I'm afraid."

Pericles was left speechless, his mouth gaping and his eyes red as fire. His mind couldn't process this harsh talk. His heart couldn't endure the darkness of all he heard. He thought, perhaps Calliope saw things this way since her father has been imprisoned. There might be a better way to look at things. He wanted to believe that things were the way his grandfather had described to him.

He mentioned this to Calliope who gave a little laugh and said.

"Perhaps there was once a world out there such as the one your grandfather described to you, but even that is questionable. We live in the twentieth century" she reminded him, "and life has changed a lot since the days your grandfather left Hellas."

At that moment the train made an abrupt movement from one side to the other and she literally fell on him. He held her tight feeling the warmth of her body. He wished he could feel this warmth in his heart but it wasn't. His heart was injured. He felt its ache. He shivered at the thought. He moved his body on the seat as if shifting his life from a dark image to a positive and warm one.

Moments passed silently. She took her pen and a piece of paper, and wrote her address and telephone number.

"Remember to call me when they let you go. You can come and visit me at home. I live with my mother who would love to have you for a while."

He took the piece of paper and placing it in his pocket he said.

"Thank you Calliope. I promise to come and visit when they let me go, as you said."

"My mother and I would be more than happy to accommodate you and help you get onto your way to Crete. Don't even mention it. Just call and come, *entaxi?*"

"*Entaxi,*" he said.

Pericles got up and walked toward the bathroom and, passing by the lieutenant, he found him in deep sleep. Further on from the lieutenant's row two young men argued about something, their high pitch voices, loud enough to wake up even the dead other than the lieutenant.

It was night now and the only lights Pericles could see were the ones from towns and villages the train passed by, signs of life far away in the dark horizon. Pericles walked back from the bathroom and sat next to Calliope. They remained silent for a while. Pericles felt heaviness over his chest. A fear lurked in his mind, a fear he had never experienced before: the fear of the uncertain tomorrow. Where would the lieutenant lead him? What was lurking in tomorrow's coming? What would he do when they would treat him like a spy? Thoughts over thoughts and no word spoken, not even from Calliope. He looked at her, his eyes questioning. She understood with her concern for him written in her eyes.

"I don't have anything to say." She didn't want to tell him that she was afraid of tomorrow as well and that she was thinking of her father and when he would be released from prison, and what was waiting for him in Athens — that he could be treated like an enemy of the state like her father had been and put away for a long time.

Pericles smiled and squeezed her hand. "Everything will be alright, at the end, everything will be alright."

"Remember what to do when they let you go; when you'll be free come and visit."

"I promise. On the first chance I'd have."

He leaned close to her and their lips locked in a kiss.

Athens

Pericles remembered once in Romania he heard of the beautiful blue sky of Attica and it was confirmed to him when the train reached Athens the next morning. Light fought against darkness and the crystal clear blue Attica sky was proof. People have lived in this city since the ancient days and they have loved and respected it. They have also lived the lives of little Christians hoping for a secure after life in a faraway heaven. And at other times they have dwelled in the hell of their everyday struggle, and they don't know which of the two they've hated the most. Many a time Pericles had read in various books about the beauty he observed as the train crossed the last suburbs of Athens before reaching the terminal. Just at that moment, from where they passed by, he glanced across the horizon and saw Acropolis, sunlit and graceful on top of its small hill, an image that gave him an exulted feeling of joy, something he had never felt up to this point of his quest. The radiant light of the Attica sky reflected onto the old and modern Athens, on antiquities and modern high-rises, a radiance that spread onto the faces of the young and onto the wrinkled faces of the old. Pericles stood up to have a better view and Calliope, upon seeing him so excited, also stood up and next to each other they took in the perfect moment of the Acropolis view. The sun was just a meter up on top of the eastern mountains flooding the landscape with a warm feeling that accompanied the effect of light. Drops of dew glistened off the leaves of trees and moistened the shrubs and dry soil. The train engineer blew the whistle three times in the row to let everyone know they were passing the last suburbs of Athens and nearing the main train station. If Thessaloniki seemed to Pericles to be a very busy city, Athens was a lot busier since it had three times the population and, along with Piraeus the harbour in its south, perhaps four times as much.

Although the city was awakening at the time the train arrived, there were already lots of cars in the streets and people were lined at the bus stops, some reading newspapers, others simply talking to others. He saw girls in their high-school uniforms ready for school, workers heading to their daily destination, the vendors selling bread cookies in the shape of circle called "Thessaloniki's", from their place of origin. Everything fell into place and fitted into the big picture of a city in constant glow. Pericles was impressed with all these new images that he had yearned for all the years he was growing up waiting to undertake his quest. His voyage to discover the place where he might belong, a quest to where he could fit in this world, to just be a man and at the same time an accomplished man. It was something he was willing to search for the rest of his life.

Calliope stood next to him and Pericles held her hand, and felt her trembling. They had arrived at the main train station, their destination. Some people had already disembarked carrying their bags. Calliope looked at him as the lieutenant was headed in their direction. "You'll have to go with him," she said. Pericles nodded and kissed her. The lieutenant was by their side. They had to leave.

Calliope went toward the taxi stand and Pericles followed the lieutenant outside of the train station where an army vehicle was waiting for them. The soldier driver stood at attention and saluted the lieutenant. Pericles jumped and sat in the back while the lieutenant sat in front next to the driver.

They drove for about half an hour. Suddenly they had reached a building with a big gate. They went through the big gate. The driver drove the jeep toward a big three storey building. Pericles followed the lieutenant inside. When they got inside, they went to the second office off a long hallway. The lieutenant spoke to another officer. He gave him the papers. He referred to Pericles as 'this man' and said that the papers were given to him at the army base in northern

Greece. The major, who was sitting behind a desk, took the papers and went through them. Then he looked at Pericles with a puzzled expression but didn't speak. The lieutenant and the major exchanged salutes, the lieutenant shook Pericles' hand, wished him the best, saluted his superior once more, and left.

The major eyed Pericles from top to bottom and ordered a soldier who was in the office, "Escort the young man to his room."

Pericles followed the soldier to the end of the long hallway outside the office where they were moments earlier. When they reached the end of the hallway they descended a staircase and went along a line of rooms. The soldier stopped in front of one, unlocked it and showed Pericles in. Once Pericles went inside the soldier locked the door from the outside and left.

Inside, the room was simple: a bed, a chair, a toilet, and a sink. Pericles looked around and then sat on the bed. Was he a prisoner? Was this a prison cell?

A couple hours went by. Pericles' mind became blank as if a windless day had emptied it of all thought. His eyes fixated onto the door so intensely he thought it would open wide, that a hand would drive a key into the keyhole, two fingers would turn the lock open and the door would open to the world. Suddenly with no reason at all his memory went cloudy like a pleat of the sky suddenly covered by short ambient clouds, so that the surroundings of the room took on a gray funerary look. There was hardly any light coming from the small bulb hanging from the ceiling. A lone light bulb in the room like Pericles both left in there on their own: one to vaguely light the surroundings and the other to fear for what was forthcoming.

He was left in this room for three days and three nights without any words exchanged between him and his guards nor the officers. They brought food to him three times a day but never took him out for questioning. At times he heard the steps of the army boots walking along the hallway and the opening of a lock, then the steps of boots walking away. At other times he thought he heard yelling and moaning, voices of people being tortured, but he was as unsure of that as he was about the reason he was held here for three days and three nights.

Around noon of the third day one soldier came to get him. As he walked the long hallways shivers of horror tingled down his spine. He wondered if his time had come to be treated like the other men and if he'd be tortured. The guard-soldier guided him to the same room he was examined in the first time where a different officer, a colonel, was waiting. They told him to sit and the questions commenced like the first time: the reasons for his trip, who were his family members, how old was his mother, what has his father's work, was he a member of the communist party of Romania?

The colonel stayed on that subject for a while, and asked again and again how many members of his family were members of the communist party and how many years were they in Romania. At times a sudden question would arise such as, "What do you plan to do here?" to which he gave every answer that came to his mind, plainly and simply, a fact the colonel appreciated and he mentioned to Pericles that they would let him go very soon.

Pericles felt tears well in his eyes when he saw that the colonel was ending his examination as he put his papers away in a briefcase. He felt ready to shake his hand or even more, to hug him, but something told him not to try. Indeed, the colonel instructed the soldier to take him back to his room get his belongings and bring him back to the same office.

Soon after he was again before the same colonel who shook his hand, welcomed him to the motherland of his parents, wished him good luck and before he told him to go, asked if he had any money and how he would travel to Crete. Pericles said he had no money, but he hoped to find a couple of days of work which would provide him with what he needed until he would reach his village west of Chania. The colonel opened his wallet, took out a few bills and he handed them over to him.

"Here, take this money. It will be enough to take you to your Crete," he said dryly.

Seeing the seriousness of the colonel's gesture, Pericles took the bills, put them in his pocket and thanked him. The colonel once again wished him good luck, took his briefcase under his arm and left the office.

The soldier smiled at Pericles, he said "You are very lucky to be treated like that." He showed Pericles the door and together they walked out toward the big gate. The guard opened it and Pericles walked out with a strange feeling of lightness. He felt a strange emotion as if he could fly. He was full, he was content. He was whole: a man with a feeling of humanness like no other, a condition of wholeness. He felt incorruptible, invincible. He was free to go as he pleased.

When he passed the big gate leaving the military base he thought of what to do before he'd find his way to Peireus to buy a ticket for the overnight boat ride to Crete. He had promised to call Calliope. He searched in his bag and found the small piece of paper she had given him. He stopped at the first telephone booth he found and dialed her number.

A woman, perhaps Calliope's mother, answered and Pericles mentioned his name and asked for Calliope.

Calliope came to the phone. Her voice trembled when she realized who she was talking to. She invited him to visit. He said that he didn't know how to find her. She asked him where he was, the name of the street. He explained his location. He said he was standing just a few blocks away from the military base. She urged him to stay exactly where he was and she would come to find him.

Pericles promised to do that. He put the phone down and looked around. People were going by as if nothing was happening, as if none of them knew he was a free man in this big city of Athens. He was free and he had just arrived from Craiova, Romania, and he was in his parents' motherland. People just walked by him oblivious to all this. No one noticed his teary eyes. No one shook his hand as a welcome gesture. No one stopped to ask why he was weeping. No one asked him what he felt. No one cared about anything other than their hasty pursuit of something invisible, yet profoundly important which occupied their daily affairs.

He stood for a while observing the passersby, men and women, young and old, who were going by him with their heads down, eyes focused forward. They all walked fast, as if they didn't want to arrive late to an event.

Suddenly his eye caught two men exchanging blows with fists.

He heard curses and saw the shorter of the two men kicked hard against the crotch of the taller man who crouched down holding his torso and yelling in pain. The short man ran away as fast as he could before the tall man could catch his breath and go after him.

Pericles stood there and stared at the injured man when he realized that he was the only one of all the crowds of people who were still walking fast and faster by them but never bothered to stop and see what if anything they could do to help. Pericles talked to the man and walking close to him he extended his hand to help him up but the man snarled,

"Go to hell. I don't need your help."

Pericles questioned the man's comment but no answer was given to his question. The man just looked at him again and added, "You aren't a soldier. Did you just get released?"

Pericles replied that he was never a soldier. The man laughed and grimaced, obviously still in pain and asked

"Then why the attire?"

Pericles just said, "It's a long story."

The man shook Pericles' hand and then he walked away limping.

"Hello Pericles!" He heard Calliope's voice and turned to see her walking towards him. He thought she was floating in the air such was the first glance of her body come closer to him. He embraced her and held her tight against his body feeling her warmth. They kissed. They stopped somewhat embarrassed and looked around them to the curious glances of the passersby. Laughing, Pericles took Calliope's hand and they walked along the busy street: two anonymous young folk among the rest of the citizens who went by them.

Calliope directed their walk toward the first square they came to and after finding a small bar they sat under an acacia tree. A flock of sparrows flew out of the trees then back to the acacia branches making a sudden commotion.

Their server came with two glasses of water and took their order.

"What you plan to do now?" Calliope asked Pericles.

"Leave for Crete, as soon as I can. I need to get my ticket."

"We can go to Peireus and find your ticket. But it would be better if you stayed the night and travel tomorrow."

"I can't stay too long; it must be expensive to stay in Athens. I don't have much money. Ah, didn't tell you, one of the army officers gave me some money, enough to go to Crete," he said.

Calliope smiled at that comment.

"Some of them are still humans." She added. "You can stay at my house for one night, Pericles. My mother wouldn't mind" she said.

He was unprepared for such wholehearted proposition. His fingers were entangled with hers and she leaned close to kiss him.

Pericles felt very warm. Her proposal made him feel happy considering the circumstances under which they had met.

After they finished their food and drinks they walked toward the closest metro station. They got two tickets and rode the train to Peireus.

At the end of the subway ride they walked to the closest travel agency where Pericles bought his ticket. After confirming that his ship was due to sail next evening they walked along the docks observing the longshoremen doing their jobs.

There were many people walking about on the dock, some just passing by others waiting for ferries to take them to the innumerable Hellenic Islands.

They walked back to the station and got on the metro train to return them to the city. Calliope led him from street to street until they reached a six storey high-rise where her family's apartment was. She took a key out of her purse and opened the front door. A small elevator took them to the third floor to her apartment's door which she opened and they walked inside. Calliope's mother greeted them and Calliope introduced Pericles to her.

"Mama, this is the good friend who I met on the train from Thessaloniki. I told him he could stay overnight until he goes to Crete tomorrow. Pericles, this is my mother, Urania."

Her mother responded with a smile and welcomed him to their house. It was a small flat no more than a hundred square meters with two bedrooms, a living room, dining room and a small kitchen; and like all such apartments in Athens it had a good size balcony with a big awning which was opened during the hot hours of the day.

Calliope led him to the small living room furnished with contemporary items, very clean and with a lot of pictures on the walls one of them of the whole family. Calliope said the man in the photo was her father. Pericles noticed a resemblance between the father and Calliope which he mentioned to her and she laughed. Urania, her mother, brought in a welcoming tray with a sweet made of grapes and a few cookies. Calliope told him they were traditional things most women in Hellas bake every Christmas and some of them, like her mother, throughout the year. The cookies reminded him of sweets his mother baked in Craiova, the same taste of ginger and plenty of cinnamon. The thought of his mother filled his eyes with tears. It brought him back to his home with images of celebrations on birthdays, name days and other religious holidays which were traditional among the Hellenes of Craiova. Although Pericles didn't always observe the religious celebrations he remembered well all the other occasions.

The phone rang and Urania spoke to someone while Calliope and Pericles enjoyed the sweets. Their glances met numerous times as if they conspired to commit something no one else should know. Urania finished her phone call and told Calliope she had to go out to meet a friend so they would be left alone for a while.

After her mother left and closed the apartment door Calliope led Pericles to her bedroom. She hugged and kissed him and pulled him onto her bed.

A little later and exhausted she leaned next to him. His arm was under her neck, her galloping breathing slowly relaxed into a passive sweet acceptance. He turned his head and saw the heavenly expression on her face.

Time lapsed. They got up and dressed. Not too long after they were sitting in the living room Urania came back from her meeting. Pericles asked Calliope if it was possible to make a phone call to his family in Craiova and she gave him the receiver.

"Yes, of course," she said and got up to leave him alone.

He dialed the number and the line opened. The voice of his father was heard.

"Hello."

"Hello father. It's me; I'm in Athens and I'm *entaxi*. Tomorrow

I'll travel to Crete. How're you? How're my mother and my old teacher?"

"We're all *entaxi*, son. I'll let you talk to your mom in a second, but tell me, is everything *entaxi* over there?"

"Well, not so dad. I'll tell you at some time. But I'm well and I look forward to going to the village tomorrow. Let me say hello to my mother."

"*Entaxi*. Keep well and please keep in touch."

His mother's voice, faintly heard on the other side of the line.

"Hello *poulaki mou, ti kanis*?"

"*Kala mama*, everything is *entaxi*. How are you?"

He heard her light sobbing.

"*Kala poulaki mou*. You've forgotten of us."

"No, I haven't. I just couldn't call you earlier. That's all."

"*Entaxi...keep well poulaki mou*."

"Bye mother. Love you."

He put down the receiver and tears flowed down his eyes. Calliope found him teary and hugged him in front of her mother's surprised eyes.

It was evening when they said good bye to Calliope's mother and went out for a coffee at a nearby bar. Enjoying a cold frappe each and holding hands Calliope said.

"My father came from a big family of merchants. He was educated here and abroad. In fact he received his basic medical diploma from the Stanford University in California. Then he did his specialty in surgery. After he received his specialty diploma he returned to Hellas to serve what he thought was his duty, although he had plenty of opportunities to stay in the USA and thrive as a surgeon."

Pericles was looking into her eyes absorbing all he could from her beautiful expressions while his mind ran to his father, a grocery store owner.

"You're very proud of your father." He said.

"Yes, wouldn't you? But what did he accomplish when he came back here? After a practice of twenty so many years and at the top of his productive career this monstrosity, the dictators, took over the reign of our motherland and for all his good service they arrested him, and they exiled him in the island of Yiaros."

"It's hard to understand the logic behind these actions of the military government. Don't they appreciate their highly educated citizens who offer greatly to the improvement of people's lives?" Pericles interjected.

"Absolutely. It's insane to think of a country that punishes her good citizens instead of rewarding them. So, to carry on with my father he was forced to stay idle, away from his people, his clientele, his world, because they said he was a leftist. Can you comprehend this nonsense? The system puts away people of that calibre because they had a leftist relative. And they expect this country to get ahead? And do they deserve to get ahead when they treat the best members of their society in such an anachronistic and stupid way? Some say my father was an enemy of the state, my father, who was a saint, a man of unparalleled qualities."

She stopped for a moment to observe his reaction and as if approving his attention she smiled, and kissed him. Pericles held her hand as if he didn't want her to get away from him, not even for a moment, he returned the smile and waited for her to continue.

"So is this the Hellas you wished to discover? Is this the homeland where you wished to relive your parents' and your grandfather's life? This place is a hell on earth," she told Pericles. "This is a country that knows very well how to devour her own children. This is the country you are mistaken to believe is a Paradise."

Pericles added.

"What also surprised me was the expression on the people's faces. They walked with their heads down as if bowing to someone, as if asking for someone's forgiveness, as if they depended on someone's decision or order as to what to do and where to go, what to think or who to follow."

Calliope looked into his eyes and said, "This is another story, a long story, Pericles, but now it isn't time to talk about it. You'll find out soon enough."

Pericles answered that he was alright with that, although the strange behaviour of the populace made him re-examine his feelings and beliefs. But he still believed things would be different in Crete where he was destined to reach the day after tomorrow.

When they had finished their coffee Calliope suggested they go for a walk before they went home. It was still early and her mother was preparing supper.

Pericles held her hand tight in his as they strolled from street to street. Some stores were still open at this time in the evening and store owners were eager to sell some of their merchandise.

"I still find it hard to believe that you walked all this way," Calliope said, "to come here because of the way you were brought up and the way your grandfather prepared you for this quest of yours. What about your parents? Did they approve of this or have they lived in agony for all this time you've been on the road?"

"Yes, they reluctantly approved my voyage but of course I've talked to them first when I entered Hellas," Pericles said. "The army people opened a phone line for me and I talked to both of them. No, they didn't like the idea of this trip much, to tell you the truth, but I made sure they understood and didn't object it too much. I know that my mother would prefer I had stayed put and never started this trip. Then I talked to them again earlier today. I'll call them in a couple of days when I'm in Kolibari."

"I wouldn't have expected anything else from your mother, she's a mother after all," Calliope added.

"Yes, but my belief in what we call motherland, homeland convinced me that I had to try. I had to come although given today's circumstances and the military government having the upper hand, if I knew what it meant perhaps it would had been different, perhaps I would had given it more thought."

"Aha, yes, the concepts of motherland and roots, how easily they control our way of thinking and making our decisions. It's truly fascinating to think about how these concepts influence us and how easily we decide one course or another based solely on them."

"Of course, but that is what we are Calliope. These concepts make us different from the animals." Pericles observed.

"So true, yet, they're just words, Pericles. They're just words yet powerful words and we base much of our lives on them. But I would describe another scenario to you."

"What do you mean?"

"We talk of motherland and our historic enemies, the Turks, and every time someone mentions that name our back crawls up as if we got stunk by a wasp. Yet let us suppose that in the foreign land you've lived you had a Turk neighbor. Let us say he was a good family man, went to his work every day, exactly the way you did. He earned his wages and raised his children just as you did or your parents did for you. Perhaps it could be possible that you would be the Turk's friend. If you thought such a scenario was possible, and if you think that you and he have lived side by side for years, how would the concept of our motherland and our historical hatred towards the Turks interfere with the life you'd lived next to him and his family?"

Pericles answered, "Perhaps under these circumstances I could live a happy life next to this neighbor regardless of him been a Turk."

"Of course it could be possible and that shows that the concept of homeland is nothing but a word. Just an invented word, Pericles, used to separate people, to make them believe they are different from others. It also gives a reason for some to attack others and for some to declare a war against another. They are just words."

"I agree Calliope, and yet we hang onto these words and make them an inseparable part of our lives," Pericles added.

"Yes, and for this reason you have come all this way from Craiova just because the word 'motherland' was so much entrenched inside you by your grandfather that you couldn't resist the desire to come and see for yourself."

"Wouldn't you have done the same under the same circumstances Calliope?"

"Ah, yes perhaps I would have, Pericles, but now let us face reality. Now that you have come and have seen and have experienced quite a bit, as I have found out from your words, tell me, was it worth the dangers, the tiredness, the loneliness, the pain you have endured to be here today walking with me along the streets of Athens?"

Pericles looked at her eyes and felt a short-lived lump in his throat, as if he had difficulty swallowing. An awkward smile appeared on his face when he said.

"I've enjoyed being with you and although certain things didn't prove to be close to what I've wished them to be, I'm still happy that I've started my quest to get here. On the other hand I've met you, and we're together and I like it very much too," he said. He turned toward her and kissed her.

They had reached a park and found a bench under the trees. Pericles hugged her and Calliope leaned her head onto his shoulder. Suddenly time refused to count itself, the empathy of the universe turned coincidence, an effortless on their behalf effort, the universal agreement on something as serious as their feelings developing slowly since that day in the train. Pericles felt the trembling of her hands to which he responded with a light touch of her cheek followed by a soft kiss on her lips. Truly nothing else mattered at this moment.

Then Calliope's glance became serious and she stared at him with lips tightened, her head held straight up.

"I want to remind you of your comment about noticing the submissiveness in the people glances, a fear in their behaviour, a servitude you didn't expect to find."

"What goes through your mind Calliope?"

"You said that you had waited for so many years to come and meet your proud ancestors, the people in your grandfather's stories who walked and talked with the gods the ones who danced up in the air like eagles, the ones you haven't met so far."

"Yes. What is your point?"

"They behave the way you noticed because they feel inferior; because someone else has always been above them, the one who has turned them into peons, into anthropoids, animals resembling humans."

"Who do you mean, Calliope?"

"I mean the people behave the way you've seen them because of the one who has graced them with that servitude. Now they bow their heads as if seeing one superior than they are. This is nothing else but the organized religion: the church that sucks their blood, their money, their brains and their minds for the last seventeen centuries."

"Are you sure of what you imply, Calliope?"

"Of course I'm sure. And you might as well say that there is no way out of this catastrophe unless they close them all, the churches I mean, and turn their lives around one hundred and eighty degrees. Then perhaps after a long time you may again see true Hellenes walking along these streets: only then and not a single moment before it."

Pericles listened to her attentively absorbing all she said, letting it sink in his mind. At first contemplation he realized she was right. When one has been told by someone that he is inferior and the first one is above him it places so much fear before the eyes of the second it would be impossible to feel free and stand upright. For this reason they've always been bowing, as if waiting for their saviour to come from above, while all along their survival and safety has lain in their own hands though they couldn't see it due to that constant fear in which they have dwelled for such a long time.

Pericles remembered the members of the Hellenic Community in Craiova and how their most important function was their church and the various church holidays that ran all year round and at regular intervals as if someone had filled each day of the calendar with a different holiday, a different church event the members had to attend. And of course, every time they went to one function they had to place some of their hard earned money in the church basket that resulted in the members of the congregation having less and less and the church amassing more and more every day of the year.

Calliope raised her head again and looked in his eyes. She kissed him and felt content as he did too.

Time went by slowly and later in the night they got up and walked slowly through the busy streets of Athens until they reached the proper bus stop. A short ride brought them a few blocks from her apartment and walking in they greeted Urania who like any other mother in the world had prepared their supper and within minutes it was served. All three enjoyed the food over a glass of wine.

The next day found Pericles and Calliope totally immersed into each other: they felt as one. Pericles wished he could stay with her but time had come for him to leave and pursue his quest. Yet he hoped he would meet her again someday.

Evening came. It was time for Pericles to go to Peireus to take the ferry to Crete. Calliope went with him to the harbour.

They took the subway together and reached the designated dock.

Before he climbed up the ramp he hugged Calliope tightly. She held him close for the last time. He didn't want to let her go yet his mind went to what he had come from Craiova for. He let go of her as one lets his favored bird fly away into the clouds. Minutes later he leaned onto the ship rail and waved at her for the last time.

"*Am I ever going to see her again?*" his mind tyrannized him. He smiled at her for the last time knowing he was going to Crete. "*If it meant for me to meet here again, I shall,*" he thought.

The whistle of the ship sounded and slowly as the ship was untied from the dock he tried to untie himself from another attachment. Next stop: Crete.

Crete

The engines hummed their song, a muffled sound as if coming from the depth of the ship creating light vibrations Pericles felt on his soles as he walked from place to place trying to find a corner to lay down and stretch his legs for the ten hour overnight trip. He located an empty chair. He decided: this would be his bed for the night. He sat and remembered everything that had passed and what he had experienced during his quest. His parents' faces came to his mind, sad image that almost brought tears to his eyes. His old teacher and how he wiped his glasses again and again to hide his nervousness and anxiety and his mother who went from the table to the sink numerous times although there was nothing for her to do. His dad who tried his best to avoid eye contact out of fear his son may sense his grief at this time of separation.

Pericles' eyes swelled with tears but he kept them to himself. People walked by him trying to find a spot to sit and relax as he did earlier. Everyone was consumed by their own thoughts and memories. It was a voyage after all and every one of these passengers had left someone behind. He had too: Calliope and Penelope further north in the Bulgarian village. He visualized Penelope, in her bed, like the first time he saw her with the help of the mirror. His body felt a jolt of adrenaline and he felt excited. He tried to move his mind to other images and slowly he relaxed enough to fall asleep, leaning his head on the back of the chair and waking during the night until they had reached the port of Souda around 6:00 in the morning.

He headed to the exit along with the foot passengers holding his back sack on his shoulders. As he stepped out to the ground, the Cretan ground, he felt as if he wanted to lean down and kiss it. His chest felt heavy, as if a big grave slab was resting onto it. The unease of who will he meet and how will he be accepted crawled into his mind, *"who is my uncle whom I'm about to meet?"* he wondered and yet a sweet emotion made him feel at home, *"this is my homeland"*, he said to himself aloud and upon hearing the words his eyes swelled with tears. He turned around. He looked at the people. Has anybody noticed he was teary eyed?

He walked away from the dock and searched around to locate the proper bus that would take him to the main bus depot in Chania; shortly after his bus entered the main depot of Chania where a dozen busses were parked and were ready for their destinations. A lot of passengers walked around with their bags on hand, some had suitcases, others holding the hand of a child, others hugging and saying their goodbyes before separation from a loved one or a friend, or an acquaintance. There was quite a commotion around and among all those people Pericles who also looked for his bus to take him to Kolibari. It didn't take too long to identify the proper bus which he boarded.

Deep in thought, he didn't even notice when the bus started until they were almost out of the city. They passed one after another the villages straddling the land along the sea. He marvelled at the sights of the houses along the way, the farmers riding their donkeys or their mules as they went about their daily affairs. He noticed a few cars that passed them or the ones coming from the opposite direction, the road wasn't as busy as he thought it would be. Half an hour passed when suddenly at a turn of the road the village of Kolibari, the village of his grandfather and father, came into view: as if smiling at him being flooded by the morning sunshine. It was located at the foot of a mountain, as if it wanted to protect its back from the invisible enemy, as if the mountain kept an open eye on this small village in this parched part of the globe. It was a village, nothing more, but a village and its people. Its houses which from afar looked as if they were built touching each other, as if they had built them glued to each other, houses among which the north always created havoc, stood as if supporting each other.

Above the houses, the mountain rose a few hundred meters against the blue background of the sunlit sky, that blue, unlike any other, this Hellenic blue adorned by the painters' brushes. Upon getting closer Pericles saw narrow paths leading up the mountain where almond trees strewn and yellow flowers bloomed among the thyme shrubs onto which the busy bees foraged.

If one looked down from a high point over the village one could on the right side the plain with pieces of marsh land, full of insects and turtles where the children of the village explored and learned. The drier spots separated into pieces, each belonging to one of the villagers where the owner would graze his animals, a cow or calf, and most likely their two or three goats or sheep and their donkeys and mules.

The fields were full of a shrub called *agoustros* which the farmers gathered to feed their animals during the cold days of winter. The owners of each piece of land defended it against any enemy foreign or domestic intruder. It was part of their lifeline a part of who they were.

Pericles remembered a myth his grandfather had told him about one of the uprisings of the populace against the Turks, those difficult days they struggled for their independence and the union with the free Hellas. According to the myth, a large number of Turks were killed and buried along the sides of this mountain and since then the almond trees got very angry and stopped producing their delicious fruit. The buried Turks, the myth went, being angry that they had lost the island, would rise every night and throw stones chasing away every night traveller.

His grandfather said that when one climbed up this mountain and sat on a big rock to look downward one could see on the left the blue sea, which was sometimes angry and dressed in its dark blue colors, and other times peaceful and serene, so the light blue of the sky made it almost impossible to separate one from other at the edge of the horizon. The sea rumbled day in and day out. At high noon and at midnight one could listen to its secret anguish, just like the people's anguish when they narrated their toils and struggles. The sea sometimes looked angry, like a woman in need of a man. Closer to the shore, one could see the small harbour where the fishermen tied their boats, a small harbour they had built after years of soliciting and begging the politicians in Athens.

This small harbour played the role of their window to the future. Some of these villagers earned their living from the sea. Their boats were moored in this harbour. Everyone knew the owners of these boats which were given glorious names, such as *Salamina*, and *Navarine*, and *Aegos Potamoi*, glorious names from ancient and modern naval battles. One could easily relate those battles with these fishermen who fought against this sea when she was dressed her dark blue color.

Pericles got off the bus at the main intersection and placing his backpack on his shoulder he walked the five hundred meters to the village. He passed the only paved road with the trees on each side and plenty of potholes. "*Not much different from the roads in Craiova,*" he thought and a smile appeared onto his face. With that inexplicable smile he passed a few stores, the bakery, the general store, the post office, a notary public office, the butcher shop, a small store full of souvenirs for the tourists. Soon enough he reached the village square where two cafes were established.

Pericles entered the first café and sat at a table. The owner walked to him with questioning eyes as the rest of the patrons also looked at him the wonder written on their faces.

"A frappe," he ordered.

"Do you want milk in it?" the café man asked.

"No, just sugar," he answered.

His eyes searched around the rest of the patrons. They were sitting two in each table except a group of four playing cards who were also very vocal in their game. His coffee was served. He addressed the café man.

"I'm looking for Aristarchus," he said.

"Oh, you know him?" the café man asked.

Pericles smiled at the man. "He's my relative."

The eyes of the man showed surprise, "relative?" he wondered aloud and waited for something more from the visitor.

"Yes, he's my uncle."

"Your uncle?" the man was even more surprised this time.

"Yes, I'm from Romania. I'm looking for my uncle Aristarchus."

"Oh, I see. Well, welcome to Kolibari," he said and extended his hand for a handshake. Then while squeezing Pericles hand he asked the other patrons, "Have you seen Aristarchus today?"

"Yes, he was at that café earlier. He's gone home," said a man showing the café across the street.

"How can I find his house?" Pericles addressed the man who showed the café across the street.

The villager showed him the way.

"At the end of this road, the last house to the right," he said.

"Thank you," Pericles said and drank a sip of his coffee. Minutes later he paid the café owner and got up. He walked to the road the man had shown him along the houses of the village. He passed outside a yard with a beautiful jasmine fragrance. He stopped for a few seconds and savoured the wonderful aroma which reminded him of his mother's jasmine right outside their kitchen. As soon as he would step out of their kitchen to the yard, to his left the jasmine was most of the time full of flowers filling the air with their beautiful aroma.

A couple of minutes later he was in front of the last house, as the man at the café said, his uncle's house. It was part of an old, castle-like building with a gigantic arched gate leading to an open area with a number of doors to rooms all the way around the square courtyard.

Pericles called his uncle's name and a man appeared at one of the doors.

His uncle, Aristarchus, a man about seventy years old with a slender body stood gazing Pericles. Other than his wrinkles Pericles could see that he was healthy and vigorous for his age. He greeted Pericles.

"Good morning young man. Come in, who are you?" His voice had a light soft tone as if life had passed over him and had slowly softened his rough edges. Forbearance glinted in his eyes. It was evidence of the simple life he had lived up to now and Pericles discerned a sign of wisdom in him just like his grandfather.

"I'm Pericles from Romania, Alexander's son" Pericles introduced himself.

"My cousin's son? Your grandfather, my uncle's name was Pericles, wasn't?"

"Yes."

"Your mother, who's your mother?"

"My mother's name is Aspasia. She was born in Romania to Hellene parents."

His uncle opened his arms and embraced him, holding him tight for a good moment. He invited Pericles to come inside. The young man stepped in his heart pounding wondering what would come next.

"I remember your father was a young man when they left. How long ago did my uncle die?" Aristarchus asked.

"Five years ago." Pericles said and his eyes ran around the space.

The room smelled of herbs and the poverty was overwhelming. An old table straddled the middle, three chairs with loose, creaky joints making them move unevenly as Pericles discovered when he sat down. Most noticeable was an oil lamp hanging from a hook on the wall, the only light that flooded the room. Shadows in every possible shape invaded each corner of the room, each wall with a different apparition, as if it was time for the fairies and the night rascals were ready to commence their stage play. The house had been Aristarchus' dwelling for a long time and one could smell abandonment in every little piece of the two rooms. Here it was where only relatives visited and not too often. There wasn't any radio or television.

The house had a dirt floor and a ceiling made of wood sticks and over them a layer of soil, from a special place outside the village, a special blend between clay and slate that kept the rain from dripping inside. Pericles sat at the table and his eyes fell on the dirt floor. His uncle noticing Pericles' attention to the floor explained to him all the rooms of this old building were of dirt and so was the roof.

Often during the stormy days or nights, Aristarchus told him, he had to place his casseroles and saucepans in two or three spots on the floor to stop the dripping water from spreading although he was accustomed to the sound of those drips and he could even say he liked their cadence especially in the darkness of the night, "one would feel as if someone else was here keeping him company and he also knew that after the weather system would go by, he would have to climb up to the roof and seal those spots of the roof with extra soil."

Turning his head around Pericles noticed his uncle was cooking his meal at the hearth. He told Pericles, that he found the food tasted better than the food cooked in the gas stove he had in his kitchen.

Aristarchus offered him tea which he had just boiled. He filled two cups from a teapot sitting in the middle of the table. As they sipped their tea Pericles told him about his parents in Craiova, his grandfather's passing at the old age of ninety eight. He talked about his father's work, and the way of life in Romania. Aristarchus listened attentively and also told him about life in the village and how the days went by. He added that for an old man such as him it didn't matter, he had lived all his life resigned to his fate; He said that he gazed life through the lens of suspicion. He said he was like most of villagers who mistrusted the politicians, the priests and their own beliefs.

Like most others in Crete, the Cretans let their memory lead them to painful remembrances, memories that reminded them how ephemeral life was. A fact they had accepted with serenity and doubtless with a sense of resignation.

"For this reason," Aristarchus said, "we have lived our aching nights without knowledge of anything better and their excruciating high noon hours under the merciless conflagration of the sun with a perseverance one could always admire."

Aristarchus went on to tell him how these villagers with their brutish hearts were mostly uneducated, yet as wise as other people who have been educated in the school of life. There weren't any diplomas, but the simple acceptance of anything life brought their way, and although they were the most wretched of people, they still retained an indescribable value most people with diplomas never attained. These villagers could grab a sack of fertilizer, one hundred kilos heavy, and place it on top of their shoulders as if it was filled with feathers.

"The evening twilight has the imperceptible softening of the light that gives to us, who have been abandoned by fate, a reason to smile and an excuse to contemplate the beauty of life here." Aristarchus said "Every single man of this village can turn himself into a Zorba and without hesitation he can stand up and start dancing as if he has wings."

This was the life of people in Crete. Pericles absorbed every single word like a sponge.

"They are divided in two camps, the villagers," Aristarchus said, "Half of them frequent one café, while half were regular patrons of the other. They frequent these cafes since they don't have any other form of entertainment and also because the liveliness of the cafes stands opposite the loneliness and boredom they feel in the solitude of their houses."

"Which of the two you frequent uncle?" Pericles asked.

"I go to both, one day to the one the next day to the other. I treat both the same way." He said with a smile. "But we'll go there later on and you'll meet some of the villagers."

And they did so. The same evening they went to the cafe and Pericles wondered why the villagers were divided into two camps. He had seen the two café owners. They were both short and stocky with balding heads and red noses like beets. He had noticed that they seemed ready to pierce one with their sour eyes. They looked as conniving as foxes. Even their aprons were equally dirty. Yet, they differed in one thing, and it wasn't their names. The owner of the café to the left as one would enter the village square was called Elpinor and the owner of the café to the right was named Aegeas. Both had glorious and dignified names. Yet the owners and the villagers were still split in two clans: those who loved the military government of the day and the others who hated it. The first ones had as their excuse a stupid reasoning that the country needed a strong governing hand and the military brass was the ideal hand to deliver it. The others were democracy lovers who wanted a simple, plain democracy, the bittersweet myth called freedom. These two camps couldn't tolerate one another and often one bunch would isolate someone of the other camp and give him a good fight. And there were a few like Aristarchus who didn't give a hoot about politics and didn't care to observe the differences between the two clans of the village. The local police, who didn't really care to get involved, let them find their own ways since it was in their blood. The Cretans liked to fight amongst themselves, as if this was the only way a Cretan could show his strength and affection to one or another.

There was something in the island Pericles had felt from the first time he stepped onto its soil, something like a little craziness, something different from the rest of Hellas. He couldn't name it, but one could easily be afraid of it. There was a Cretan word that described this craziness, the word *kouzoulada,* something unexplainable. And it was unexplainable to the rest of Hellas but something that meant a lot to the Cretans.

The people here felt free of the fear of death and they would do anything to dare it, like his cousin Akratos. His uncle told him the story about his cousin.

"Akratos," the shepherd was once up on the mountains and along the great Samaria Gorge when a friend dared him jump from one side of a very deep ravine to the other. Akratos with a smile on his face and without ever thinking of how deep the chasm was between the two edges or how easily he could fall in and die, jumped and made it to the other side. He dared his friend to do the same but this other man didn't have the nerve to do so."

Pericles laughed at the wild demeanor of the man called Akratos, one of his further out relatives. Yes, Pericles knew it, there was something in the attitude of these villagers which defied logic and made them feel strongly about life which they loved to the extreme as they loved their women and their food and their wine, the simple satisfactions people have, a good word, a good meal, a good glass of wine or two, a good friend, an honorable enemy although sometimes these weren't enough around. And during those times they would go out of their way to exhaust their Cretan craziness, their *kouzoulada* by fighting each other. That time one group would grab a member of the other just to start the feud once again. Many years ago, when the Turks were in Crete, the villagers always had a reason to fight, since some of them didn't mind the occupiers as long as they had a few benefits coming their way, while the rest were adamantly opposing any close relationship with the 'enemy.' Therefore they would always find a reason to keep the feud in full bloom and although they were two creeks of the same river, and they would eventually merge into the same sea, they kept on fighting. In later years, when the Germans were in Crete, the same dispute was going on. Finally, during the civil war, they didn't need to find any excuse. They divided in two camps with one fighting the other for years on end.

This was the way Pericles observed the villagers. Only at this time they were divided between the supporters of the dictatorship and the opponents who called the first ones fascists and the fascists who called the second ones communists. Even when they went to church, they stood on opposite sides before the altar. The women in the back of the church sat anywhere they could, while one group of the men stood or sat on the left side facing the altar and the other group opposite them. In the middle was the priest, father Konstantinos, who for years had followed the actions and reactions of these brutes with inexhaustible patience and dedication. Thank God there was only one pulpit therefore it couldn't be divided in two fractions. In this atmosphere the church was doubtless not the place of the Lord. Upon entering it one would find the women in the back of the church eyeing each other and murmuring various comments about one another and *what she did, how she dared.* The other similarly gossiped while one group of men eyed the other. The priest tried every Sunday or holiday to futilely serve his Lord.

Truly, father Konstantinos was in the middle almost all his life since he had been appointed to this parish back in the day when he had graduated from the Theological School of the University of Athens. Soon after he had married his beloved wife Adrianne who he was allowed to touch once a week, on Saturday night, with every single light shut off and without his clerical collar, according to the advice of the older priest, Gervasios. The old priest had just retired and had in mind to stay around for the rest of his life. A single man in his seventies, he had already bought his burial site from the parish. He had already sat on the marble slab and had taken a photograph which he gave to father Konstantinos and advised him that upon his death that picture was to be placed on his tombstone.

Villagers and the Priest

The next day after supper Pericles with his uncle Aristarchus were sitting by the big arched gate of the compound of rooms and they enjoyed the view of the sea on the left side of the horizon. Aristarchus narrated some stories about the villagers just as he wished to make his nephew familiar with the villagers and their way of life. On top of the list of important people, of course was the priest of the parish father Konstantinos.

"A very meticulous man, focused in his task" Aristarchus said, "always careful as to how he could handle each situation the best way possible. He has managed all his religious responsibilities the best he can, and he had buried his predecessor father Gervasios in his designated burial site and taken responsibility in executing his last wish regarding the picture. He regularly visited the burial site and lit the candle and the incense and said the proper hymns allotted to dead people."

He stopped for a minute and looked at Pericles who was listening attentively with a smile upon his face. The story reminded Pericles his grandfather and his stories; a sweet emotion ran through the young man's spine as his uncle carried on.

This was the life of father Konstantinos, up to a day, two years ago when the good Lord took away his wife, his sweet Adrianne. From then on everything changed for father Konstantinos, because his late wife was still a very young woman. They never had any children however Adrianne was a very vibrant woman in every respect.

She was his errorless advisor when time came for him to deal with the brutish Cretans, full of craziness in their blood, something he never truly understood, being a northern Hellas boy."

"Why there is such a difference between the northern Hellas men and here in Crete, uncle?" Pericles asked.

Aristarchus gestured his hands as if trying to explain with a movement of hands rather than by words. Sometimes words didn't come easily. Other times they didn't explain much but rather they complicated things.

"This difference, as you called it, is something you have to live and experience. It's not something I can describe in words. But I'm sure now that you are here and you'll stay for a while you'll come to know it."

"For two years," Aristarchus carried on with the story of father Konstantinos, "the priest kept his neutrality as his beloved Adrianne always had advised him. 'You have to keep it even Steven,' she used to say to him. 'Be good with both camps. We only need a little longer and the fish tin is almost full of money. You'll need to find a new one soon,' she would say, referring to the money they collected from both sides of the isle. Yes, his fish tin, where they kept their money, was full of bills, but he often thought God was unfair, because He had taken his beloved Adrianne, a good, young Christian woman and a very obedient wife who would go out of her way to please him. His Adrianne was basically an uneducated woman, which was good to begin with, but she had a brain that could convince Lucifer to get into a jar and have him sealed in it. Her ingenuity was proven when she had been proposed to become the wife of this young priest, father Konstantinos. Adrianne knew how to deal with people and she would often apply herself when it came to dealing with the issues of the parish and the responsibilities of the priest and the parishioners, these brutes, as she called the Cretans. Being a Peloponnese girl, she was right every single time when she suggested to him to take a stand regarding this or the other issue in hand. And by forcing father Konstantinos to follow her advice, she kept a balance he always admired. She was the one who had devised means and measures unheard of up to her arrival at the parish: the weighing and skimming the oil given to the church by the villagers to use to make candles, and all other church functions, and the smart way of burying people. Rumor had it that the corpses of many villagers were put to their graves with no clothes, because she would strip them, and with the help of the undertaker, and after modifying them a bit, she would sell at the flea market."

"Very practical and devising," Pericles said with a smile.

"Yes, very much so," Aristarchus said, "there were other conniving schemes too, that always resulted on her getting some financial gain and with little outlay of funds to her undertaker-helper. Some people said that all these smart inventions cost her life. People also rumored that the year the corpse of Homer Balouka was buried naked she got sick; and he was buried naked because the priest's wife, Adrianne, kept the shroud for her own use. And as a result people rumored the bad disease spread in her body and within four months she was gone. The doctors talked of maternal issues, although she never had children. The people talked of the cursed disease. In truth, she had gone quite fast."

"Most unfortunate" Pericles interrupted.

"Yes, most unfortunate, as they are sometimes the ways of the almighty" Aristarchus added, "time has passed by since then, and nature turned father Konstantinos into a wild animal, because when nature works its wild craving into a man's mind he is capable of doing unheard off things. This was the way father Konstantinos suffered the last two years, a hell on earth as one could call it, and since he was in the prime of his age his eyes always fixed on every woman of the village, until the men smelled his intentions. Three of them cornered him once after the Sunday mass and in a frank and straight way, well known to Cretans, they told him to make sure he kept his equipment tight in his pants or else. Which father Konstantinos took as an insult and promised himself to pay them back and in the most appropriate way."

Pericles gazed the dark blue sea and felt serene and calm, as the sea seemed to be from where they saw it. His uncle stopped his narration leaving the young man time to digest all the discussion, until a later time when he would tell him something else.

This was the way Pericles found the villagers and the priest whose he got to shake the hand the following Sunday when Aristarchus took him to the church. Pericles found the liturgy as boring as the one he attended back at home with his parents. He promised himself not to be a frequent church visitor. However this time he shook hands with father Konstantinos who welcomed him as a new comer to the village, from a faraway land relative. Pericles as he expected, found father Konstantinos aloof and devoted to his Christian demeanor.

And this was father Konstantinos who got up in a bad mood this morning, because sleep didn't relax him during the night. As he tossed and turned in his bed he knew well what he was missing, an unbearable craving he just couldn't take out of his mind. He had hardly slept two hours when the cocks of the neighborhood woke him up with their morning cantos. "Even they are trying to find their morning chicken to jump," he thought and that aroused him more than ever.

He walked to the front door and opening it, he gazed the eastern horizon where the sun was almost peaking from the top of the mountains. He felt the need to have a cigarette although he had given up smoking four years earlier. Then upon realizing he was still in his pyjamas, his eye caught the rooster with the brown reddish plumage, the sexual machine of his neighbor having a willing participant chicken under it. He felt his skin crawling.

"To hell with you," he thought, and went back inside. He walked to the kitchen and absentmindedly to the mirror. He smiled at the 'good morning' written on the top of it with calligraphic letters. He heard the cocks making havoc outside his house in the neighbor's yard and felt the urge to run and grab them by the neck and just twist them a little to see how fast they might stop calling the next chicken to be mounted. But he remained absorbed in staring at his face. His eyes were full of dark circles. His nose looked to him a bit longer than before, his forehead, with his hair falling onto it, his hungry lips longing to mix with female lips, his unkempt beard. There was a time his Adrianne would spend time looking after his beard, stroking it with her fingers. He got up and almost ran to the sink. He threw a couple handfuls of water onto his face then he decided to go out to his small orchard down toward the river to water his plants and gather a few vegetables which he would boil for his lunch later in the day.

He grabbed his bag and walked out heading to his orchard with his mind running to the brutes of the village and how he was kept in the middle when even the village patriarch was against him.

Yes, the president of the small community with his whore in Chania, why was he so against father Konstantinos? Was he concerned that the priest might take his whore away from him? He thought of the widow of the village, Ariadne, and his face brightened. It was as if she was for him and only for him. He had to present himself the opportunity to get close to her and in a private way. Perhaps he would suggest to her to come for a communion or even better for a confession, although those days people didn't observe much of that.

The fools, he thought, *they thought they knew everything and confessions weren't as necessary to them as they were in older days; but time would come, and they would realize that they have to observe such functions otherwise they would go to hell.*

Many a time he had pondered whether such place as hell ever existed, but he left the pondering unanswered, since the current scenario fit his goals better than the unraveling of such issues; especially with agnostics and brutes such as these villagers. Yes, the widow might be a good woman and being deprived of a man. She might be as hungry as him, although she looked after the old seaman, and people talked of her giving him every comfort her imagination would device since he was in the late days of his life. Even the village patriarch often visited her bedroom, the villagers gossiped.

A light breeze was coming up from the shore, an inexhaustible spring of salty fragrance and femininity he found quite invigorating, although he preferred thoughts as far away as possible from anything feminine. Walking toward his orchard he took notice of the sky that had acquired its regular vibrancy with colors between the light blue and light green as if reflecting all the trees and vegetables people had planted in their orchards. He reached his small plot where he had his ten tomato plants which already had started producing, and his cucumbers, his leek, and Swiss chard and beets, arugula and lettuce, parsley and thyme, and basil and oregano, his favored herbs. There were two rows of potatoes, green peppers and eggplant which he used to cook in his oven with plenty of feta cheese and lots of parsley. He put his stuff on the side and after taking his spade he diverted the water supply from the main ditch and guided it to his orchard. It was his day to water as the water was scarce and each villager had certain days of the week that he would water their orchard. He watched the water flow as it turned from the main ditch to the one leading to his plot, a slow flow that finally reached the beginning of his land where he diverted it to the first line. He had eight lines of vegetables to water. It would take him no longer than one hour to water the whole orchard. When he looked up from his chores, he noticed Agesilaus walking toward him. Agesilaus was a man of strange manners, sometimes polite and willing to assist in whichever way the situation might require, and other times rough and laconic, man of a few words, who would spit on the face of anybody even if that person was the priest of the village. Agesilaus, a man in his forties who never had the pleasure or misfortune to marry, lived next to the widow's house and rumor had he also visited her from time to time, visits the priest wished he could make too although he never got the courage to pursue it.

Doubtless this is why he felt jealous of this man who, if the rumors were right had slept with the voluptuous widow.

Agesilaus greeted the priest when he got closer. "Good morning, father Konstantinos."

The priest responded in the same pleasant manner and the conversation, perhaps not as laconic as other times, started blossoming as if today was Agesilaus' good day of the week.

"I see you got here first. But you only have a few lines to water, I'll wait for you to finish and then I'll water mine." He pointed at his own plot, as he was the owner of the orchard next to the priest's.

"Yes, I won't take too long. Come, let us sit here and have cigarette," the priest proposed.

"You smoke, father? I thought you quit smoking long ago," Agesilaus said.

"Yes, I quit long ago, but today I would like to have one. Can you spare one?"

"Of course father" Agesilaus said and opening his pack he gave the pries one; he took one for himself and they lit up together.

The priest inhaled the smoke, but being off smoking for a long time, the first puff choked him and he coughed a lot, to which Agesilaus laughed, and told him perhaps he shouldn't smoke so many years after he quit. But the priest managed to get a hold of his breathing and he truly enjoyed the cigarette to the point of deciding it was time for him to start smoking again. After all, his Adrianne wasn't around to complain about his smoke stinking breath. He thought of his wife and suddenly melancholy clouded his thoughts like a black shroud.

"Lord, you were unjust, when you took my Adrianne." He thought of her ethereal body that he had so much enjoyed.

As if reading his mind, Agesilaus said: "But what is it father, suddenly you look absentminded."

"Oh, nothing really Agesilaus; but could I ask you something more personal?"

Agesilaus nodded and the priest carried on, "Is she good?"

"Who, father Konstantinos?"

"You know, the widow? Is she good?"

Agesilaus turned reddish, puffed his cigarette and said nothing. The priest took this as a positive reaction and was ready to carry on with his questioning, but Agesilaus turned the conversation to a different direction and said, "Let me turn the water to the next watering line"

Giving no time to the priest to say anything more, he got up and with the spade he guided the water flow to the ditch that ran along the first row of potatoes. When he got back, instead of sitting next to the priest, he said, "Let me bring you a watermelon from my orchard." Two minutes later he was back with a good size watermelon for the priest to take home a gesture that forced the priest to stop asking him personal questions.

Soon after the priest finished watering his orchard he left Agesilaus to water his plot and taking the watermelon underarm he left.

Conspiracy

The rest of father Konstantinos' day crawled slowly and when the sun got tired lighting the earth he made space for the night to come and commandeer the people's minds and bodies. And it was as painful for all villagers who would rest their tired bodies of the day's toil as it was for father Konstantinos who was awake as if this was the beginning of the day rather than its ending. The night invaded the priest's room inch by inch: a slow invasion as if suddenly the swimmer lost his stamina, as if suddenly the sea resisted his unprecedented advancing. He tossed and turned in bed, sweating and fuming, unable to relax and fall asleep. Terrible thoughts controlled his mind like a myriad of bees buzzing their crazy dance in the air leaving him no a moment of relaxation, of privacy. He closed his eyes and for a moment he could see the image of a naked woman laughing her provocative laughter, teasing him to get close to her and take what he wished. Who she was he didn't know, yet the image was there every time he closed his eyelids, a punishing image as if the sadistic instrument of Satan had turned one after the other his nights into nightmares. He opened his eyes to the pleasure of the absent naked body and, with the wish to close his eyes again, hoped that he would meet her, to enjoy if only visually her exquisite lines and provocative secret contours.

"Oh, God, please help me" he prayed as he raised his body half up in his bed. His eyes ran around his room hoping to truly see her, the woman who had waged war against his patience, the woman in his dream. But alas, she wasn't there and his eyes turned to the window through which the night glow came in.

A strange power was evident in his room, a power coming from outside and precisely from above from the enticing moon which was as bright and as seducing as a woman.

"Thank you Lord, you've wakened me up. Help me forget her!" With that thought he sat up and almost instinctively his hand ran under his pillow in search for his cigarettes, the first package he had bought after four years. Grabbing the pack, he took a cigarette out, he lit it and inhaled his first drag, letting the smoke dive deep into his lungs. He felt he was taking in the woman he had seen in his dream, a thought that forced him to get out of bed. He stared at his bed before he stepped out of his bedroom. A lonely bed it was, deserted like an orphan, a bed with no peace, a bed without a woman. It was an unfortunate bed where he was destined to spend the rest of his life craving a body he would never have, craving the lust 'his Lord' had taken away from him.

He walked to the front of the house, opened the door and sat on a step by the entrance. His eyes looked around the surrounding images clearly visible under the moonlight while the night moist touched his flesh and cooled him. He decided to walk around for a while.

It was a quiet night, as silent as his bed since his Adrianne left him along with her sweet moaning, a sound he craved to hear again. Only the breeze sounded its erotic murmur, like a woman begging for more. The breeze danced amid the wild osiers and the small tangerine tree in his neighbor's yard.

"Here is another well- off man." He thought of his neighbour, Aristides, who was the richest man of the village making his fortune during the war days, by stealing and cheating. He got help from the occupiers, as the rumors had it, and after the war was over he had a head start on every other villager. He had his wife, and a very pretty daughter who studied at the University of Athens to become a doctor. He was a successful man, his neighbor, what more could he ask? And to top everything else, every time he needed something special his first hand, Hector, would do anything for his boss.

By then the walk of the priest had lead him just outside the church court yard. He absentmindedly walked into the yard and through the cemetery next to the church. Almost by instinct he walked out again, because although father Konstantinos was a man of God he had always been scared of walking around the graveyard alone in the dark, the graveyard of the village located next to the church courtyard. He had heard a lot of stories from the locals who described strange things that had happened in this graveyard. Once a few villagers with the crazy Minoas as their leader, after a good night of partying and drinking and after they all got drunk to the rim, they bet who would dare go to the graveyard at midnight. Upon sitting on top of the marble slab of the most recently buried person, he would sing a *mantinada*. Of course Minoas, the craziest of them all accepted the challenge and at midnight he walked to the village graveyard, located the grave of Aristotle, the one who had died a month ago at the honorable age of ninety eight, and with the others as witnesses he sat there alone and with no hesitation he started singing. Suddenly a strange subterranean roar was heard as if the whole earth was revolting and before long, while his companions ran away, the earth opened and the grave slab was so strongly shaken that it opened and Minoas fell inside it. Next morning they found him dead and they didn't question the reason. Deep in their hearts they knew it was the anger of the recently departed person, Aristotle, and they simply moved the new body close to the half dissolved other so it looked as if they were embracing, as if they had become friends. They sealed the slab with fresh cement to make sure it wouldn't ever crack open again.

Father Konstantinos shivered as he recalled the details of the story. He distanced himself from the church yard until, at the turn of the narrow village pathway, he reached the house of Demetrios, the church hymnist. Demetrios was a man with a good education, a retired high school teacher who sang the hymns at mass, an honorable man with a young wife whose erotic demands the hymnist couldn't take care of, so the rumors had it.

Suddenly father Konstantinos thought he heard voices. He tuned his ears and yes, the voices were coming from behind the house. He couldn't figure out what was said, but he was certain that a couple of persons were whispering behind the house. He decided to walk slowly to the back yard and upon reaching the back side of the property he lowered himself to the height of the stone wall fence and peeked over. He saw two figures standing by the lone eucalyptus: a man and a woman. She was leaning against the tree and they were kissing. It was Helen, the wife of his hymnist, with Agesilaus who gave him the watermelon.

The sight of two figures fondling and touching under the gleam of the moon drove the priest to hell and back in a flash of time. He gulped his saliva as he stood there motionless seeing what was taking place. The tension was so powerful that the eyes of the priest couldn't see anything anymore but he heard them arranging to meet again the next day in the early afternoon hours when her husband was having his afternoon siesta.

Agesilaus walked to the other side of the pathway, Helen walked back into her house and father Konstantinos was left in the agony of unfulfilled desire. Suddenly he realized he better leave just in case the hymnist woke up and perhaps sniff his presence. Who knows what he would think?

"Dear Lord why you sent this martyrdom to me tonight? As if I didn't have enough in my loneliness you wished to try my patience once again. Thank you, Lord, for trying your servant."

As father Konstantinos distanced himself from the place of sin, he thought, *"They plan to meet again tomorrow afternoon at the barn, but which barn?"* He pondered with glee that he would do his best to catch them in the act again.

He walked absentmindedly thinking of the couple when he realized that he had arrived just outside the widow's house.

"Everything has conspired against me tonight," he thought. He raised his eyes to heaven as if looking for an answer from the stars that gleamed in the firmament and the lonely moon that craved what father Konstantinos also craved. He walked around the widow's fenced garden and stood opposite the window of her bedroom. The thought of her always drove him crazy and his imagination was creative drawing various stances and positions he wished he could enjoy

with her body. He imagined her right there in front of him, naked and willing. The thought of her drove him even crazier because the men of the village talked of her as being easy rather than objecting. But while a few of the village studs enjoyed her, she always refused to lean toward him, the head of the village, father Konstantinos who could not only grace her with fantastic lovemaking but could also deliver her of all her sins. This, he felt, was the worst embarrassment for him — to think that even to the old seaman, a human husk she would give her sexual pleasure and yet she always avoided coming close to him.

A dog started barking as if the thoughts of the priest disturbed its sleep. Father Konstantinos didn't care about the barking and took a cigarette out of his pack, lit it and took a good puff, inhaling the smoke deep into his lungs. He exhaled a cloud of smoke along with his intensity and the dog started barking again as if it had seen the priest's cigarette smoke rising toward the sky.

He decided to walk back to his house, but before he took the first step he gazed the window. He thought that he noticed a shadow of a person moving from one side of the window to the other.

"It must be her!" He thought of her alone in her room and in a second he felt aroused. He took another puff of his cigarette and just then the light of her bedroom was turned on and the shape of a woman came to the window frame. He knew it was her!

His heart raced like a horse galloping in an open field; the woman took a quick look outside, and must have noticed the red tip of the cigarette and that someone was there looking at her window. The priest stayed motionless, although he thought she had seen him. Then the shape of her body left the window opening and he cursed the fear that had held him back from talking to her. In anger he threw the cigarette to the ground and stepped on it putting it out. Then as if by instinct, he gazed toward her window and saw her standing naked in the middle of the window with her arms wide open. His legs started to tremble and his jaws rattled as shivers took control of his body. He stared at her clearly now and she knew who was there.

"Ariadne, Ariadne…" he called her first name softly, but loud enough for her to hear him.

"Who's there?" she asked.

"I am here. It's me" he answered, his voice quivering with intensity.

Before she could say a word, the dog started barking. From inside the house, father Konstantinos heard the voice of the old seaman.

"Ariadne, sweet girl, did you call me?"

The widow let a loud laugh float inside and outside her window as she closed it.

"No, I didn't captain, go to sleep."

The light was turned off, but the priest stayed motionless like a dead man hoping that she would come back and he would find the courage to talk to her. Better still, to tell her how much he loved her and how he desired her.

Time passed. She never came back, although his imagination showed her to him naked as she had been earlier in the frame of her window; she was there with her arms extended as if she was ready to take him in her arms, ready to grant him his wish, ready to guide him into his heaven. A futile thought it was. She didn't come to him, and he was still out there craving her while she was in the comfort of her bed, perhaps enjoying her femininity, perhaps relaxing from the intensity of the night under the exciting moonlight.

"Oh Lord, please help me get away from this sin. Please Lord, help me forget her. Please help me," he kept saying while he walked away and without noticing, his steps, as if listening to his plea, guided him to his house. He entered, but to sleep was impossible after all the sights he had come across in his night walk. So he sat on his front steps waiting for the sun to rise and send the morning star to sleep.

He thought back to the early years of his life before he entered the Theological Faculty of the University of Athens, even before that to his teen age years. He remembered what he had followed after high school, the constant concern of every youth wanting to find something they liked to do, but also something they were good at. Something that would not only provide the means of a career and a livelihood, but also something that would make their parents happy. This was the constant thought in the minds of every young man and woman in their tender teenage years.

Father Konstantinos had been influenced by two different and equally powerful forces: that of his father who wanted him to become a captain on commercial boats and travel the world. He could earn a good living, while his life would unfold in foreign lands and ports away from this miserable place, his motherland to which his father had not much respect.

On the other side was his mother's influence with her religious beliefs and background. Her father was a priest and she knew it was a good and secure way to earn a living when most people struggled to make ends meet. His mother was the winner between the two. He had made up his mind to enter the Theological School of the University of Athens and upon his graduation he was appointed as a priest to this parish. Before he even got his position arranged, he had married his beloved Adrianne. They weren't graced with children, yet he never questioned the will of the Lord. He only felt it was unfair.

The roosters woke up in his neighbor's yard and stood on top of a post or the edge of the fence. They would claim their right to a number of chickens which they would mount on the first opportunity. The rest of the village had also woken up to the sounds and smells of the morning: sounds of animals, echoes of poultry, chirps of birds introducing themselves to the new day; father Konstantinos got up from his front step and walked in to his kitchen where he washed his face at the basin. He put two spoon-fulls of chamomile into his tea pot and boiled it. He added one scoop of sugar as his Adrianne always told him that too much sugar is bad for the pocket and for his health. His wise Adrianne had taught him to drink his chamomile with only one scoop of sugar.

He took his cup and went to the same spot by his entrance where he sat at the exact position he had sat in earlier. He noticed Hector, Aristides's helper, loading things onto his mule. Aristides was by the entrance of the house giving Hector instructions as to what was to be done today. When he noticed the priest, Aristides turned his attention to him.

"Good morning, Father Konstantinos. How are you?"

"Good morning my good neighbor; I'm very well, thank you. God bless you."

Hector, Aristides' first hand, had finished loading his mule and grabbing the reigns of the mule, he started away. He nodded his head down as he passed in front of the priest. This was his typical way of addressing father Konstantinos. He never asked for his blessing, never went to his church; never said a word except a nod of his head, an acknowledgement he observed only when he was in a good mood.

Father Konstantinos didn't like this man at all, first because of Hector's behavior which was always disrespectful and rebellious, but also because of all the rumors that went around the village that Hector would stop at nothing when it came to serve his boss's requests or needs. Hector would do anything in order to execute his boss's orders, even if that meant the death of someone. When this happened his boss had a way of taking care of the authorities who would leave Hector alone. Above all these details, father Konstantinos never liked Hector because he always flirted with his beloved Adrianne. With a comment or a meaningful glance or an imperceptible signal, he always showed his attraction to father Konstantinos' wife. Sometimes Adrianne reciprocated as if attracted to his brutish ways or to his manly stature. Hector stood a meter and eighty centimeters up, with wide shoulders and huge hairy arms. He had beautiful blue eyes for a brute of man he was and he was delicate and swift for the size of his huge body. One could call him attractive as well which always made father Konstantinos feel uncomfortable and insecure. And more than anything, this brute of a man always smiled an ironic smirk every time he met the priest as if enjoying the priest's uncomfortableness.

As if by instinct his glance turned toward the man who rode his mule and disappeared at the turn of the narrow pathway.

"I hear your orchard is doing very well this year, father," Aristides said.

"Yes, it looks very good this year, my good neighbor. How are your orchards?"

"They're good but not as good as yours. Did you use fertilizer this year?"

"No, none at all," replied the priest. "But I had a good load of manure which I spread over it. That obviously had a positive effect."

"But, of course, father Konstantinos," Aristides replied, "The manure is always better than any fertilizer."

At that moment Aristides' daughter, the girl with the scimitar eyebrows came to let her father know that his tea was ready. She was at the house because of a break she took from her studies at the University of Athens. The old man didn't answer, but left the priest and walked into the house cursing, "To hell with the stupid tea."

Father Konstantinos was still standing by his front step when he heard a familiar voice.

"With your blessing father," the widow's voice resembled the sweet chirp of a chickadee, and her body looked like Aphrodite's as she walked by him without waiting for his answer. Her buttocks moved from left to right and elevated his blood pressure to the stratosphere. Smiling, Ariadne, always provoked him, teased him by showing to him what he couldn't have, what he craved but wouldn't ever get.

He only managed to utter, "Good morning." Her name, Ariadne, came to his lips but he didn't call out to her as he enjoyed the sight of her behind.

The villagers were coming and going like any other morning, some to their orchards, others to peruse the shape of the olive trees and how this year's crop night turn out, some to meet their lovers.

"*Ah, yes, Helen will meet Agesilaus at the barn,*" father Konstantinos thought. He had heard them planning a tryst outside Helen's house by the eucalyptus.

The priest went inside the house and got properly dressed. It was early for him, truly very early in the day. He headed for the café where his hymnist was a frequent patron. As he walked along the narrow pathway of the village his footsteps kicked up yellow dust, as he thought of the lovers and hoped they would get caught.

Finally he reached the café and entered and without answering to the greetings of the regulars who were there he glanced around. He noticed Demetrios, his hymnist, sitting close to one corner of the café and reading the daily news. The priest went to sit next to him. He leaned close and made Demetrios aware of what was about to happen come siesta time. The hymnist, upon hearing from the priest what was to take place later today, raised his eyes from the newspaper showing something between anger and condescension, an apologetic glance that said, 'I don't know what to do. I can't do anything about it.'

Father Konstantinos let himself absentmindedly concentrate on his coffee while the other man closed the newspaper as if determined not to commence something he didn't even know about himself. Yet something was about to happen, and father Konstantinos wished that that would be a violent act of revenge.

Demetrios stood up, straightened his aching body stretched his rubbery arms as if to strengthen his muscles to make them firm and with no word, he walked out.

He took the pathway that led out of the village and toward the fertile plains where he had his orchard. The most appropriate was not to get into a fight with Agesilaus. He knew this was out of the question since old men never win against muscular types like Agesilaus.

He reached his orchard, went to the edge of the property where he had hidden his spade, took it, and started digging here and there uprooting the weeds. He picked them up and threw them to the edge of the field. From there he would bring them to the edge of his orchard where eventually one day he would burn them. This tedious task took most of his morning.

By noon he hid his spade under the usual shrubs and headed toward his house. Upon reaching it he went inside. His wife, Helen, wasn't surprised to see him home since it was almost time for their lunch and their siesta.

She prepared everything while he took a quick shower and when done he joined her at the table.

"Were you not a bit early today?" Helen asked him.

He shrugged his shoulders. He looked at her.

"I got restless and left the café early. "I went to the orchard. Let's eat."

He poured a glass of wine for each of them. Helen put food in two plates and sat next to him. They clinked to health, they ate. When they finished Helen took the dishes to the sink.

While she was cleaning them, Demetrios went behind her and hugged her in the way he used to do in the old days, a signal of his so familiar to her. With his arms around her they walked to their bedroom.

"My dear husband, I have missed this so much," Helen sighed.

"I know, my dear wife, I have too," Demetrios answered.

He left things the way they were, and they both had their siesta, hugging and being next to each other, as if they were young, as they used to be in the old days. Demetrios felt the tenderness a man would feel for his woman, a sensation rejuvenating him and they finally fell asleep leaving Agesilaus alone at the barn.

Haves and Have Nots

Thus was the way Pericles found the villagers according to what Aristarchus told him and with no doubt his uncle was an endless river of information flowing slowly but steady on a daily basis which the young man enjoyed the most. Today they were sitting at their usual places by the archway entrance of the housing complex where Aristarchus' room was and looking at the dark blue sea to the left of them the uncle narrated details about the *haves* and the *have nots* of the village.

As Pericles already came to know that the villagers were separated into two camps — the ones supporting the dictatorship and their opponents there were also in two different camps when it came to riches; in the same manner the citizens of this Cretan village were divided into the poor, who were the most of them and the rich ones including Ephialtes, who was also the president of the Community.

Although not the richest villager, he was comfortable since he had a couple good pieces of land: one good size orchard where he produced vegetables not only for his own use, but also produce which he sold to merchants. And he also had acres of olive groves that produced a few tonnes of oil which the co-op of the area bought every year for a very good return to the grove owner.

The other rich man was father Konstantinos' neighbor, Aristides, who had vast land holdings that included grapevine fields, olive groves, grain fields and animal food products such as clover which grew abundantly. And even richer than these two was the monastery with its vast parcels of land consisting of orchards, olive groves, grape vine fields, almond tree orchards and thousands of animals the monastery shepherds were taking care of up on the mountains.

"How did these men and the monastery ended up being so rich, uncle, and the rest of the villagers aren't?" Pericles asked.

Aristarchus sighed, "There is a story for each of them, son, but let's take things slowly."

Of the three the one none of the villagers liked was the president of the Community, Ephialtes, a man of a few words, a divorcee who would go out of his way to gather information about everything and anything that happened in the village and the surrounding area, which he passed on to the official representatives of the dictators. Ephialtes, the president as everyone addressed him, stood thin and light against the wind, a man resembling a lone tree blown in every direction. He featured long thin arms like long leafless branches, long thin legs like canes and his hair thinning too. His demeanor was even more acidic than all his other characteristics.

Another reason why the villagers didn't stomach Ephialtes, were the stories of what he did during the years of the German occupation. Rumors had it that he was a German informer and nothing could escape him, nothing that the Germans wouldn't learn thanks to Ephialtes. There was word that the Darridis family was wiped off the face of the earth thanks to him. Every member of that family was shot by the SS point blank as they stood against a rock fence wall right in the middle of the village, as an example that the occupiers wouldn't tolerate resistance.

However, one member of that family, Achilles Darridis, a school teacher was smuggled out of the village in the darkness of the night by a good friend of the family. Homer, a shepherd, guided Achilles to the mountains where he has stayed for all these years. Being against the dictators, he was also in the cross-hairs of the current occupiers who would arrest and exile anyone who stood to oppose them. Hellas consisted of a lot of islands where they sent the dissenters. Some of the small islands were totally populated by exiles.

This man, Achilles, was expected one day to come down from his hideaway in the mountains and take care of the traitor Ephialtes.

Everyone in the village knew this, and everyone believed that one day it would happen that the guerrilla, Achilles, would come and avenge the blood of his family which had been shed because of the traitor's actions. Although these days he was protected by his military godfathers, the villagers knew that Ephialtes' days were numbered.

The president of the Community was once married then divorced because just two months into his marriage his wife *'got on top of the broom stick'*, as the saying went those days about any woman who would go out of her marriage and sleep with another man.

In this case, Ephialtes' new bride was caught having sex with a clerk of the local co-op, which prompted Ephialtes to file for a divorce which was approved right away as it always was in such cases. Ephialtes went from being a newlywed to a divorcee in a few short months and he never even tried to match himself with anybody else. He had suffered a lot in his first trial and it wasn't the financial issues involved not even the pain in the dealings with lawyers, but the scorn of the villagers that cost him the most, especially from the person who witnessed the infidelity and narrated in detail the whole thing to a full house café. His ex-wife ended in Chania in a house where everyone could go and have their sexual hunger satisfied, as long as he held tightly in hand the proper fee which those days was about one hundred drachmas. Ephialtes managed to get appointed president of the Community by the military rulers. He was to be theirs as long as he kept an eye on everyone around, and as long as every shred of information was reported straight to the junta.

The rest of the villagers were poor. They worked for any of these three landowners. Each land owner parceled his properties in pieces, depending on their location, and the product expected from it. They rented it to one or two families of the villagers, depending on the size of the family. The tenant family seeded or planted, fertilized or worked the land until production which they would split in two: one for the owner, who didn't do any work but provided the land, the seed and the necessary fertilizer and the other to the working family, until the next year when the process would repeat itself.

A lot of rumors circulated about another rich man in the village, who was also the priest's neighbor, Aristides. He also stood high, a huge man that he was, taller than anybody else, and with shoulders as wide as the whole island of Crete. He had a hairy chest and long strong arms. He resembled the tallest oak in the forest, the one every other tree aspired to. He was a smart man, almost cunning, a good organizer and truly good decision maker. The villagers called him 'epidemic' since he managed to outsmart the villages and buy out everybody's property during the days of the German occupation. Aristides had a brother in Athens, Xenophon. The currency of those days had lost its buying power due to the war, and people needed carry a lot of money to just buy coffee.

Xenophon conned many citizens out of their savings with promises of the new currency, due to appear soon, and after he gathered a chest full of these bills he travelled overnight to Crete where the money still had a relative value. Rumor had it that the two brothers went on a buying spree before the war spread all over and they managed to own more than a thousand goats which they had sheltered in their old barn, and a lot of other items such as machinery, equipment of every kind, stored on their property. When the Germans had advanced to Crete after a bloody invasion, the two brothers were equipped with plenty of things they could sell to the first buyer, which they did. In the first two years of the German occupation they amassed properties one after the other from the villagers who sold whatever they held in order to buy food. This resulted in the two brothers owning every piece of land and housing and after the war ended they were the richest villagers at the expense of all the others. This justified the term 'epidemic' that the villagers had attached to their names.

Three years after the liberation, Xenophon died leaving Aristides with everything they had amassed, the richest man of the village.

"During those years of the war, our family lost our small orchard and olive grove to Aristides," Aristarchus said. "And since then, we've worked in the fields of the monastery under the half and half verbal agreement that governs such arrangements."

Pericles looked at the old man who looked resigned and almost cynical, "and you still work the monastery orchards, uncle?"

"Yes, of course; I make some money and also get my food."

One couldn't describe the wealth of the area without mentioning the dark blue sea that licked the feet of the village and turned the whole area into a natural paradise equally enjoyed by the locals and the throngs of tourists who visited the island during the summer months. Tourists from northern Europe made their homes in every little inch of this'sacred soil with its bucolic atmosphere and the hospitality of the locals which was known all over the world. This sea, which at times turned dark and fearful like an angry woman ready to punish and to do justice for anything unjust done, this sea with its fragrance and salinity that was immersed into the foundations of most houses as if they stood firmly on earth as if their base was their steadfast love for this sea with its immense treasure of fishes and octopuses, turtles and small sharks. The sea's smooth swells and angry waves provided recreation for the villagers and food, not only for this village but for the most villages in the surrounding area. It was famous for its best fresh fish. Hundreds of visitors came daily to taste the freshly barbequed fish and octopus in the restaurants and tavernas located right on the water, providing a good source of revenue for the locals.

The villagers felt a strong dependence on the sea. Three families were fishermen who would go out when the weather allowed along the length of the Spatha peninsula and cast their nets and fishing lines. They would spend three hours on a secluded cove where they moored and perhaps catch a shut eye, then go and pick up their equipment and the catch of the night coming back to the small harbor in the morning twilight to display their catch where it would be sold to the villagers or the tavernas and restaurants.

There were a few of the villagers who had family members abroad, the ones who dared go away to search for a better future for themselves and their children, like Pericles' grandfather and father did. In such cases, the only way of communicating was via correspondence, a slow process. There was a telephone connection to every part of the globe, but it didn't mean they were talking to each other, except the exiled to the ones who had remained behind.

Pericles heard of exiled villagers who died in foreign lands and had made arrangements to be transported to the motherland to be buried in the family gravesite. Such was the case of Varanis, who had travelled in a coffin all the way from the central United States to this village and was buried to the amusement of the locals who said,

"Varanis was a dedicated traveller who never stopped seeing the world, not even after he died."

The village was also known for its mariners, the seamen who embarked on commercial boats and worked all their lives travelling and seeing new places such as Pericles' relative, Odysseus, who worked as a second captain for many years. When he retired, he took his pension from the nautical pension fund — a good amount of money coming to him via mail at the first of each and every month. He was always full of stories, a man of innumerable images from places the locals couldn't even imagine. He would often narrate to them to the point that sometimes it would turn into a monologue often repetitious and that disappointed his listeners.

Many of the villagers enjoyed his stories, except the youngsters who only cared for television and how to bet on the national sports lottery, the PRO-PO; although more often they would offer the old seaman a drink, usually moonshine, which the seaman would down in one gulp; when that happened nothing would stop him from starting his endless narratives until one by one the men around him would distance themselves from him giving him the signal that it was time to stop. The old captain had seen so many places and met so many different people of all nationalities, and he would finally conclude his narrative with a reference to his good buddy Yuto, a Japanese athlete who he had befriended. He said he almost married the athlete's sister, Sakura, but since he could have any woman in the planet he decided not to get tied up to a woman in Japan. So the wedding never took place.

For all the other villagers who never got the will or the opportunity to travel or to emigrate to a different country, all these stories were not only informative but also their chance to familiarize themselves with the ways and things of the foreign lands and their people. This compelled them to sit around the old captain and listen to him for hours. The old captain, having so many listeners, would always start a story at the end of another thus mixing them up and presenting to them whatever came to mind. Drinks were available, time was available, the locals liked the stories; it was a win-win situation for everyone involved.

There were times when he narrated to them his sexual adventures with Swedish or Norwegian girls. He liked the Northern European women, and he never ran out of stories about them while all the men around him would salivate as their imagination took them to beds undone and bodies willing to be taken. Only the luckiest of men could have these precious bodies and they were the lucky men who let their imagination run wild.

This distant relative of Pericles' was the celebrity of the village and as such he was also invited to all official functions, let that be a national holiday such as the 25th of March, the day of the Commemoration of their Independence from the Turks or the 28th of October commemorating the strong "NO" their government under Metaxas said to the ludicrous demands of the Italians before the German invasion of 1941. Odysseus was always invited to attend and sit with the officials. He remembered to shave and groom himself to present the best he could just to honor the celebration. There were times he would also get up and give a short speech regarding the particular event.

Pericles even heard from Aristarchus that their ex-captain relative, Odysseus, gave a speech one time when for some unexplained reason, old age was the culprit more than likely he lost track of his papers and jumped from page two to page four but he was the only one who knew of this. The attendees never knew any better, the officials didn't either, but the old captain confessed his mistake to Aristarchus and he cried like a baby. Needless to say that Aristarchus consoled the old captain and promised never to disclose to anyone the old captain's mistake.

This was the way Pericles found the village of his origin, Kolibari, and the inhabitants who he got to know not only from the stories his uncle Aristarchus told him, but from his daily interaction with them. What impressed him most was the suspicion of the villagers towards him. Even his relatives, except of Aristarchus, saw him with the same careful eye and kept a distance from him. This disappointed Pericles and made him wonder why they displayed this behaviour. He tried to get an explanation from Aristarchus who not only stood by him but also provided him with his house and food. However whenever Pericles asked why the other relatives avoided him Aristarchus said he didn't know, and it was better if they didn't talk about it. Pericles also noticed a policeman always trailing him, keeping an eye on where he went and who he met, although most of the times Pericles was with Aristarchus or alone.

Yet the eyes of the law constantly followed him which, to a certain degree, he understood since he had come to this country from Romania a communist country under the influence of Russia. Yet in his mind he expected something different, something better; something he had dreamed off when he was back in Craiova.

Aristarchus and Pericles went to his orchard everyday where Pericles help his uncle do the daily chores, slowly learning a few things pertaining to growing vegetables, their regular watering, the digging out the weeds, the clipping of the unproductive branches, tying stems on a firm piece of cane. It was all detailed work that proved to be beneficial to the produce. This made Pericles feel better, since he was accommodated and fed by his uncle so at least he could help him with his work.

Pericles was also impressed by the pictures his uncle had on the walls of the house, black and white pictures of relatives but only pictures of men. One of them was of his grandfather who stood against the front entrance of a house. His black eyes were exactly as Pericles remembered him, his forehead where thunder and lightning emanated. He was dressed in the traditional Cretan costume breeches and heavy coat, a scarf over his forehead. In his belt there were two bandoliers in a criss-cross fashion with shining bullets and two Cretan knives, as if he was ready for a battle, ready to start a war against every enemy foreign or domestic. This was Pericles' hero, his grandfather, the god of his family, there on the wall commandeering the rest of men to the tasks before them. Pericles felt proud, an indescribable pride so much so that his eyes got teary upon seeing the stature of his grandfather. Aristarchus noticed his reaction.

"Yes these were the men of our family, son, but don't forget they were men first and foremost they were men with families and descendants. Nothing more."

Pericles turned and looked at Aristarchus. In Pericles' eyes one could see the surprise at the comments of his uncle.

"Yes, I know, uncle, but they were also the heroes of our family, weren't they?"

"Yes, yes," was the whimsical answer of Aristarchus.

What Pericles also noticed there weren't any pictures of women anywhere in the walls.

"My uncle, I don't see any pictures of women along with these men," he asked Aristarchus.

"Why you think women belong there next to these men?"

"It's simple my uncle: did they not get married to women? Did they not have any children with women?"

"Of course but that doesn't mean women have to be in a picture there," Aristarchus said in a stern way, "look at my father, your grandfather's cousin, you believe a woman deserves to be next to that man with the huge moustache and his bandoliers and his Cretan knives? No, I don't think so Pericles." He said and shook his head.

"But," Pericles started saying when his uncle interrupted him.

"Women, ha! What do you think, son? Do you expect women to be next to these beasts? Ha, no, of course not!"

With that Aristarchus left him alone to examine the pictures while he went to sit by the front step of the house where he looked out over the dark blue sea, the fields and the eternal and omnipotent sun, sovereign and unquestionably potent even at this time of the evening.

It was a sweet human evening, and suddenly at twilight darkness spread over the sunlit blue sea. The bright hills reflected on the surface of the water which had grown calm. Even the breeze refused to disturb such equanimity and ran away to the sea caves where it kept company to the little seals that found their night beds on top of rocks. The cicadas had gone to bed and the animals had been put away in the barns with their hay spread before them. Even the dogs of the village were quiet.

To the north and just outside the small harbor, the three fishing boats were going out for tonight's fishing with their captains on the rudder eyeing the dark blue sea.

Pericles went out and sat next to Aristarchus. He felt an inexplicable heaviness on his chest as he looked at his uncle who was absorbed into the sounds and images of the approaching night. He took a deep breath.

His uncle sniffed the air and said "Something will happen tonight" as if warning him of an upcoming disaster.

"What do you mean?" Pericles asked.

"I don't know. I just feel it." Aristarchus' eyes were still fixed onto the bright sky as if trying to discern the signs of the stars. "But let us drink another glass of wine. Don't worry whatever is meant to happen will happen."

Pericles got up to pour wine in their glasses. Aristarchus grabbed his and took a good sip which Pericles replenished with a little more.

"You feel better now?" he asked his uncle.

"Yes, now I do, although I still believe something unexpected will happen tonight. I remember this quietness. It's always there every time something comes unexpectedly, as if it was meant to be. And always it happens on a night such as tonight. The fishermen say 'Tonight is a female night,' when they have a good catch or a male night if the opposite happens. And tonight is a female night and something is about to come along. Frankly speaking, we might see Achilles Darridis come down from his hideout up on the mountains to take care of his responsibility."

Pericles stirred in his chair as he remembered what Aristarchus once told him. Achilles Darridis' duty was to avenge the blood of his family: he had to come and make the traitor pay with his life for the deaths he caused on the Darridis family.

"You meant he'll come down and kill Ephialtes?"

"Yes, this was allotted to him by the Fates. He has to come and do justice to the blood of his family; because these have been the rules of our existence on this earth. One has to obey and act. Sometimes, without asking too many questions, one has to act according to tradition, and Achilles Darridis isn't one who would disobey such tradition. Believe me son, it will happen because of the roots from which he has sprouted. These have been our traditions and beliefs from the old days. Listen to this story because it has to do with his father, Ajax. When Ajax was young, during my youth, he was a rascal. There wasn't any occasion on which people would gather that he didn't try to create some trouble, some mischief. He was well known for that. One year during the Saint John celebration away out and over the mountains on the west side of Crete where the Saint John church was located, people from all the surrounding villagers would go to the church celebration where they would camp for two days and two nights and then after the event finished they would go back to their villages. The evil spirit tempted my good friend Ajax, to do something only a cunning mind such as his could devise. It was customary those days for the people of the surrounding villages to walk to the church of Saint John, an exhausting walk over the mountains that took four hours. A few of those had promised to walk barefoot and enter the church to light their candles before the regular mass took place. My friend decided to go and gather a bunch of blackberry branches full of thorns and spread them on the final part of the path leading to the church so the girls would step on them and injure themselves, while he would have a good laugh out of it."

Aristarchus stopped and grabbed the wine bottle to fill their glasses to the rim. He took a good sip again and turned to see whether Pericles was listening. Then he carried on.

"He executed his plan in detail, spreading over one hundred meters of the pathway with thorny branches. Of course a few of the people, men and women, young and old had a hard time dealing with the thorns. Ajax laughed at the misery he had caused them. Until that evening, when all of a sudden he felt a strange pain all over his body and he didn't know what had hit him. People said it was Saint John who punished him for what he devised regarding the pathway thorny branches he had spread. Indeed, only after he went to the church and divulged to the priest what he had done, and only after the priest gave him communion, did he felt better and the pain went away."

"Do you really believe it the Saint John who punished him?" Pericles asked.

"Doubtless!" Aristarchus said. "People believed those days that even people in love caught doing things inappropriate during the two days of the celebrations would run into trouble with the Saint. For this reason they abstained from engaging into anything while they attended the church functions and all other celebratory events. Also, I remember it was customary those days to devote a child to the saint and have it baptised during the two days affair. The father would take the child and at the time of the mass he would offer it to the priest who in turn would offer it to the congregation. Whoever would go first and touch the baby in the arms of the priest, that person would be his godfather or godmother and the christening would commence. After the sacrament would end, the parents of the baby would meet and get acquainted with the godfather or godmother, as the case might be."

Pericles listened to the story while occasionally sipping his wine glass and imagining himself in one of those events. His face glowed with an obvious affinition to the story and the role of the people in it. He refilled their glasses with a little more wine and said to his uncle.

"I wish I would get the chance to attend one such a festivity now that I'm here, my uncle."

The old man looked at Pericles and his face showed his satisfaction. He knew this young man who was raised in a foreign land felt as good as any of the young men of his family who grew up in this island.

That thought satisfied him and taking his wine glass he clinked against Pericles' and they both cheered and drank.

Time went by; the deep part of the night blanketed the earth and a dog started barking as if it sensed a stranger coming closer, an unknown person walking about in the narrow pathway of the village and slowly but steadily nearing the house. Suddenly, in the darkness their eyes discerned the stature of a man coming through the big archway of the outside building. He looked like a giant who had just sprung out of a mythology book, a giant who could make the most daring heart palpitate. The nails on the bottom of his boots made an abominable sound over the slabs of the courtyard. Pericles felt as if he was seeing an out-of-this-world giant who step by step came closer to them. The man had a rifle over his shoulder and two bandoliers criss-crossed over his breast. Pericles saw two Cretan knives with distinct black handles shining in the starlight. The man came closer. His eyes were fiery as if an ever-burning flame was lit in them. He had the look of revenge on his tightly pursed lips. He was a determined man, and he was here for his mission, and his mission was to avenge the blood of his family.

It was Achilles Darridis. Aristarchus got up and opened his arms accepting him in his house. He kissed him three times, placing his left arm on the right shoulder of the giant. This was a sacrament taking place between two Cretan men who knew their purpose in life, the oracle of which the ancient temples never stopped pronouncing. When the giant tried to say a word, Aristarchus stopped him. Men such as these didn't say any word in such encounters. It was all said by their silence and emotion, by their glances meeting. Words didn't have any place in their embraces and understanding.

Achilles eyed Pericles and Aristarchus reassured him there wasn't any reason to be alarmed since the young man was a family member.

"Indeed," Aristarchus explained, "he is a family member who has come from a faraway place to become a useful member of our family."

Achilles eyed Pericles suspiciously and said, "Aha, yes, you have come from afar, but why?"

Pericles answered, "To find my roots, to find the relatives of my grandfather and father, to discover the motherland, Crete." He couldn't take his eyes off the giant.

Achilles Darridis seemed about forty years old to Pericles who noticed that his boots were clean, his traditional Cretan attire well kept.

Achilles took the rifle off his shoulders and put it next to him on the ground while Aristarchus went inside and brought another glass of wine which he offered to Achilles. They clinked glasses, eyed each other, and drank. Pericles sighed as if releasing a burden he carried, as if relieving himself of unwanted anguish.

"I couldn't get it out of my mind that you would show up tonight, Achilles" Aristarchus said. "We talked of you a little while ago. But what would be the reason of your visit?"

"You said it right, Aristarchus. I had word that the traitor is due to go and water his field very early in the morning and usually when he does that he stays overnight at the small shack he has built at the edge of the field. Well, time has come to give him what I have promised him. Only, I wish my visit here tonight to stay between us. I don't want to put you in trouble."

"What you have promised to him, you do tonight my son. It's your destiny," Aristarchus said.

Pericles admiration for the giant was mixed up with sadness at the prospect of a killing, yet he knew this killing emanated from another evil done to the family of this man, and that Achilles felt it was his duty. Nothing else mattered to him or to Aristarchus, or to anyone who truly knew this was the way Cretans keep their word given to slaughtered family members.

"Even if someone told me that I would meet a man such as you, Achilles, I couldn't have believed that the time would come for me to sit here with you two enjoying a glass of wine."

He eyed the giant of the man who sat next to him who was calmly sipping his wine as if nothing else existed anywhere in the world. It was as if a rule beyond and above all worldly things was written in the hearts and minds of such men, like Achilles, whose only purpose was to avenge the blood of his family, blood that was shed because of the Ephialtes' actions. This was the only course of action a man such as Achilles could take because this course of action would be his deliverance, his transcendence to the realm of the beyond.

"What would be my purpose?" Pericles wondered. He couldn't find any answer. He wished he could discover one. His eyes met Achilles' and an imperceptible shiver ran down his spine. Truly, this man could evoke the worse fear in a man. Truly, this man could stop even the thinking process of one because of the intensity created just by looking at this man.

"How have you found your motherland, Pericles?" the giant asked him.

A faint smile appeared on the lips of Pericles though it proved to be hard for him to answer. Yet it wasn't proper not to, therefore he laughed, giving himself time to ponder what to say.

"It has been my wish from a very young age to come back to the motherland and meet my relatives, to meet Aristarchus and you, Achilles, and everyone else. I have always dreamt of meeting true Cretans like you and my uncle." He pointed to Aristarchus and smiled. "I remember my grandfather told me so many stories about life in Hellas and especially here in Crete. I wanted to come and experience it firsthand."

"Oh, I see," Achilles said with a stern look. "But I didn't ask you to praise me or anyone else for that matter. My question was referring to life in general and how you saw the villagers. Did you enjoy talking to them? What impression did they make on you?"

"I was saddened by their division," Pericles said, "that they have been in two camps, the ones who support the dictatorship and the ones against it. It reminded me of stories I heard from my father and grandfather that Hellenes have always been divided and always fought against each other."

He took his glass, and raised it into the air. With a cheer he sipped a good gulp which travelled slowly down his throat. It calmed him down and gave him time to examine the giant's reaction to his comment.

"I believe you wouldn't like to tell the truth about these people, because these villagers aren't people, they're animals, donkeys and bulls and cows, and goats; anything other than human beings. They might look human but they don't think like humans do. Since the day I could first remember, they have been eating each other, they have been killing each other they have behaved not different than animals, since the old days. First it was the war when thousands were killed. Then the occupation years with more thousands who died of starvation and a lot who were executed. Then the civil war when everyone found a reason to kill someone they didn't like. Then the dictators came to power and that gave the people another reason to be on constant vigilance, each person keeping an eye on the other, what they say, who they meet, why they do this or that. Endless! Yes, it has been endless and the hatred has been always among them, a situation with no end."

The giant was agitated by his own words and he gesticulated moving his hands in every direction just to emphasize his message. Even under the light of the night one could notice his eyebrows and his lips tightened. Even under the influence of the wine one could sense the anger of this man, the giant who came down from his hideout to commit a killing and that only to avenge the shed blood of his family.

Suddenly Pericles's lips uttered the unexpected words: "But you have come tonight with the same purpose in your mind."

Achilles Darridis glared him but remained silent. Aristarchus sensed the tension between them and said to Pericles, "Yes, Achilles has come to kill someone. But this is different. This is his duty to his family's blood which was unjustly shed."

Achilles got up. His shape was almost to the sky and with no words spoken he placed his bandoliers over his chest in his traditional fashion, his rifle over his shoulders and stood in front of Aristarchus who had also stood up to wish him farewell.

"Uncle, your blessing," Achilles said.

Other words weren't necessary between the two men who could read each other's mind and wishes even in their silence.

"You have my blessing to avenge the unjustly shed blood of your family. Do what is due. No mercy."

It was as if they took an oath together and it was the balance between what the Fates and luck had blended, for this man, Achilles who was just the instrument meant to carry the weight of the act, a weight he was mentally and physically ready to undertake, the weight of being called a killer for the rest of his life and the weight of his family's curses thrown against the man who was the cause of their undoing. This was an event about to happen which no one ever would be able to cleanse. Nobody would ever grant this man a forgiving blessing as one day when his days would come to an end he would join the immortals in the Elysium, the abode assigned to the blessed and the demigods after their death.

Aristarchus kissed him three times as when he arrived and after he placed his arm onto Achilles' right shoulder, he gave him the customary blessing.

"Farewell and may the souls of our ancestors escort your days and nights."

"And you, as well, my uncle." The giant said. Then he turned to Pericles, extended his huge hand, and squeezed Pericles' hand. As if shot by lightning Pericles felt an unprecedented power going through his whole body. It was as if all the Cretan Gods had awaken up as if the angry dark blue sea was rising to gulp everyone in its passing, as if the earth groaned in anger and shook its foundations. It was as if the hand of Minos was squeezing his hand and the emotion was completely overwhelming. He felt ready to cry, ready to dance like the proud Cretans do in such occasions. It was an experience he had never felt before.

The tall man, Achilles, walked toward the archway and before going out to the darkness of the night, before heading toward the dark act he had to commit, he turned back toward Pericles for a second. From under the huge archway he let a laughter float in the air as if laughing at life, at his Fate, at his duty. He laughed, a strange laughter, an abominable laughter familiar only to the brutes of men who act what their Fate demanded of them, and when his laughter ended, he cried out: "And you think I'm not an animal?"

The dark night engulfed him and he disappeared behind the archway of the old Cretan building.

Duty and Passion

Far out to the right of the Spatha peninsula the morning light decorated the fields of the plain with rosy colors and the stars paled as the village woke up to the things people were to do for another day. Some had to go and water their orchards, some to go and feed their animals, others to go and gather their watermelons as the days were ripening for that seasonal chore. Like all others, Pericles and Aristarchus got up to their day's work. His uncle prepared the necessary things which he put in a traditional Cretan bag and slinging it on his shoulder they started down the narrow pathway of the village toward the plain.

One could smell moisture in the air because of the light fog that dominated over the plains, which slowly dissipated leaving the earth and the air clear and sunny. June was the time of year for the gathering of the watermelons and melons to be followed by the grains end of June beginning July and then the grapes in August and later in the year the olives.

On the narrow pathway where they walked Aristarchus reminded Pericles to keep to himself last night's visit from Achilles, since today was the day they would discover what their giant visitor had accomplished.

Pericles nodded although he had doubts the giant had committed his duty. He turned to the direction of his uncle and asked how sure he was about Achilles' actions.

"When such a man promises to do something it isn't any different from the law," Aristarchus said. "He must see it to its completion one way or another."

Soon after that they reached the watermelon patch and started their daily chores. Aristarchus went about the orchard and followed line after line, hitting each good size watermelon with his fingers, a special hit making a sound that told the ripened ones from the unripen. He cut each ripened one from its stem and placed the watermelon into a cylindrical coffin which, when filled, Pericles carried to the shack at the edge of the field.

About one hour later, the bell of the village church sounded its melancholy rhythm, the familiar sorrowful chime used when one had died. Aristarchus raised his head and signalled to Pericles that people had probably discovered the body of Ephialtes. He gazed around focusing toward a field where people were running about and shouting.

Pericles and Aristarchus walked over toward it and upon reaching the field where people were gathered Pericles realized the giant's promised course of action was completed.

Ephialtes' body lay motionless on the ground with his throat severed as if he was a goat or a sheep expertly cut by a butcher. His blood stained the soil a strange red color, the symbol of life, of rejuvenation, of renewal, like Achilles' life which was renewed after he executed his plan.

A few people stood around whispering sad words and a policeman from the local precinct was walking around, observing whatever details he thought were important. As he stepped around the body he heard Achilles' name mentioned by one of the onlookers.

Turning toward that direction he said: "Who of you might be the smart one who mentioned the name Achilles?"

The people started to walk farther away from the crime scene without answering his question. A few minutes later the superior police officer came, and after he diagnosed that the body was that of Ephialtes both policemen walked away. The undertaker, who was waiting for the examination to finish, lifted the body with the help of his assistant and placed the dead Ephialtes on the back of a donkey as if it were a heavy sack of potatoes. Then they took him away to their office where they would embalm him and ready him for his final destination.

Aristarchus and Pericles stood there all along the police investigation and diagnosis and the undertaker doing his job. Both their faces gleamed satisfied that the giant had avenged the blood of his family. At one moment Pericles turned to his uncle and with a faint smile said.

"I guess we can go back to our daily duties too, my uncle."

"Yes, we have our duty too," was Aristarchus' answer.

They went back to their field and worked for another two hours gathering all the ripen watermelons. They placed all of them under the protection of the shack except for one that they wanted to take home. When they reached the house Aristarchus suggested they clean up a bit and go to the house of Ephialtes where the coffin with the dead man would be on display as it was customary. They prepared themselves and upon reaching the mourning house they found almost the whole village gathered there. The women were going back and forth bringing food and wine that belonged to the dead man, and the men were partaking in all of it. This was their way of saying *kalo taxidi** to the recently departed Ephialtes.

Four ancient crones dressed in black sat together in a separate room where the coffin was placed and whispered, not to disturb the celebrants in the next room. They wailed the traditional mourning songs to themselves. After all, this man was a loner and as a loner he must go to the afterlife along with the dirges of the mourners. The old captain was there among the villagers with his maid, the widow, who went back and forth taking care of the serving and arousing in every young or old man of the group a silent sexuality. Every one of them would love to have the widow or any other woman, especially after they had consumed a few more glasses of the dead man's wine.

Father Konstantinos was there making sure the blessing of the man was done properly and also making sure he could manage to send his signal to the widow. He had to force this woman under him at some time in his life, even if this was his last brave manly act. But

---

bon voyage

his advances and secret glances weren't as private as he wished them to be, and almost everyone kept an eye on him instead of the exquisite behind of the widow who was enjoying all this attention.

The traditional servings, first almonds and dried figs, then pan fried sausages and a whole assembly of the goat's intestines along with three or four wine flasks were consumed. Everyone's mood was in full party mode. Then half of a goat discovered hanging from the truss of the cellar in the basement was boiled by the women and presented to the still hungry men along with the traditional pilaf. The wine was used more than the water and the flasks were filled again and again. Then suddenly the priest stood up wanting to say a couple of lines as it was customary. His mind was confused by the excessive wine and by the sexual thoughts he observed on seeing the widow's ample buttocks but it was his duty to say a couple words, so he started uttering some gibberish such as "Dear departed…the forgiveness of the Lord may escort you…Dear departed may you always be remembered…" until a low tone "boo" was heard and he was forced to sit down. But he did so only for a moment and then, as if he remembered something very important, he got up again, made the sign of the cross and added, "Dear departed, the Lord may have mercy on you and may the Gatekeeper Peter open the gates of Heaven for you."

With those last words he had done his duty and he sat down letting a long and tired sigh float over the room, a sigh of relief because from now on the only care he had was the food, the wine, and the behind of the widow.

The actor was there as well: a groomed man in his early thirties who they called 'actor' since he resembled one of the most famous men of Hellenic cinema. He was the one who got caught in the back office of the co-op with Ephialtes' wife the reason for his divorce. He was enjoying every minute of the event since he never liked Ephialtes.

He also hated the fact that he had to travel by bus to Chania to visit his beloved and even worse the fact that he had to pay the regular fee in order to enjoy his five minutes in bed with her. She had become such a professional, that woman, that she wouldn't give him his short sexual pleasure free of payment. Every female of the village was under his scope and he would do anything and everything to sleep anywhere he would find a willing bosom. In fact as lately the villagers talked of him being interested in the richest man's daughter, something her father Aristides didn't like at all.

Like most fathers in such situations who didn't like a prospect groom for their daughter, he was willing to exterminate each and everybody who he wouldn't approve as his daughter's husband. But the 'actor' was oblivious to such threat and kept on courting the young woman who wasn't putting much resistance to his advances. In fact, a few people had seen her talking to him and touching in a way inappropriate for the richest man's daughter. But today the 'actor' just walked around the coffin, as if he imagined Ephialtes jumping out of it and chasing him, like back when Ephialtes learned of his wife's encounter with him, and a pleasant smile was evident on his face.

However the main actor of today's show was Ariadne, the widow, who had control over every man's eyes and every man's thought as the hours went by and the consumption of alcohol kept unabated. At one time, as if taking a break from serving the men, she sat aside and let her mind ran to her husband who eight years ago was laid in such a coffin. After his death she wore the black traditional garments of the widow only for a couple of weeks instead of the usual one year and although she mourned in her own way without tears and wailing, the villagers thought she didn't much care for her dead husband. Rumor had it that she was the reason he had died, since she was the never sexually satiated woman and she would put him under her and she would keep on demanding of his firmness which resulted on him to experience the fatal heart attack that took him away from her forever. Yet the days had gone by and the day came, perhaps too soon for the opinion of most villagers, when Ariadne took off the mourning black clothes and became the woman she always has been, sexual and demanding. Now she demanded her sexual satisfaction from whoever would come to her no exceptions which was the reason the women of the village didn't like her. To them she was a threat to their wellbeing, since she was the cause of the infidelity that ran amok in the village. Only lately, since she had started taking care of the old seaman, she had quietened down a little to the surprise of most women and men other than father Konstantinos, who deep inside knew what kind of sexual woman she was and he would do anything to have her.

As if by instinct, the priest grabbed the wine flask and said it was empty, and he knew of a good barrel, a mature old wine, in the cellar. He started going down to get it but not before he eyed Ariadne, and not before he signalled to her to follow him down below.

He descended the steps and groped around as he tried to locate the barrel he had in mind. He remembered it from one time Ephialtes, being a proud man, and wanting to showed the priest his wealth, had taken him down to his basement. He had not only showed father Konstantinos his selection of six barrels of wine, but he offered him a good glass of his old 'marouvas' as he called it, an exquisite wine with beautiful aroma almost turned into brandy. This was the barrel that father Konstantinos tried to locate in the dark while he waited for Ariadne to come down. But she took her time, and the priest cursed her for having him wait. Then suddenly, in the half-dark basement, he saw her beautiful behind coming down the steep ladder steps. His heart fluttered like a wild animal ready to grab its prey, which he did as soon as she was on the ground. But Adriane, a flexible woman, twisted her body and got away from him, and then with a playful laugh went and hid behind a barrel.

The priest reached her and placed his arms around her to hold her close to him. Their lips locked, and his fire wasn't a simple kindling anymore but a complete conflagration. He was ready to take her right there but she twisted her body away from him.

"Not now, not here," she said.

"I'll come…to the house tonight," panted the priest.

"No, not to the house."

"When, where?" His voice was between a gasp and a demand.

"Tomorrow after the funeral, I'll come to the church."

"In the church? Not in the church."

"Yes, in the church, why not?"

"Alright, tomorrow, but outside, not inside the church."

"Okay" she said and climbed up the stairs while the priest tried to concentrate on why he had come down to the cellar to begin with.

Finally he found the barrel and filling the flask to the rim, he also climbed up the stairs to the party room and to the whispers of all who were present.

The old sailor said to him, "You got lost in the basement father Konstantinos? It took you so long to get the wine and we've become thirsty."

"Yes, it was dark. But here is the beauty I mentioned. The departed, God bless his soul, had shown me this special barrel." And he poured a bit into his glass and passed the flask to the others.

The minutes turned into hours and by midnight the party was almost over. Pericles, with his uncle, left to go home as they still had some more work to do in the orchard come early in the morning.

But on their way home Pericles asked, "What was the meaning of all the strange comments men were making when the priest returned from the basement?"

"People always talk and always criticize, simple as that. There were rumors that the priest was after the widow, him being alone and such."

"I remember the good hearted, simple minded people of Crete my grandfather described to me in stories," he said, "but here it's a completely different world from what my grandfather told me."

"Why so?" Aristarchus asked.

"Here they're divided in two camps. They fight each other. They kill with no punishment. One sleeps with the other's woman. The priest is a womanizer. Half of them fight the other half. This isn't the place my grandfather described to me. This isn't the Crete I expected to find. God help me find my way."

"These are the ways here Pericles. Don't forget you talk of people. People are always the same everywhere one goes."

That answer didn't satisfy Pericles but he left the subject aside knowing that the opportunity will soon arise when he would dig into it a bit more.

The next day after they had worked gathering the last watermelons Aristarchus left to go and inform the clerk of the monastery that the crop was ready to be picked up by the merchant and Pericles headed toward the house. It was a magical twilight and he could see the orchards and watermelon patches all around with the fruits ready for the marketplace and lots of grapevines with the grapes already formed and slowly growing in size and sweetness. It was a quiet evening; the winds had flown away to other lands leaving the west side of Crete in its serene mood with only the sounds of evening rushing birds.

Ephialtes had been put into his grave earlier that day, but Pericles couldn't settle his mind whether Achilles was right or not for killing him. After all, who has any right to take another man's life? And was revenge the answer to this? He couldn't say.

The night was falling upon the earth like a heavy shroud that was meant to heal the wounds of the day and give the village people time to rest and contemplate on the value of friendship. Pericles reached the first houses of the village and the sounds of humanity woke him from his wandering mind. He heard the bark of a dog as if it was welcoming him back to the fold, as if saying to him he wasn't alone. He was passing outside the church which was built on a big rocky area overlooking the surrounding lands. From there the path led uphill to the highest point of the village where Aristarchus' house was located.

Pericles thought of Ephialtes and what an unorthodox way to go in an orthodox land of pious believers who loved to attend the church mass but wouldn't hesitate to take a man's life, as long as it was demanded by their customs and beliefs.

His mind told him to walk into the church grounds and pay a visit to the gravesite of Ephialtes. He entered and walked to his right. He bypassed the entrance to the church and directed his steps to his left toward the cemetery with Ephialtes' gravesite. Flowers were visible from afar and this is where he headed.

The flowers, a combination of carnations and roses with a couple hyacinths, were still fragrant. He stood for a moment motionless, as if paying attention to the memory of the departed Ephialtes. Thoughts went through his mind, serene thoughts bringing him back sweet memories of his family home in Craiova: the day they buried his grandfather and the multitude of people who had come to the funeral. He shook the hands of so many and he knew only some of them, yet it showed him how well known was his grandfather amongst the Hellenic Community of Craiova. His thoughts turned into anguish for the turn of events here in Crete since his arrival. He wondered whether he would like to stay in this place for a long time, but he dismissed this as unsuitable after what he had seen. He thought of where he could go if he decided to leave. He remembered his parents' stress and pain for leaving them to chase his dream, his utopia. These thoughts brought tears to his eyes. Suddenly, as if from deep slumber, he became aware of where he was and he overheard a discussion coming from the back of the church; it was laughter, a woman's laughter then a *sshhhh* sound.

He turned his attention to the sounds and saw the widow coming from the rear of the church. She turned her head to every direction as if to make sure no one was around, then she turned toward the main gate of the courtyard. Soon after, before she walked outside the church grounds, father Konstantinos appeared from the same place, as if he was following Ariadne. He was holding his clothes high up not to mess them on the soil of the courtyard.

Pericles stood up to make sure they saw him. When the widow passed close to him she moved her body with all its femininity present as if saying to him that was the power of a woman's body, and with a pleasant laugh, as if she was happy that she was caught by this stranger, she walked out of the church grounds. Father Konstantinos saw him and asked, "Who's there?"

Pericles walked up to him saying no words.

"What are you doing here this time?" the priest demanded.

"I would ask you the same question, father Konstantinos," Pericles replied. He recalled what had happened yesterday at the house of the recently departed.

To avoid a confrontation Pericles chose to walk out of the church grounds without saying anything else. What he had seen was enough. He needed time to digest it. He needed time with himself and his thoughts.

He didn't go home, but his steps slowly led him to the top of the hill above the village. He reached the edge of it where he couldn't go any further, because any more than thirty steps would lead him to the big crevasse which was at the far northern part of the hill. He stopped at a cement structure overlooking the bay of Chania and the plain from the village all the way to the city of Chania which, on a good day, was clearly visible from this high up point. It was said that the Germans had built this cement structure and used it as an observation point manned by perhaps a few soldiers who would keep an eye on the big bay of Chania that stretched from the west side of Crete to Chania. No ship coming from the north and heading for Chania or Souda, the main port in this side of Crete, could go unnoticed from this vantage point. It was also said that children after the war would come here and find unspent munitions and other leftover war material.

Pericles sat on the cement and stretched his legs to feel its coolness. His gaze travelled toward the north where the sea gleamed under the starlight: a dark gleam, as if mourning the death of Ephialtes and for the death of all ideals and dreams Pericles had before he came to his motherland. His jaws clenched making a macabre sound as if he was ready to chew something, anything that would relief him from the heat of his emotions boiling inside. He felt as if he was ready to punch someone, someone he didn't like someone like father Konstantinos, unfamiliar emotions inside him. A blended of disappointment and hatred he felt for the first time since he came to Crete.

Yes that's what is was — the emotion of hatred, one which he disliked the most, an emotion he had never expected to feel here in Crete. He hated someone. He hated a lot of things. He hated the priest. He hated his relatives, except of Aristarchus: those relatives who looked at him with suspicious glances and avoided talking to him. He hated the policeman who was behind him almost every day. He hated the littleness of the people who he had expected to be proud, the people with the servitude in their attitude the ones he expected to have their heads up high. He hated his breath that had become stagnant and astringent the way his dreams had turned since he had come here to face the harsh reality. Everything was dark around him and not because of the night which had fallen over the village, but because of the night of his life here in Crete, in the motherland.

To his right, the village with the gleaming lights of the houses broke the darkness into pools of light. It was as if they were pools of life, bright stars upon the immense sky. One part of the sky being lit and another being dark like the night he was living here in Crete since his arrival. Here everything looked androgynous to him. Everything laughed at him, a sarcastic laughter that heightened his agony and exasperated his mind. He couldn't find his way home while his mind urged him to walk to the edge of the crevasse. His mind tried to lead him off the heights and down to the level of this land, the land of his ancestors. But a strong instinct kept him away from the edge and led him to the opposite direction toward the village.

The thought of leaving came back to him. It was strange that this thought had gone through his mind so many times lately. His memory took him back to Athens and Calliope, and also to Penelope and the Bulgarian village. What was the answer he sought?

His steps guided him toward the village with the lighted houses and the café where he headed. From far away, from the side of the fields, a donkey declared the day done while the dogs in various yards of the village answered their agreement. He went to the first cafe and sat by the corner not even seeing two of his relatives playing a game of backgammon. He waved to the proprietor to bring him a shot of *tsikoudia.* Where had the pride of this island gone? What had happened to the glorious and the mighty Cretan men who could fight against anything and anyone who would come against them? What had become of their pride? Why did they look so little to him? Why had they become so different from what his grandfather had told him? Who or what had changed these men into the common ruffians that they were?

His thoughts were interrupted by Aristarchus who came and sat next to him.

"Where have you been? You haven't gone to the house since I left you in the watermelon patch?"

"No, I went for a walk. I didn't feel going home."

"You haven't eaten anything, but why Pericles? What happened to you? Why the walk? Where did you walk to?"

Pericles told him about his evening encounter with Ariadne and the priest and about his anger and his walk to the German observation post. Aristarchus listened to him without interruption, but when he focused on the priest and his encounter with Ariadne, his uncle stopped him a gesture of his hand.

"Why do you find it so difficult to understand? Why do you react in that negative way? They are both widowers. They need each other. Man wasn't meant to be alone, you know."

"Yes, I understand that. But in the church? Wasn't there any other place where they could do this?"

"Good point, but I'm sure they had their reasons," Aristarchus said. "Don't bother your mind with such things. They're two lonely people. That's all."

Pericles shook his head as if agreeing with his uncle. Aristarchus asked him: "What are you chasing Pericles? I would point that what you've come to find isn't here and I suppose that realization makes you very upset."

It was true. Pericles knew it. What he had expected to find wasn't here. Perhaps it never existed. Perhaps his grandfather and parents wished it to be here or nostalgia had created the image of such an ideal place in their motherland. But wishful thinking didn't always mean reality.

They got up and walked back to the house where Aristarchus revisited their conversation. Pericles talked to him about what he always believed in and what he had created in his imagination, what he had expected to find here which he hadn't met up to now. He talked about his grandfather and his stories. Aristarchus became angry and stood up, his eyes aflame and his lips tightened, and fists clenched.

"You've kept on saying things about your grandfather, my uncle. Perhaps the time has come for you to find out a few more things about him, which perhaps he never told you."

"What do you mean, uncle?"

"Did he ever tell you about his brother who died very young?"

"Yes, he told me about their dancing in those days and how his brother was injured"

"No, he wasn't injured. Your grandfather, and uncle of mine, killed him because of his stupid ideas about dancing. And not only that, but did he tell you what he did to his nephew, Alexander, my brother's son?"

Pericles was speechless since he had never heard of a story about a nephew named Alexander.

Aristarchus explained: "One good morning when your grandfather, my uncle, went to the orchard to water his watermelon patch, he found his nephew, Alexander, watering in the field next to his. Since he didn't want to wait for the young man to finish they started arguing, until word for word and punch for punch he hit him with his spade and left him breathless on the ground. Not only that, but he left the field and took to the mountains for a week. No one knew where he was, until one night he came down, packed the family, his wife Irene and his son, your father who was still a teenager, and left. That's why he ended up in Romania. And he dared send his letter to confirm to me it was him who killed his nephew over the right to water his field patch."

Pericles mouth gaped opened and stayed open for a while. He felt as if he was choking and his breath stopped. There was no hope for resolution, only the agony of betrayal, and the pain he felt in every molecule of his body. He stared at Aristarchus. He didn't know what to say under these circumstances. What could a person say when they discover that everything they believed in was a sham? What can a man do when he finds no light at the end of the tunnel but instead an endless darkness on which one floats with no hope of escape? He had come from a faraway place to this faraway misery and why had his grandfather insisted on him coming here?

Pericles looked deep into the eyes of his uncle as if trying to discover the answer, the hidden meaning of all this. "Why did my grandfather have me swear to make this trip? Why did he want me to come here and find out this horrible story?"

"The truth. He wanted you to find the truth, son. He wanted you to release him from his guilt. He wanted you to find the truth. There's no other answer."

Pericles jumped up. His face was red and fiery. His eyes had darkened and he felt the weight of the world on his chest. He wanted to say something, yet he had difficulty finding the words. He took a deep breath. Then he said.

"I'll leave. Tomorrow I'll pack my bag and go. I don't belong here."

He left his uncle at the table and went to bed but he couldn't sleep. His breath was choking him. The air was stifling. The room felt as if it was a prison cell. He wished to could get up and run, to go far away from this place. He wished daylight would come soon. The sounds of the night kept him company for five excruciating hours while outside the beautiful voice of the owl could be heard from the one hundred year old olive tree reminding him that there was another bright day meant to dawn soon.

The foundations of the house creaked and the first sunrays flooded every corner of the old building. The sparrows were already chattering their endless dialogue from the branches of the almond trees where they were already foraging on bugs. The sparrows' chirps interrupted every other natural sound of the day as Pericles and Aristarchus got ready and started their way toward the watermelon patch.

When they were outside of the rich man's house they stopped. The body of a man was laid in the middle of the narrow pathway. It was the body of the 'actor' lying there motionless, silent, a body which at first glance one couldn't say whether it was alive or dead. His clothes were partly ripped, his flesh looked dark. His body was obviously broken and he had a bleeding nose, with a couple teeth shattered, and one eyebrow slit in two pieces. One of his arms was obviously broken and pulled unnaturally far onto his back. It was the body of a man who was at other times handsome and well groomed.

Upon nearing it, Aristarchus leaned down and touched the man's neck. By placing his two fingers on the main artery he discovered the 'actor' was still alive although savagely beaten. He raised the injured body a little off the ground and tried to move his facial muscles as if imposing on him the energy to stir the desire to show life. Then father Konstantinos appeared, and seeing the body of the 'actor' in the arms of Aristarchus he tried to help to raise it up although its weight proved to be too heavy for them to lift.

"Wait, wait uncle", said Pericles, "let us try together." With a common effort all three managed to raise the injured man and place him against the wall of the near house.

"I'm sure you know who might have done this, father" Aristarchus said.

"Who?"

"Well, look at where we found him."

"What do you mean, Aristarchus?"

"Father Konstantinos, everyone in the village knew about the desire of this man toward Aristides' daughter and everyone also knew about her father's resistance to such a union."

"It doesn't mean anything, Aristarchus" the priest pointed out.

"Perhaps not in your mind, father, but I would insist that Hector, the rich man's helper has done this."

The priest touched his beard and looked sceptical. He said no word but went quickly toward the house of the rich man and called him to come outside.

When the old man Aristides saw the body of the injured 'actor' he crossed himself as if seeing something abominable. He turned to the priest and said, "God almighty: who could have done this?"

"You mean you don't know?" Aristarchus questioned.

"What do you mean?"

"You see, we found him here in front of your gate."

"It doesn't mean anything…I didn't do this."

"Of course you didn't. Your helper did," Pericles added.

Aristides gazed Pericles and in his eyes was a mixture of surprise and anger.

"You better stay out of this, you *foreign malaka*. Go back where you came from."

Suddenly Pericles' eyes felt an absolute darkness cover each and every cell of his vision and the day turned from being bright and sunny to black and fearsome. His emotions turned from been serene and peaceful to blasting rage like a volcano ready to explode.

Foreign malaka was what the old rich man had called him and perhaps many of the villagers call him the same way. Perhaps they referred to him using these words. Perhaps they called him like that in their conversations. He didn't know. But he surely knew this island was the wrong choice. He had selected the wrong place on the map. No, this wasn't where he should stay and live. No, this wasn't the paradise his grandfather had infused in his imagination with those beautiful stories of people and the Gods walking side by side, people and Gods conversing and playing and dancing together. No, this wasn't the place of his destination. He knew, this moment he knew he had to leave. Yes, today was the day. Yes, today he would pack his backpack and go.

What a fool, I have been! Pericles thought. The realization appeared as if from nowhere to open his eyes to the light of the bright day and the face of the old man he wanted to punch. The old man Aristides realized what he said and what it meant to Pericles and he walked away. When he entered his yard he shut the gate behind him leaving the others to take care of the injured 'actor'.

The priest and Aristarchus lifted the actor and carried him to the priest's house. They placed him on a couch and father Konstantinos brought a bowl with water and a towel which they used to clean the man's face. They asked him who beat him so badly he said he didn't know. He didn't see the face of his attacker.

What a fool I have been, Pericles kept on thinking. *How my longing has blinded me. How harsh fate has been on me! And my grandfather wanted me to come and live here. Why? God, I wish I could find the answer to this; the answer that made sense.*

He felt as though he was floating in a dark tunnel with no escape, a hell with no redemption, a tragedy with no catharsis. His tragedy was chasing the unreachable, his quest for the nonexistent his hope for the ideal destination of his dreams.

He left Aristarchus with the priest and walked back to the house. He saw darkness before him and behind him, above him and under him. To his right and to his left darkness was everywhere. It was in his thoughts while he put together his back-sack, his humble belongings along with his hope.

Just when he was ready to commence his new quest his uncle appeared by the door. They didn't say any words, such useless instruments in cases when the heart is in turmoil and the mind in revolt. Only their eyes spoke of what was felt and what was about to take place.

Pericles hugged his uncle, a tight squeeze, an eternal hug. He walked out of the door and into the bright day, into the day that would lead him to his destiny, the day during which he recommenced his quest.

A faint smile appeared on his face. There was a goal after all. It was there before him and he only needed to seek it.

Μανώλης Αλυγιζάκης, Κρης, εποίει...

About the Author

Emmanuel Aligizakis, (Manolis) is a Cretan-Canadian poet and author. He's the most prolific writer-poet of the Greek diaspora. At the age of eleven he transcribed the nearly 500-year-old romantic poem *Erotokritos*, now released in a limited edition of 100 numbered copies and made available for collectors of such rare books at 5,000 dollars Canadian: the most expensive book of its kind to this day.

He was recently appointed an honorary instructor and fellow of the International Arts Academy, and awarded a Master's for the Arts in Literature. He is recognized for his ability to convey images and thoughts in a rich and evocative way that tugs at something deep within the reader. Born in the village of Kolibari on the island of Crete in 1947, he moved with his family at a young age to Thessaloniki and then to Athens, where he received his Bachelor of Arts in Political Sciences from the Panteion University of Athens.

After graduation, he served in the armed forces for two years and emigrated to Vancouver in 1973, where he worked as an iron worker, train labourer, taxi driver, and stock broker, and studied English Literature at Simon Fraser University. He has written three novels and numerous collections of poetry, which are steadily being released as published works.

His articles, poems and short stories in both Greek and English have appeared in various magazines and newspapers in Canada, United States, Sweden, Hungary, Slovakia, Romania, Australia, Jordan, Serbia and Greece. His poetry has been translated into Spanish, Romanian, Swedish, German, Hungarian, Ukrainian, French, Portuguese, Arabic, Turkish, Serbian, Russian, Italian, Chinese, Japanese, languages and has been published in book form or in magazines in various countries.

He now lives in White Rock, where he spends his time writing, gardening, traveling, and heading Libros Libertad, an unorthodox and independent publishing company which he founded in 2006 with the mission of publishing literary books.

His translation *George Seferis: Collected Poems* was shortlisted for the Greek National Literary Awards, the highest literary recognition of Greece. In September 2017 he was awarded the First Poetry Prize of the Mihai Eminescu International Poetry Festival, in Craiova, Romania.